Why Should I Love You?

Ivy Symone

Chapter 1

Aisha was late as always. No consideration or respect for other people's time. She knew Abe had a busy schedule and she should consider herself lucky that he even cleared some time for her.

Looking around, Abe could see that *Batey's Kuntry Kitchen* was crowded with lunch hour patrons from different walks of life. An Asian couple sat nearby politely eating chicken and dressing, with mixed greens and a biracial couple sat behind them enjoying the tasty cheeseburger meals that came with fries and a dessert of their choice.

Really? Abe thought as he looked at the time displayed on his cellphone as if the diamond Cartier watch on his wrist couldn't be of much assistance. His watch was merely an accessory like the diamond bracelet on his opposite wrist. Both of the pieces symbolized not only his expensive taste but his status and wealth.

"If she ain't here in the next ten minutes, we gotta go," Eli snapped with annoyance in his usual, ostentatious manner. "Ain't nobody got time for her fuckery. Why you even agree to talk with the skank?"

Abe shot his younger brother a look. Eli, who was also Abe's personal assistant, always had a low tolerance for nonsense. As much as Abe hated to admit it, he knew it was time that he considered adopting his brother's attitude.

Abe was a softy and very passive when it came to personal relationships. Business was a different story. His aggression in that arena had been compared to that of a beast. Abe didn't play when it came to his money. If linking up Aisha that morning had been a business meeting; he would have been gone and on to the next.

"I just wanna hear her out," Abe said in a gentle tone.

"She cheated!" Eli said incredulously.

"I haven't been the kindest dude, either," Abe argued in her defense.

"But y'all were close to being married, and she cheated," Eli countered. He studied Abe's expression. An expression Eli had to be reading wrong. With suspicion, Eli pondered. "Are you considering calling the wedding back on? Are you having thoughts about giving this trick another chance? I know you can't be thinking of possibly still marrying her."

Abe gave an unsure shrug averting his eyes from Eli's piercing gaze. "I was kinda...thinking..."

"Thinking nothing! You ain't marrying that bitch!" Eli snapped loudly. His outbursts received attention from nearby patrons in the restaurant.

Abe frowned, "Be quiet."

Eli leaned forward, lowering his voice and repeated himself. "You're not marrying that bitch."

"I shoulda left your ass at the office," Abe chuckled. He glanced toward the front of the restaurant and noticed a very suspicious male looking over at them. "Who is that Eli?"

Eli tried to casually look over at the person. The guy was a young baby face cutie. He wasn't shy at all as he flashed Eli a bright smile. He was then joined by another suspect male, which Eli then directed his attention toward.

Eli rolled his eyes with frustration and sighed as he looked over at his brother. "Why you think I know everybody?"

"Cause, you're nosy as fuck," Abe teased.

Eli smiled deviously and said, "I think him checking for you. He thinks your pretty ass is gay. And he probably think I'm your bitch."

Abe didn't find Eli's humor very funny. Abe was worried about another man even thinking to try him like that without him instantly snapping.

Getting back to the subject at hand, Eli started again. "Abe, are you really thinking about going through with marrying Aisha?"

David Batey, the owner and operator of *Batey's Kuntry Kitchen,* came over to their table.

Good, Abe thought, *a distraction.* Eli was going to give him a hard time about this Aisha business.

"Hey fellas," David said cheerfully. Noticing that the two were missing the presence of their older brother, David asked with a puzzled expression, "Where's Ike?"

Abe answered, "He's out of the country with Tomiko."

"Oh. When is he returning? The two of you look so incomplete without him," David joked.

"Do we really?" Abe asked.

David laughed, "Well I'm just so used to seeing all three of you. If you see one, at least one other is right behind. So how are you two doing? Y'all doing alright?"

Eli cut his eyes at Abe, "I am. He ain't!" And, without hesitation, he started in on his brother. "David, tell him marrying Aisha is a bad idea."

David was caught off guard as he chuckled, "Whoa! What?"

Abe looked up at his longtime friend and mentor. If anybody understood him, it would be David. The older man had been one of the men that represented a father figure in Abe's life. It was David along with a couple of others who helped Abe redirect his life from the streets of crime to a life of earnest goodwill, honor, virtuous generosity, and hard work. It was David whose shoulders Abe had cried on, tears of emotional suffering endured over his lifespan.

"I didn't say I was going through with it. I just wanna hear what she has to say," Abe said.

"Hear it and keep it moving," David stated firmly. He frowned, "I've never really cared for that girl."

"So now you tell me!" Abe said with feigned disbelief.

David shook his head. "No, Abe. I tried telling you before, but you were in your zone. You know how you do."

Abe knew it all along; he just wanted to make an excuse for loving her. He sat there, thinking back to how this could've happened. What made her cheat?

———

Eight days prior, Abe surprised Aisha with a lunch date at her apartment. He had been so busy with work that even he admitted that he'd neglected her and all he wanted to do was make it up to her. Aisha seemed delighted by the surprise of the delicious seafood takeout from *Batey's Kuntry Kitchen.*

8

Abe felt good to know that he'd put a smile back on her face. After their nice, quaint lunch date, Aisha said that she needed to return to work. Abe also needed to return back to work as well, so they kissed, and Abe quickly made his exit with Aisha coming out of her crib behind him.

Twenty minutes, after sitting in heavy traffic and almost making it halfway to his office, Abe remembered that he'd left some of his work at Aisha's place. He had meant to grab it while he was there but was caught up by the quality time that he was squeezing in with her.

Abe re-routed to Aisha's. Upon his arrival, he was surprised to see her Range still in the driveway. Abe figured that maybe she had forgotten something, too and had to return. He parked his car, and then glanced in the side-view mirror, noticing a green, late model Jaguar backed up across the apartment lot. He knew only one person that drove a car like that. He scowled at the front license plate which showed the initials, *MW*. So what was Aisha's boss' car doing across from her condo apartment?

Abe immediately assumed what he had been suspecting for a while. He tried giving Aisha the benefit of the doubt when everyone said she was no good. He really did.

Quietly, like a feline in the wild sneaking upon his prey, Abe let himself in Aisha's place using his key. Reverting back to a time when being sneaky and undetected was a requirement in his street craft, Abe's movements were soundless. He heard them. He smelled them. Their aroma mixed with Aisha's hollering and moaning; it was nauseating, to say the least. He couldn't believe that her nasty ass would have somebody else digging off in her pussy just minutes after he'd left. It was like her boss had been hiding in the closet while Abe had been there.

Since they weren't expecting guest, Aisha didn't bother having her bedroom door locked, let alone shut. Abe stood in the doorway and observed with his own eyes as Aisha was being fucked from behind by her boss.

Mixed emotions went through him as he watched another man pounding in the woman he was prepared to marry. First anger settled over him, but it was quickly replaced with hurt. She seemed to be enjoying the rough aggression Michael delivered, but she would always tell him to be gentle and just to make love to her. She acted fragile when she was with him, saying that it was because of his size, trying to manipulate his ego. From the looks of Michael fucking her, she was taking dick like it was what she was built to do.

She was even talking to Michael. "Fuck this pussy."

Michael was definitely giving her what she wanted. "Whose is it?" He asked as he slapped her on the ass.

"Yours!" She screamed out.

Abe interrupted her as he cleared his throat to talk. "I thought it was mine."

They both jumped about ten feet high and screamed. Abe smugly laughed and turned away. It was either that, or he was going to jail for murder. Aisha tried to cover herself and come after him, explaining at the same time. "Baby, it's not what it looks like."

Abe didn't want to hear it. He retrieved his work off of the countertop in the kitchen. He looked to his left and saw her keys sitting next to her purse. He picked them up and removed the ring of keys that allowed her access to his world, and then he tossed the keys at her as they fell to the floor by her feet.

"Baby, please," Aisha called out, but Abe didn't want to hear it. At that moment, he was now able to see what everyone else had been warning him about.

"We're not getting married." He said, and then just that quickly, he left.

Upon getting in his car, he was thankful that his past had led him to being a much calmer man. He was a man that now cautiously practiced a resistance to anger. Had it been years prior, Michael would've caught the wrath of Abe's deadly hands and so would his now ex-fiancé. However, at this point in his life, he was okay with just being able to walk away.

––––––––

Abe's thoughts had him caught up thinking about Aisha and the foul shit she did. So much was coming to light like her never mentioning why she needed or even wanted to be with him. She never broke down her love for him. No type of sincere nothing that would've given him a second thought. The only thing she screamed or cried was that she was sorry and that she didn't want him to call off the wedding. Listening to her made him realize his own revelation; he wasn't really in love with Aisha.

David noticed that Abe had wandered off and changed the subject in an attempt to revert his attention back to them. "Don't forget about my niece and her kids coming tomorrow night."

"I haven't forgotten," Abe said. "I've already instructed Lulu of everything."

"I need me a Lulu," Eli joked about Abe's housekeeper. "She may as well be a personal assistant, too since she handles every other thing that I don't."

"That's what she gets paid for, dummy." Abe coolly stated then looked back at David as he continued. "Lulu knows to expect them since I might not be there upon their arrival. It's time for our Singles Mingle night," he said, feeling enthused.

"Yep, I'm gonna be there, just to be nosey," Eli stated with a grin. "Actually, I love hearing what these crazy people have to say on Singles Mingle night. Plus, TAV is always packed with a nice crowd."

David smiled. "Takes a Village," he said just above a whisper, which is what the TAV stood for. "It actually takes a real man to find himself and leave the street life alone while making a positive difference in the community."

David's thoughts reflected on how Abe took an old abandoned building that was once was a private school and redesigned it. He kept the original structure and turned it into a state of the art, high tech and very modern Center for the community. It turned out to be TAV, and it was an ingenious idea.

After the center's reveal three years prior, Abe had been quite busy with everybody wanting him to design their buildings or homes and some even contracted him for various construction work.

"My brother is certainly a smart man." Eli boasted since he was also very proud of Abe for changing. "He's educated and skillful in his trade. He became an architectural engineer, holding a doctorate's in building technology."

Abe smiled. "Eli, not now," he said, already figuring that Eli was about to give a rundown of his resume like David didn't already know.

"Don't act like you don't like me bragging on how you've stepped your game all the way up while specializing in urban land development. I mean, you've cut out the middleman by being the broker that seizes the land, designs the house or building, constructs it, and either sells or rents it out. Let's face it, brother. You are indeed one wealthy man, and I'm just blessed to be related to you." Eli teased with a huge kool-aid smile on his face.

"Yeah, I bet you are," Abe responded, knowing that Eli was definitely spoiled and got paid hefty checks just for being his right-hand man.

"Well, you know I'm proud of you," David cut in, just feeling good at the moment to see Abe doing so well for himself. "And, I appreciate you letting Kiera stay with you for a few months until she gets up on her feet. If Vanessa and I didn't already have our bedrooms occupied with her daughter and grandkids that we can't get rid of, then she would've been more than welcome to come there." He said.

"No problem," Abe commented. "My house is so big that I probably won't even see her and the kids." They laughed.

"No, but you're probably right." David chimed in.

"That's my brother for you. Good ol' Abe," Eli said matter-of-factly.

Abe flashed a Colgate smile, "Yeah. Good ol' me."

Eli smugly grinned, ready to joke. "What does your niece look like? Abe could use a distraction."

David laughed. "Oh no Eli, don't get no ideas. Besides Abe has that to take care of." He said, and then nodded towards the front entrance.

Abe looked over and saw Aisha casually coming through the door.

"Let the bullshit begin," Eli whispered.

Abe's eyes fixed on Aisha as she walked over to the table with a huge grin plastered on her face. "Hey Mr. Batey," she spoke.

David gave her a friendly hug. "Hey, Aisha. It's nice to see you." He said, and then looked back over in Abe and Eli's direction. "Abe, Eli...I'll talk with you two later." With that, David walked off, not wanting to hear any part of that disturbing conversation.

Aisha turned to Abe, gesturing with a raised eyebrow as if all was still good. "You're not gonna--"

"No," Abe cut her off. He pointed to the seat next to him. "Have a seat." He sternly stated. How dare she expect respect and chivalry after what she had done?

"No manners today...Okay," she mumbled under her breath as if nothing serious had happened like her being caught getting fucked by her boss. Eli shook his head with disgust as she sat down next to his brother because he knew what type of bitch she was and he didn't like it.

Aisha Davis considered herself a diva, a dime, a bad bitch. She had a high paying executive assistant job at a reputable insurance company. No crumb snatching ass kids in her life.

14

She wanted it that way for a while. She and children just didn't mesh. Even her nieces and nephews sickened her.

Aisha drove a Range, wore designer clothes and shoes, had a fat bank account, and had her own condo.

In addition to all she had to show for herself, she was also five feet seven inches of fine. Her long Beyoncé weave framed her slender face and highlighted her cat-like, green eyes. She was a slim size eight with just enough curves in the right places. She worked out on a regular basis and didn't have time for fatness. What real man would want all of that jiggly cellulite flesh in the same bed with them?

She felt that she and Abe complemented each other. She was the perfect woman for him, and she felt that he was the perfect man for her. Yes, they had flaws, but who didn't? Dr. Abe Masters had become her king, and she didn't want to lose him over a mistake she'd made. All she wanted to do was make amends and as soon as possible since he'd called off their wedding.

———

Eli stared at her. His disgust and disdain evident by his turned up lip.

Without acknowledging Eli, Aisha looked over at her ex-fiancé. "Why is he here?"

"He's always with me. He's my assistant or have you forgotten that, too? I don't know what you can remember these days since it seemed you forgot that you were also engaged." Abe said, with an unsatisfied expression on his face.

Aisha looked around, still as if all was good. "Can I get me something to eat? I'm famished."

"You hongry. Say hon-gree," Eli mocked. "Only bourgeois bitches say 'famished.' Didn't you grow up out south in the projects?"

Aisha rolled her eyes upward, showing her aggravation. It hadn't been two minutes yet, and Eli was already about to get slapped.

"You can get you something to eat, but Eli and I will be leaving," he hesitated as he looked down at his expensive watch. "In about five minutes," he said.

"Five minutes? I just got here."

"And I got a business to run. You asked to meet me, and I agreed, but within the timeframe I allowed. You decided to show up when you wanted to. Now say what it is you wanna say. Your five minutes are ticking."

Eli snickered.

Aisha grimaced. "Does he really have to be here?"

"He gon' tell me whatchu say anyway," Eli scoffed.

"Whatever," she mumbled.

"Abe tells me everything," Eli boasted. "So go head, say whatchu wanna say. Speak your heart girl."

"Abe!" Aisha called out. "Please get rid of him. I can't talk while he's around with his faggoty fairy ass," Aisha snarled.

Abe sighed with grief as the two went at each other's throats. Abe sat there patiently while they slung insults like two immature teenagers.

"You're not going to tell him to watch his mouth, Abe?" Aisha incredulously asked. "I can't believe you're allowing this foolishness. You know he doesn't like me."

"And now, no one have to wonder why," Eli stated, with a roll of his eyes.

Abe sighed and got up from his chair. He stood six feet, four inches tall. He had a solid, thick build of rippling muscles. His golden complexion contrasted with the deep black of the hair on his head and on his face. He was biracial, so he had fine textured hair that he currently wore in a neat, low even cut. His facial hair style changed often. Nowadays, it was a modest beard at his chin, a thin mustache and the hair in the dimple right under his bottom lip.

Aisha immediately regretted her decision as she watched her handsome man slip right out of her hands.

"C'mon Eli," Abe said as he walked off.

"Abe!" Aisha called as Eli got up from his seat with a pleasant smirk on his face.

"Bitch," Eli spat under his breath as he followed his brother.

Abe went up to the counter to speak with one of the food prep ladies. "Where is David?" He asked her.

"I'll go get him, Dr. Masters," the lady responded.

"I'll see you in the car," Eli said as he exited *Batey's Kuntry Kitchen*, but he had to cut his eyes back at Aisha one more time to see the cut look on her face. He enjoyed seeing the bourgeois bitch sweat.

"Okay," Abe said to Eli as David came out the back. Aisha got up from the table and began to walk over in their direction.

"Everything straight?" David asked.

Abe cut his eyes at Aisha. "As straight as it can be." He said as Aisha now stood behind him with her arms folded like she

17

still had it like that. "Anyway, I just wanted you to know that I was leaving."

David then came from around the counter to give Abe a warm-hearted hug. His short, stout body was nothing compared to Abe's height, and muscular frame as Abe towered over him. "Well, you take care and be careful, son. Love you, kid."

"I will. Love you too," Abe returned, continuing to ignore Aisha.

The *Batey's* staff bid Abe farewell as he walked out with an irate Aisha following behind him. She was determined to get his attention one way or the other.

Chapter 2

The next morning, Aisha was starting to feel the regret of what she'd done. How could she be so stupid? She risked her relationship with Abe, all for what? Michael had been after her for the entire time she had been with Abe. As a matter of fact, a lot of men had been after her ever since she hooked up with Abe. It must have been an ego thing. A man would feel pretty special if he could take Dr. Abe Masters' woman away. And to think, she catered to Michael's ego along with hers.

Aisha stared over at a sleeping Abe lying beside her. He was such a beautiful man. He was nice to her. He was just kind period. It was a privilege to even be the woman on his arm, but it was no secret that Abe had a past and a darkness that he refused to let Aisha know about. She needed to know so she could understand the reason behind his nonchalant mood swings and how he would shut her out for days and be so distant. She had to keep telling herself that his unpredictable behavior was the reason why she did what she did, but it was a weak excuse.

Aisha watched his bare chest rise and fall as he lay on his back, and then Aisha noticed the thick piece of meat outlined under the sheet that was over Abe. Aisha lifted the sheet to sneak a peek at his partially erect tool. He was thick and longer than the average on soft. Aisha had to do all she could to get back in Abe's good graces.

Abe stirred out of his sleep to the sensation of warmth and wetness on him. He looked down and saw Aisha doing what she does. For his size, Aisha was the only woman he'd encountered that could give him head properly. Maybe that was why he fell for her. She sucked his dick with superb skill. She was waking all of his senses. A moan escaped his lips as she was taking him there. He reached down to move her hair out of the way so he could watch her mouth slide up and down on his meaty dick. Within the minute, he'd erupted in her mouth. He watched her drain his snake, and then swallow like the freak she was.

Aisha smiled up at Abe. "Good Morning, baby," she spoke, hoping that the amazing blowjob she'd just given him would make him think about what they had.

"Morning," he nonchalantly spoke. "Get up here and poke it out," he ordered.

Aisha was eager to oblige. Anticipating what he was about to do, she giggled. He positioned himself behind her but didn't enter her right away.

"What are you doing?" She asked.

"I need a condom," he said, reaching under his pillow.

Aisha frowned. "A condom?"

"Ssh. You're gonna ruin the mood."

Aisha sighed with an attitude. He was making a statement with that condom move. She knew she would have to earn his trust back, but it wasn't going to happen overnight.

Once the condom was on, Abe eased inside Aisha. Her walls seemed to suck him right in just as her mouth had done. She let out a soft moan. The rhythm picked up, and he went deeper, causing her to cry out to God. This was the first time he fucked Aisha since he caught her with Michael. Her pussy was about to be punished, and he was going to try his best to fuck her up mind as well.

Aisha thought he was trying to kill her. She pulled away from his dick, but he wouldn't let her get away. "Ain't this how you like it?" He questioned, and then slapped her ass so hard it brought tears to her eyes.

"Abe!" Aisha screamed. "It hurts."

"Exactly."

Now, this was the evil, vindictive man she didn't like. Treating her like this, reminded him of how he'd been in his younger, more unruly days. He thought the shit was quite funny. He enjoyed delivering this kind of pain. He wrapped his hand around her neck and shoved her face down into the mattress as he pummeled her. Aisha was ready for it to be over. He had never treated her in this matter, but all she could think was that she hated the way he used his dick as a disciplinary tool.

Aisha was so glad when he stopped. She wanted to cuss him out, but her throat hurt from all of the screaming.

"We can't do this anymore." He said, immediately getting up.

Aisha finally moved, flipping over on her back. She looked up into Abe's discontented face. "Abe, we did this last night. Can we please move forward, baby."

"That's just it. I can't move forward. I need some space to clear my head. I said I didn't want to do this with you and I can't. I mean, I loved you, and I was willing to make you my wife, but you didn't want that."

"I did want it. I just made a mistake. I love you Abe, and you love me. I know you do."

"I do, but not like I thought I did," he said. He removed the condom as he walked in the bathroom to clean himself up.

Aisha had to admit, Abe's body was the truth. She had never been with a man with a body so sculpted to perfection. His abdomen area looked manufactured. He didn't even work out on a regular basis. It was just a genetic thing because even Eli had a nice body on him.

Aisha got out of bed to follow him into the bathroom, but her legs were too weak.

Abe looked back at her. "You okay?"

"I'm fine," she mumbled, easing back down on the bed. He pushed the bathroom door partially closed as she called out to him. "So what do you want, Abe? You wanna be free so you can see other people?"

The shower started. Abe stood at the doorway to the bathroom as he responded. "This isn't about that. I just wanna be alone to sort things out."

"But Abe, you always wanna be alone, and you never tell me what you're thinking." Her eyes wandered over his body. Even though she had seen him naked numerous times seeing his dick always amazed her.

Abe got in the shower as he ignored Aisha talking to him.

"You hear me, Abe?" She called out. "You never tell me what you're thinking." She repeated.

"I'm telling you now!" He yelled out over the shower water.

"No. You're telling me you wanna be alone so that you can think which is usually around the time you shut me out."

"We're not doing this again," Abe said as he tuned out her ridiculous plea, so he could peacefully wash off her juices since he wanted no more parts of her anymore.

Aisha let out a groan. This was the exact thing that bothered her. He would never let her in.

Abe didn't need to date anymore. At least not until he figured some things out, but then again, there was nothing wrong with making new friends.

Before he knew it, Aisha was joining him in the shower. Abe had already predicted that she'd show up.

"Abe, are we going to work through this?" Aisha asked.

"I don't know." He responded while washing over his muscular frame with the sudsy washcloth.

Aisha sighed. "We can still make this work. The wedding can still go on. The invitations can still be sent out. I have family coming from two different states." He didn't' respond. "Abe! We've already paid for everything. We can't get our money back."

Abe rinsed his washcloth, and then looked her way. "Aisha, first of all, *we* didn't pay anything. I did. I've already had Melissa cancel everything. And why hadn't you notified your family, yet?"

"Because!" She exclaimed. Realizing her frustrated tone, she lowered her voice. "Abe, I'm your wife. We're getting married in three months. We're not calling off this wedding. Do you know how fabulous this wedding will be?"

Abe shook his head with pity. Aisha was that self-centered that her psyche was oblivious to her denial. He didn't know why he even agreed to let her come over.

"Look, you need to be leaving here. David's niece and her kids are coming today or did you forget that, too?"

"I wish you'd stop with your corny ass jokes."

"I don't see anything corny about it. The only corny thing I see is a selfish ass woman who cheated on her fiancé, but won't take any kind of responsibility for fucking up nor does she seem to have a heart in sincerely wanting things to work out."

"I do want to be in this relationship. I want things to work out."

"I can't tell." He said and then got out of the shower. "You know I have to attend the Singles Mingle later, and I have other things to do prior to that."

"The Singles Mingle," Aisha said, rolling her eyes up in her head. "I'm not going tonight. I don't even know why you're attending that meeting with us going through this crazy mess."

Abe shook his head at how delusional Aisha really was. She spoke to him like he didn't catch her with another man's dick in her pussy. "Aisha, this relationship is over." He spoke sternly. "Make sure you take anything that belongs to you when you leave." With that, he walked out of the bathroom to get dressed so he could leave.

Aisha let the water run over her face to wash away the tears. Abe was definitely not falling for her bullshit. She couldn't help but think that with time, he'd get over her. It was a part of her that hated him being a woman magnet. She knew they'd be drawn to him and especially now with him being single. She thought about David's niece moving in. Was this a plot that David and Eli were setting up? Only time would tell if it was, but she wasn't going out without a fight for her man.

––––––

Kiera hoped moving to Tennessee was a good thing. When her uncle suggested she stay with a Batey family friend Kiera thought, how nice but she didn't want to impose. David insisted it wouldn't be a problem and that the friend, a Dr. Abe Masters eagerly extended the welcome to stay at his place. David and his wife Vanessa were unable to really take all three of them in being that Vanessa's daughter and her kids were already occupying their two secondary bedrooms. David never bother suggesting anyone else in the family.

Upon arrival at 1056 Magnolia Drive in the wealthy elite area of Grand Ivy Estates Kiera asked, "Is this right? This can't be the house."

Bryce looked out of the backseat passenger window. He saw two grandiose lion statues on either side of a big iron gate. "Is this a mansion Mama?"

"So this what a mansion look like in real life," his twin sister Bria said gazing out of her window.

Pulling up to push the intercom button the gates suddenly opened. Kiera moved the white Acadia forward. A driveway wound around to a majestic contemporary modern home. It was dusk, so the floor to ceiling windows allowed a view inside the home. The lights were on, and no curtains were drawn. From the outside where there was no white surface material, it was nothing but glass giving the house a very fragile appeal like it should come with the precaution: handle with care.

Now eight-year-old Bryce was awestricken and amazed. "This is not the house we're staying in! It can't be."

The house was magnificent; almost proud. Just looking at it and its different levels prepared them for the maze inside.

As Kiera pulled the car under the portico, a petite Asian lady exited the huge wooden double doors. She didn't seem too pleased; at least not by looking at her expression.

Lulu ushered them inside. "Come, come. Move car later." She gave them a quick once-over. She frowned but proceeded to lead them inside.

They stepped into a lower level white marbled floor foyer. It was like stepping into a white Emerald City. As they neared the top of the steps to the main floor, both Bryce and Bria noticed the two gongs on either side as decorative wall pieces. The mallets hung along beside them. Bryce was so tempted to bang one. Kiera shot him a look. Bryce resisted the urge.

Lulu wasted no time showing them where they would be staying. She gave them a very quick tour of the house with brief commentary. The eight-year-old twins were the most excited, to say the least. Lulu gave them all quick lessons on accesses, codes, and how to operate the different systems within the house. After she finished, she gave Kiera an envelope and retired to the pool house. Her job was done for the day.

Kiera widened her eyes, "Ooh, it feel like a card in there. Nice handwriting too."

Kiera was right. It was a credit/debit card. There was also a note. Kiera read: *Kiera and Family, Sorry I'm not there to welcome you properly however in my absence, please feel free to make my home your home. Anything you need or want Lulu will assure you get it. I'll see you soon...Abe*

Kiera wanted to look around for clues of who Abe was. Kiera went inside the glass-encased home office. The first thing that caught Kiera's eyes were the dozens of photos scattered around the room. They were photos of various people at various formal events and various casual family outings. The one person most common in the photos was the tall fair-skinned man with beautiful icy blue eyes. Things just got interesting as Kiera thought aloud, "Fyah?"

TAV, Takes A Village was an enrichment center founded by Abe and Pastor Marc Thomas. It was a not for profit organization and privately operated. It was also a community and recreational center. It was open to anyone, no membership required. Originally it was strictly for the inner-city youth, but different organizations started requesting use of it for a fee to do various things such as seminars, art exhibits, and fundraising events.

Aside from Abe being one of the area's wealthiest sexiest eligible bachelors, he was recognized as an affluent and influential member in the community. Abe was a giver. He gave and gave and gave. He was recognized for his humility and rewarded with high regards from city officials. People knew him to be mannerable, respectful and had an amiable personality especially when it came to the benevolence he bestowed upon the community. Needless to say, people loved Abe.

That evening, Abe and Eli sat in seats on a stage surrounded by an auditorium of three-thousand empty seats inside of the TAV facility. They were discussing the event for the night. Abe looked down as his personal phone started buzzing. It was a text from Aisha.

I know I messed up Abe but I'm sorry. I've looked past the things you've done so why can't you look past this with me? I'm not seeing him, I don't want him. I want you and only you. I've shown you this. I love you and I want to do all of the things you wanted. Call me...

Abe sighed. *What things? Marriage? Children?* He'd spoken to her about those things a long time ago. He pushed Aisha out of his mind and focused on the impending Singles Mingle.

"What's wrong Abe?" Eli asked with concern. "You've been kinda sad all day. You still wanna get married?"

Abe shot him a blank look.

Eli laughed.

Abe's administrative assistant Melissa, who was multitasking in the chair beside Eli was still tuned in to the conversation and asked, "You really loved her huh?"

"I did. But not like I needed to I guess. I'm not really feeling the Aisha type anymore."

"See that's because the way you look, your money, and the class of people you're associated with attract a certain type of woman. I mean that attracts any woman, but those things put you around only the women you're used to dating. You get what I'm saying? There could be a perfectly good woman working at McDonald's, but you would never know because you overlook her." Melissa reasoned.

"But that makes me seem shallow," Abe stated.

"It does. You are," Eli laughed.

"I'm not shallow Eli, and you know it," Abe said defensively.

"You are to a fault. You kinda just fall in that way of being." Melissa interjected.

"Y'all act like we don't know what being regular is. We haven't always lived like this," Abe argued.

"No we haven't but c'mon now, would you go shopping in the Dollar General?" Eli asked.

Abe didn't say anything.

Eli added, "Hell Abe you don't even shop; you send me."

"I pay you very good to do so," Abe shot back.

Abe loved his baby brother to death. Most people thought Eric Barnes was Abe's best friend, but it was really Eli. They shared all of their secrets. Ike was close with them too but since Eli was Abe's assistant they were a tad bit closer.

The thing Abe appreciated about Eli the most was that he never complained. Even if Abe was in a funky mood, and he decided to call Eli right when his head was about to meet pillow at night and requested something that was right down the street from his very own house, Eli would trudge right back out to the midnight plum Escalade in his garage and do whatever Abe asked.

Even though Abe couldn't stand his brother's cattiness sometimes, Abe wouldn't trade him for anything. A long time ago Abe held resentment for Eli and didn't have much to say to him. Eli used to think his brother hated him because he had little to say to him. One day Eli confronted Abe about it. Abe was about twenty-three and Eli was twenty-one. Eli went to Abe for money for school. As he did with all the people that meant anything to him, Abe didn't hesitate to give Eli what he needed. When Eli opened his mouth to tell Abe thanks, Abe cut him off and told him to leave. Eli was near tears because he was tired of Abe treating him that way. Eli asked, "Abe what did I do to you? Why do you hate me?"

Abe was too familiar with that cry. He was familiar with the hurt and confusion in Eli's eyes too. Eli felt the way Abe felt with their parents. He had cried that cry many times to his mother. To his father, he stopped crying to years before that. Esau would always respond by beating Abe. So Abe learned to steer clear of Esau. Abe didn't want Eli to feel that way, and he certainly didn't want to be the one to inflict that kind of emotional pain on someone. Already tormented and haunted by his past, Abe broke down before Eli and explained. "I don't hate you. It's just Daddy loves you, and he hates me. Hell, he even thinks you're gay. I don't get it. You would think he would be more disappointed about that than to hate me because I'm not biologically his."

Eli understood. From that point on their brotherly love grew. Eli began being Abe's personal assistant around that time.

Ike, their older brother, was a different story when it came to Esau. Ike didn't like Esau and Ike steered clear of Esau. Ike's respect for Esau went down the drain when he would witness Esau hurting their mama. When Ike was old enough to know better and picked up on the mind games Esau played on Sarah, he developed a profound dislike for the man known as his father. Ike knew deep down their mother didn't want to feel that way about Abe. She just went along with Esau because she was afraid to go against him. It sickened Ike to watch Abe give their parents the world just so Esau can tell Sarah that Abe was still unworthy to be loved.

Ike had asked their father, "Why do you accept his money and all the gifts then?"

Esau's reply was, "Because it's the debt that he owes us. All the money in the world can't erase the pain of his existence."

Ike stopped trying to understand Esau's logic.

The older Masters couple didn't acknowledge Abe as their son however they reaped the benefits of his wealth. There wasn't a thing that Sarah and Esau Masters wanted for. Abe retired the two of them years ago. He afforded them a nice five bedroom home, luxury cars, fine jewels for his mother, vacations...any and everything to make them happy. Yet they barely spoke to him. It was heart-wrenching at times to witness Abe begging his mother to look at him and simply say hi.

It was hard being the second child wondering why he was so different and was treated differently. He resembled Sarah which made him look like his siblings, but there was no way Abe resembled Esau. Everyone had medium brown eyes. Sarah was half Hispanic which gave her a fine texture of natural coily hair. She passed that trait to her other boys. Abe's hair was much straighter. Abe knew as a little boy he was slightly different, but it never mattered to him. He just wanted his mother and father to love him like they loved Eli and Ike.

Abe's grandmother Jolene Delgado raised him the first six years of his life in Nashville. He saw his parents and siblings during the summer and holidays when they came to visit from Jackson. Right after Sarah gave birth to Abe, Esau moved them to Jackson for a job opportunity, or so that's what they told everybody. Jolene died suddenly of a brain aneurysm when Abe was six. The only reason Sarah and Esau were willing to take him in was because of Jolene's life insurance policy and what was in her will. Abe didn't learn that until he was an adult. They returned to Nashville to Jolene house that she left to Abe. They got their money, got Abe, but that's when everything started. That was the baggage Abe carried around.

Chapter 3

In no time, as Abe, Eli and Melissa sat there going back and forth about what he should do with his life, the people started coming in. TAV's auditorium filled up quickly with single people looking for answers from the opposite sex in how to have a more successful relationship. TAV in partnership with GVBC had a mission to empower people of color. It was about the youth and young adults and knowing their worth but what good was that if solid home foundations didn't exist. The singles ministry encouraged and promoted unification of people of color. First, they wanted to pinpoint where a lot of people went wrong in relationships then concentrate on repairing the broken homes, so many troubled youth come from.

The Singles Mingle would have a panel of men and a panel of women. The single's in the audience would ask the questions, and the panel would answer. It was a way of everyone hearing what both sexes would reveal in hopes of finally realizing the answer to the most dreaded question in the world... Why were they really single?

The women's panel led the discussion with Debra Wilson immediately announcing Abe's new relationship status as single again. The women in the auditorium cheered. It made

Abe blush just a little. He modestly shook his head, knowing that the future advances from women would triple. Older women would be either flirting to get their groove back or wanting to introduce him to a niece or daughter. The younger ladies would, for sure, pretend to be something they aren't just to capture his attention.

A young lady stood up from her seat, ready to get the Singles Mingle started. "Why do men have to cheat when they can just be single and keep it real with a sista?"

Eli quickly answered from the panel. "Y'all don't want real. Y'all want lies. Lies make y'all feel better. Most of you can't deal with the real."

A noisy murmur of objection came from the women's side. "How does he know what women want?"

Eli heard her and stood up from his seat. "Oh, trust me, I know." He said.

Abe looked over at his brother and shook his head. Eli was always straightforward and didn't give a damn what anybody thought of him or of his sexuality. "Eli, maybe someone else should answer that." He leaned in with a whisper.

"They want the truth don't they?" Eli asked.

Debra grinned a little because she too knew that Eli was a handful. She then decided to counter his claim. "Well, don't you think it's fair that we're given the option to determine if we want to deal with real instead of y'all just lying from the jump?"

Applause came from the women's side. A man stepped up to the microphone on the men's side. "Y'all will act like you can deal with the real when all y'all tryna do is figure out how to change a man's perception of love. Y'all try to force what we

34

don't want on us, so then we're put in the position to lie to you."

"Nonsense," another woman stated from the panel.

"Y'all expect too much from us," a man from the audience responded.

"Asking for honesty and respect is too much, huh?" Debra asked from the panel. She had to defend the women in the audience no matter what was said.

Abe had sat silently listening for about fifteen minutes as he listened to the panel go back and forth with the audience on who's right, what's wrong, and why nobody is getting any sex. Then he stood up to address the audience with his thoughts.

"Women, I know you may not want to hear this, but from my experience; you can make a good man turn bad."

"How do you figure?" Debra immediately cut in.

"Because of your expectations for him," Abe answered.

"Oh, no he didn't," a woman said from the audience. "Since when have you been on the men side?" She pondered.

Laughter filled the air. Abe had always been the antagonist for the men side. He always set the men straight and advised them of their errors. For him to agree with the men was a shock.

"I'm just saying that if we are honest and we tell you that we don't want a serious relationship or that we don't want to be tied down, but after a few rounds in the hay or a few romantic dinners, you will later think that our feelings have changed. However, you knew what it was from the time it started because we told you." He said, shaking his head. "Now you've gotten caught up in your feelings because we've not met your expectations."

"Sadly, to those women, most men then become the dogs," Eli whispered with a slight roll of the eyes.

A woman quickly stood up from her seat ready to ask the million dollar question. "So what happened with you and Aisha?" Everybody was dying to know what had happened since word had gotten around that the wedding was canceled.

"I'm not here to discuss that. Besides, Aisha is not here to give her point of view on that matter, but I will say this... I'm not perfect nor is she. It was just one of those things that weren't meant to be."

"Thank God for that," a random woman sitting in the audience shouted. It was followed by laughter, and then another said.

"I know that's right!"

The two sides went back, and forward debating different topics common in relationships from jump offs to finances and stepchildren. By then a line had formed on either side to speak. Of course, there were more women than men. Most of the women questions were the same. Abe assumed they kept asking until they heard what they wanted to hear. He pointed that out, too.

"Hearing all of these same questions, however, worded differently takes me back to what my brother said earlier. It's many of you that don't want to accept the truth for what it is. Since you don't agree with certain answers to questions that have already been asked, you keep asking, hoping the answer will change."

For the first time in a TAV Singles Mingle discussion, Abe got booed. The women were certain the difference in his state of mind was because of his break up with Aisha.

"My question has nothing to do with that I can assure you. I understand the truth when it's given to me. One thing I've learned is that I can't change people, but I can change me. If things are not to my liking, I will definitely remove myself from the situation. I've had to adopt that way of thinking, not just with how I relate to men, but with how I relate to anyone. Now my question is why do men have this high standard that women have to meet? Why does every woman have to be a dime? Why not a nickel? These men be asking for so much, but they don't fit the bill themselves. Some of them have big guts and small Vienna's in their pants. I mean what's up with that?"

The women roared with laughter. The statement made Abe smile and even laugh a little. But when he focused in on the young lady at the microphone, it was shocking to see that she was everything that those high standard setting men wanted. Her beauty was beyond what words could describe.

"Good question," Abe responded as he walked back and forth on the panel stage, now with the microphone in his hand. "Let me think for a moment." The woman smiled, but all Abe wanted to think about was getting to know her better.

He loved her short black hair that swirled in messy loose curls and how it hugged her perfectly shaped head and framed her heart-shaped face. She had a funny complexion that he couldn't describe as light or dark. It was more of a honey almond, almost golden copper color. She had big round, medium brown eyes that had an exaggerated slant like the beloved animated Bambi. She had cherubic cheeks when she smiled, a straight, slender nose, and full lips that reminded Abe of the actress, Kerry Washington.

The woman stood about five-five with a medium curvy frame. She was wearing a sleeveless, sheer lavender blouse with a big floppy tie at the neck. Underneath it, she wore an ivory cami to match the ivory wide leg pants that hugged every curve of her lower half. Although he couldn't see her from the back, he was sure she had a nice size ass because he could see it from the front. She had a very natural simple beauty that Abe seldom encountered with most women within his circle. From the noises made by some of the men on the panel and coming from the men side, Abe knew he wasn't the only one that found this woman very attractive. For Abe, there was something else about her that he couldn't quite put his finger on.

Eli looked out in the audience and smiled upon seeing the woman. "Someone has finally gotten my brother stumped, huh?" The audience laughed. Abe grinned at Eli's comment, but more so, at how the woman stood patiently, waiting for his answer with a bright smile spread across her face.

"One second, little brother," Abe responded.

"I have all night," the woman spoke, still smiling. Abe was impressed with her confident posture as she stood about five-five with a medium curvy frame. She had a very natural, simple beauty that Abe seldom encountered with most women within his circle.

"Where have you been all my life?" One of the men spoke from the audience, admiring the woman's beauty and wit. "I'll be whatever you need me to be, and I don't have a big gut or a Vienna." The panel and audience laughed. "If you saw me on the streets and I wanted to holla at you would you give me a chance?" He said, looking down at his dirty construction work attire that he should've changed before he came there.

A man at the microphone said, "So are you saying that because your expectations of a man should be a dime too because you don't look like that type that would want anything less."

She said, "No I'm saying that because y'all need to lower your standards and look for somebody that's just like you. Stop shopping around for women out of your league and take a chance with that average woman who may not be able to get her hair weaved up every week or fake lashes or tight designer jeans because she struggling and doing things on her own like raising kids that one of y'all abandon."

Applause followed her statement.

The man said, "So are you the spokeswoman for the average woman. If you are, then I'll take average any day."

"I expected that. I'm not the average and won't pretend that I am. My thought process is different from most women walking around with low self-esteem and no confidence. Esteem and confidence that's been ripped from them from the cruelty of our black men. I have more than the average and won't make an excuse for it. I will not lower myself to be a spokesperson. Instead, I want to uplift them. Encourage them that they don't have to take no mess from hot dog head, Vienna packing beach ball belly men!"

Abe was tickled. He liked this girl's spunk. Besides she was definitely nice to look at.

Another man asked, "Miss Lady, just to see where you coming from would you give a man like me a chance or would you overlook me to pick one of them up there?" He pointed to the panel.

Here we go, Abe thought. He couldn't help what he looked like, but most men always brought up his looks stating women went for his type right away and wouldn't give them the time of day.

The woman smiled, almost with a smirk. "Well, I can't see you, to be honest." The audience started to whisper. "By definition, I'm legally blind. I don't see a man for what he is by sight. I see him for what he is by heart. That is all." She reached out for the woman standing off to the side of her as she looped her arm through hers, but before they could walk off from the microphone, Abe spoke up.

"Hey, what's your name?"

The woman turned back to the microphone. "Lovely," she answered. "And, it was nice to have come here. I've enjoyed the discussion."

Abe was definitely intrigued because he never realized that she was visually impaired nor did he realize that she had a nice plump ass until she turned to leave. He smiled, but said no more, allowing Debra to close out the meeting as he sat back down next to Eli. He looked down at his personal phone as an incoming text message came through.

She's here. Lulu

Eli looked over at Abe and smiled. "Seems Ms. Lovely caught your attention," he said.

"She did," Abe smiled back. "It seems that David's niece has made it to the house, too." He informed him.

Eli chuckled. "And just that quickly, two women enter the picture as the other bitch is being tossed out. Things are looking up for you already, big Bro."

Lovely was a great person, friend, and mother. She tried to overcome the adversaries life had thrown at her. Most of it was tied to a night twelve years ago. She didn't like to even think about the events of that near-fatal night for her. She lost her parents, her dignity, and her normal sight.

One thing that was never cleared about that night was how she got to the hospital while her parents bodies burned in the fire that burned the house completely down. Lovely should have burned too, but her body was found outside of the house with a hole in her head. They assumed she made it outside before collapsing in the driveway.

Unsure of her safety it was neither confirmed nor denied that there had been any survivors because clearly, it was a homicide and intent. The authorities didn't want the murderers to know she had survived and would come after her to finish the job. Luciano, her godfather, showed up and insisted Lovely go to live with her mother's people in Alabama. That's what she did. Luciano was the only person she communicated with.

After what happened Lovely survived with some brain injury and memory loss. The memory came back gradually although some things were still a bit fuzzy and there were gaps of time completely missing. The bullet crashed into the back of her head but then decided to wrap around to the right at an angle and exit her right cheek. It was a true miracle. The doctors said if a high-velocity weapon had been used Lovely would not have survived. The doctors were amazed that the bullet even exited. Normally it would have stayed inside and left a path of destruction along the brain.

If she pulled through the doctor's main concern was how much damage Lovely's brain suffered. She had been induced in a comatose state while her brain recovered. They patched up the back of her skull with a plate where it fractured. Her cheek had been repaired and was left with a scar. She passed every test except her vision. Lovely can remember trying to blink over and over, harder and harder to bring everything in focus. The reality was that would be the way she saw everything for the remainder of her life. She had cortical blindness. Her pupils dilated with light perception; therefore, it wasn't damage done to her eyes and how they function, but more so to the cortical vortex of the brain where the damage took place. It controlled how images were perceived by the brain.

It wasn't until Lovely was in Alabama with Aunt Livy that she noticed she hadn't gotten her period. Alarmed, Lovely told Aunt Livy. During this time Lovely was unable to recall what took place that night of the invasion. She wasn't sexually active. Lovely barely went outdoors. She was insecure and still afraid. Her face was still messed up, and the back of her head was shaven with scars.

After a doctor's visit, it was confirmed Lovely was pregnant. No one was more devastated than Lovely. She couldn't even remember how it could have happened. She didn't want to remember. But that was the only explanation. She had been raped. Lovely was frightened of the idea of having an abortion. Livy suggested adoption.

When Lovely gave birth to her baby, she was confused. She wasn't sure if giving her baby girl away was the right thing.

Aunt Livy told her to really think about it all the while she was raving and fussing over how beautiful the baby was. The baby's cries warmed Lovely's heart. Seeing the weariness in Lovely's face, Aunt Livy said, "Things happen to us for a reason. Sometimes it's just not for us to know why they just do. If you're considering keeping her accept what happened to you and move on from it for the sake of your child. Once you're okay with that, find peace with the decision you've made and look for the joy in it. She don't have to ever know how she got here. Loving her will erase the wrong that was done to you. Shoot it was only by the grace of God that both of you even survived."

Lovely kept her and named her Grace because of what Livy said. She never regretted her decision. Grace thought her father was a young boy that Lovely was "fast" with when she was a teenager. When she moved to Alabama, Lovely lost track of him. Grace accepted that explanation but said that she would look for him one day. Knowing Grace, that meant she was dead serious about it too.

Lovely thanked God every day for Grace. If it were not for her, Lovely would forget to enjoy life. Grace helped Lovely to live and look for the positive in everyday life. It was Grace that gave her the sense of humor that allowed her to get up before all of those people and talk crazy.

During the mingling time, several men had come up to her trying to show their interest. She gave them each a little attention as not to be rude.

"You know, it's some really nice looking men here Love," Robin said. She was Lovely's close friend and acted as an assistant/caregiver.

"I'm sure it is," Lovely said. "I want some more of those boneless wings though."

"You want me to get them for you," Robin asked.

"No, cause I don't want to be left by myself," Lovely snickered.

Robin looked around and grinned. She said to Lovely, "How about I get someone to stand right here with you, and I'll be right back with those wings."

"No. I don't trust these people," Lovely whispered.

"Oh, girl hush. Do you want the wings or not?"

"Get someone else to get them for us," Lovely suggested.

"You're gonna come off as pretentious. Ain't nobody tryna wait on you but me. And that's cause you pay me."

"Keep on I'll just get them myself."

Robin laughed. "I wanna see that."

"You ain't said nothing," Lovely said matter of factly. "Watch me. Now if I look like an idiot, you gotta come rescue me."

"Nope smart ass. Go on and get your own wings. The table is straight ahead."

Lovely started for the table hoping no one tried to stop her to talk. It would ruin her concentration. Lovely had light perception, she could see color and shape. Her impairment was the inability to make out details. She could look at someone and follow them during a conversation, but she couldn't give a description of what they truly looked like although she could get a general idea from shape and feel.

When she got to the table, she realized she made a mistake. There was different selections, and they all looked alike to her. She wanted the boneless honey barbecue wings. She looked over to the left where a group of people were talking. She said, "Excuse me." She could make out Robin laughing in the background, and it tickled her.

"You need some help?"

Lovely recognized the voice as one of the men from the panel. He sounded nice enough, and she felt like she could trust her food selection with him. "Yeah. I want the honey barbecue boneless wings, but all of this look the same to me. My friend sent me out on my own. She's not a very good friend now is she?"

"No, she isn't," he said. He proceeded to fix her a plate of everything she desired. He handed it to her. "You need anything else?"

"No, I'm fine. Thank you…uhm…?"

"Abe."

"You were on the panel getting booed weren't you?" She smiled up at him.

"Yeah. Lovely isn't it?"

"Yeah and please don't say anything cheesy like 'indeed you are.' That works my nerves."

"Okay. I won't. Are you from around here? I've never seen you before."

"No, I'm not Abe. Wait before I go into that do you know half the men in this place has asked me that question. Ask me something else."

Abe gave it some thought. He asked, "What makes you smile?"

Lovely smiled big. "That question makes me smile. Also my daughter Grace. She's a very goofy gal...Let's see. When the sun wakes and rise. When I wake and rise. When I can put a smile on someone else's face."

"You know what you could do to put a smile on my face right now?" he asked. He thought he'd try his luck. Lovely was different, and her beauty despite the scar was doing something to him.

"What?"

"If you would say yes to me asking you to join me tomorrow."

"Good one. I like that. Very direct and straight to the point...Well if I say no that won't result in a smile huh? So I guess I accept. Now take me to Robin so she can get your number for me."

Chapter 4

The next day, Kiera was up at the crack of dawn as always. It was early Saturday morning, and Lulu was assuring the order of the house. She helped Kiera in the kitchen by having her sit down so she could toast Kiera's bagel, and then she poured her orange juice. Kiera was surprised that Lulu allowed her to spread her bagel with honey nut flavored cream cheese by herself.

The sound of heels against the hardwood flooring made Kiera turn around.

"Good morning Lulu," Aisha said brightly as she stepped into the kitchen. She then looked over at Kiera. "I don't know who you are, but I'm Aisha, the woman of the house."

Lulu scoffed, rolling her eyes.

Kiera smiled, "Oh yeah? I'm Kiera. It's nice to meet you, Aisha."

Where she come from? Kiera wondered, because to her understanding Abe was single. Kiera grinned inwardly. Aisha was a nice looking woman, she thought.

"Lulu, I need some coffee," Aisha ordered.

Lulu turned up her nose. "Get it yourself."

Aisha chuckled as if she was clueless about Abe calling off the wedding. "Now Lulu, what does Abe pay you for?"

"I'm Abe housekeeper. Not your maid," Lulu said, unmoved by Aisha's behavior.

"Same difference," Aisha said like that meant something to Lulu. "Besides, when we get married, you will be both our housekeeper."

"He no marry you!" Lulu exclaimed angrily. "He said, he no marry you! So happy he no marry you."

Kiera stifled her giggles by covering her mouth.

"What are you hollering about, Lulu?" Abe asked as he entered the kitchen. His cologne, *The One,* by Dolce and Gabbana could be smelled instantly from his presence.

"You heard her, right?" Aisha said with a frown on her face. "I told you, baby, Lulu be getting besides herself."

Abe looked at Aisha like she was crazy. "What are you doing here? Who let you in?"

"I have keys," she said, jiggling them in her hand. "I had extras, remember?"

Abe looked at her sideways then cautiously grabbed the keys out of her hand.

"Not anymore," he said, causing Kiera to laugh under her breath.

"You no marry her, right?" Lulu desperately asked Abe.

"Lulu, don't worry about her," Abe said dismissively. "I don't know what her problem is, but she better get it together." He had noticed Kiera sitting there, but Aisha being there had completely thrown him off. He quickly cleared his unpleasant

48

thoughts, and then stepped over to Kiera, reaching his hand out. "Good morning. I'm Abe, and you gotta be David's niece, or I'll be wondering what the hell you're doing here, too." Lulu grinned, showing that she had a sense of humor as Abe stared at Kiera like he knew her.

Dear God, Kiera thought as she exhaled in her mind. *This man has done nothing but gotten finer since the last time I saw him.* She smiled at him, thinking that the photos did him no justice compared to seeing him in the flesh. His presence was almost still intimidating, except he looked gentler and not at all ruthless. He stood there like a big oak tree waiting for someone to climb him. His body was delectable as she stared.

My sister must've been foolish to let this nigga get away. She thought as it seemed that time had stood still for a moment, and then finally, she reached out her hand. "Dr. Abe Masters." She politely dragged out then smiled again.

Abe's eyes widened as he stared at Kiera with a sideways look. "Keke," he said.

"The one and only," she said, jumping up off of the stool and hugging him around the neck. Lulu smiled as Aisha looked at them with menacing eyes. Kiera stepped back and looked him up and down. He was a walking, mixed message, through and through. The low haircut and corporate suits he wore in the photos were conservative and professional. The tatted sleeve hidden by his shirt, on his left arm, spoke bad boy and hardcore thug, and then his tantalizing eyes screamed, pretty boy. "Hey, Dr. Masters."

"This was unexpected." He said, scratching his head.

"I didn't know you were a doctor. I damn sho didn't know your name was Abe. What kinda corny shit is that?" She asked, only knowing him by his street name.

Abe snickered. "Same ol' Keke."

Aisha looked displeased. "Oh, so you know her?"

"Yeah. We go way back. I used to date her sister, Kenya, about nine years ago." He said, causing Aisha to really turn up her nose. "But wait, if Kenya is your sister, then how is David your uncle? That seems like something I would've known."

"Kenya and I have the same daddy, so she never knew David," Kiera informed him. "However, David is married to my mama's sister, and he has always been good to us. He's like the mentor and uncle I never had. Back when Kenya and I met you, we were both staying with--"

Abe cut in. "Y'all's grandma, with her shit talking ass," he said with a light chuckle. "Oh, my bad, I'm sorry to hear that she passed away."

Kiera grinned. "Thanks, but that was six years ago." She said, really liking this new guy that was standing in front of her.

Aisha frowned at how close Abe stood next to Kiera.

"You have a really nice home. I never thought you would've turned out like this. I knew that you were doing your thing on the streets, but to turn it all around to this," she said, looking around the immaculate home. She asked, "Where are your brothers?"

Before Abe could answer, Aisha rudely invaded the space between he and Kiera.

"How long will you be here?" Aisha interjected. She didn't care for Kiera already. Not only was Kiera's sister once fucking her man, but she knew a part of Abe's past that she didn't know. She looped her arm through Abe's to pull him away. "I don't care for other women being around my man. It's bad enough Lulu gotta be here."

Abe didn't budge. "Aisha, are you kidding me right now? What the fuck are you thinking about? I said we're over. What part of that don't you understand?"

"We need to talk." She said firmly.

"We've talked," Abe said.

"Please, hear me out, and I'll go," she whispered, cutting her eyes back at Kiera. She hated that another woman knew about Abe, now being a single man. It was bad enough that Lulu probably was in on what happened between them. "Please," she said again, tugging on his arm.

"Come with me," Abe said and then looked back at Kiera. "I'll be back."

When they got to the gathering room, Aisha asked, "How long will she be here? I don't know if I want to see her every morning?"

Abe looked at Aisha as if she had lost her mind. "You don't live here, and Kiera and her family are welcome to stay as long as they need to."

"No!" she responded like a spoil brat.

"Have you been put on medication, yet?" He asked in a serious tone. "Because you need it."

"Abe, this is not funny."

"I know. The mental issues you have aren't either. If you need me to, I will accompany you to see a therapist."

Aisha smiled. Abe always had a playful side that she loved as she gently hit his arm. "I'm not playing."

"I'm not either," he said, thinking that she was cute when she'd pout.

Eli walked in. He cut his eyes at them and then turned his nose up at Aisha. He didn't even bother speaking as he headed straight to the kitchen.

Abe turned back to a glaring Aisha. "I'll talk to you later. I need to be leaving in a minute."

"Abe, I need to know where we stand."

"The same place we were last night and last week. I'll see you later."

"Maybe we can do lunch," Aisha said in an upbeat tone.

"Maybe." Anything just to get her out.

Aisha raised on her toes to give him a peck on the lips. "Love you, baby."

"I hear you," he said. He did love her, but he couldn't see himself being with her anymore.

———

Eli walked into the kitchen seeing Lulu in the kitchen doing what she did best. He didn't see Kiera right away until she turned to face him. He looked her over as she eased up off of the bar stool.

She was in a pink velour short-short strapless romper giving off a Megan Good look all day long. Same hairstyle with it combed over to one side and bangs falling flirtatiously in her eyes. She wore a seductive smile as she gazed up at Eli. "Hey."

Eli was speechless. Never in a million years would he expect to see her in his brother's house.

"Keke?"

"It's me, baby," she grinned.

Eli wrestled in his head if he should give her a hug or not. She was sneaky and wicked, so he thought it was best if he stayed away from her. "So you're David's niece?"

Kiera nodded. "Small world, huh?"

"Indeed it is," Eli said, turning his attention to the food Lulu had prepared.

Abe returned to the kitchen as Kiera walked towards him with her arm outstretched to give him something. "Uhm... I wanted to give this back to you."

Abe saw it was the debit card he left with them. "Did you use it?" He didn't bother taking it from her.

"No, but I appreciate the gesture," Kiera said.

"Keep it," Abe said, gently pushing her hand down.

"We don't need it. We're fine. Besides you're doing enough just by letting us stay here."

"Keep it," he repeated.

"We really--"

"Kiera," Eli interrupted. "Keep the shit. From the looks of that tacky shit you wearing you could use it." He then looked beside him at his brother. "Abe how come you didn't warn me?"

Looking at Kiera's lips, Eli could see a little orange juice residue right along her lip line. If he could kiss her, he would lick it right off. He wondered if her lips were as soft as they looked. How would they feel against his skin? And why was he thinking like that? He hated this girl!

Kiera arrogantly smirked. "Still catty I see."

Snapping out of his daze, Eli miserably shook his head. "I'll be catty." He said, causing Abe to laugh. "But Keke...do me a favor and stay away from me."

"Eli, get over yourself. It ain't that serious," Kiera laughed as she walked out of the kitchen.

"When it comes to me, it's always that serious. Or have you forgotten?" Eli called out, going after her.

Turning around before she disappeared around the corner Kiera grinned wickedly. "Oh trust me. I remember all the hot, spontaneous things we've done. I know you remember when I was riding you and GOOD LAWD," she said, thinking about his long thick dick.

Abe looked over at Lulu whose mouth was hung open in shock as he laughed. "Yes, Lulu you heard right."

"She not right type. She ghetto," Lulu commented.

Abe continued to laugh.

Eli went behind Kiera to have a few words, but she cut him off and started. "What are you doing?"

"What's up with you? Why are you even here?" he asked.

"I needed to get away from Georgia. Besides my granny's house burned down and I had nowhere else to go," Kiera explained. She admired the way his eyebrows were always perfect like he'd gotten them cleaned up. All of his facial hair

54

seemed painted on against his dark caramel complexion. Besides Abe and their oldest brother, Eli was one of the most beautiful men Kiera had ever seen. His light brown eyes and pretty looks were the reasons Kiera fell for him nine years prior, and the fact he had been so challenging enticed Kiera even more.

Like everyone else, Kiera was unsure of Eli's sexual orientation. He could fuck like no other, but he didn't seem the least bit interested in her at times. However, she had been so attracted to him that it didn't matter. Gay, bi-sexual or whatever, Kiera wanted Eli. He had been hesitant at first.

Kiera stared at him, thinking about that night they'd gotten drunk after Kenya and Abe had left them alone. The truth was that being with him was the best experience she'd had thus far. She hadn't quite met another since.

Kiera looked up at her daughter, Bria, as she skipped towards them coming from the upstairs bedrooms. "Hey, Mama. Can I get something to eat?"

Eli stared at the little girl in complete shock. Bria looked back at him, batting her big light brown eyes.

Kiera looked at Eli, waiting for his reaction. This had to be the most awkward situation ever because she never mentioned that she had a kid. If God had a plan, he was definitely working it out at that moment as Eli continued to stare at Bria. The obvious didn't have to be spoken, but Kiera knew how dramatic Eli could be. Kiera looked at Bria. "Sure, Lulu got something already prepared. Is your brother up, too?"

"He's coming," Bria said as Bryce made his way downstairs.

"Okay, y'all both go in there and get something to eat," Kiera said. Bryce walked up to her to give her a hug.

Eli stared at the look-a-likes. "Twins?"

Kiera nodded.

"You're not going to introduce me?" He asked, feeling mushy inside.

Kiera sighed but knew that their meeting up this way had to be fate. "Bria, Bryce...come here real quick."

The two kids walked back to where Kiera and Eli stood in between the great room and the foyer. "I want y'all to meet Eli. He's an old friend of mine, and he's Abe's younger brother. Eli, these are my babies Bria and Bryce."

Bria shyly smiled. Bryce just blankly looked at Eli.

"It's nice to meet both of you." He spoke.

She smiled at her children, "Y'all can go on now."

After they left, Eli frowned while looking at Kiera. "So what's that about, Kiera?"

"Nothing Eli," Kiera answered as she began to walk off.

Eli grabbed her by her arm. "Kiera, I didn't know you'd had kids."

Kiera stared at Eli's clean-cut fingernails as he gripped her arm. "Can you let me go?"

"I'm 'bout ready to choke you."

"No, you ain't, either."

"How old are they?" he asked.

"Damn, why you asking all these questions?" Kiera said playfully. She walked off. "I gotta make a phone call to their daddy and let him know we straight."

"Their daddy, huh?" He said, feeling like Kiera had definitely kept a huge a secret from him. "How old are they?" He called out.

Kiera shrugged him off and went to her bedroom. Just as she was afraid of; she knew Eli would suspect the twins were his as soon as he saw them. His suspicions were probably right, but as far as Kiera was concerned, the twins had a father already. It wasn't Eli.

An hour later, Eli drove in a discombobulated state. Nine years, Kiera had been gone. Nine years had passed, and he hadn't heard a peep out of her the entire time. It was weird that she ended up being this niece David spoke of and ended up in Abe's house. Maybe that was a sign, but a sign for what since she claimed that the kids had a father.

"Are you okay over there?" Abe asked from the passenger seat.

Eli mumbled something inaudible.

"Is seeing Kiera upsetting you?"

"Yes it is," Eli said. "I can't believe that bitch is in your house. Put her out, Abe."

"I can't just put her out Eli," Abe chuckled. "But what I will do is probably put her in one of the company's rental properties."

"Good," Eli huffed. He pulled the SUV into TAV's parking lot and into a reserved parking space. Today was the day of

TAV's annual Family Day Fun Racer. It was a fundraiser for the center in which the kids participated in a pretend derby using Go Karts. With a monetary contribution, any business could advertise on the side of the karts. Then the races themselves were wagered on by those in attendance.

Eli and Abe met their circle of friends on the tracks where tons of TAV's families and friends were gathering in the bleachers. The young drivers were getting prepared and coached.

"This is a better turn out than last year," Eli commented.

"That's because it's fun," Melissa said. "And everybody heard the good time we had last year."

"Is Mekhi racing?" Abe asked Melissa.

Melissa gave Abe serious side eye and a twist of her lips. "Now you know my son is scary."

Turning to Eli, Abe asked, "Did you tell Kiera to come out and bring the kids? It slipped my mind."

"I'm sure that Lulu has informed her." Eli dryly said. "Did you know that her twins are eight years old?"

"Nah, I didn't ask. Why is that important?" Abe asked as he thought a little. "You don't think--"

"I don't know what to think with that crazy girl. She said that they have a father, but who knows.

"Now that's crazy for real, if you ask me." Abe said as he searched his surroundings as if he was looking for someone. "And there she is," he said with a kool-aid smile on his face.

Watching his brother walk away, Eli said to Melissa, "Did you know that Kenya's sister was the one David asked Abe to take in?"

58

"Who? Karen?" Melissa asked, eagerly wanting to know.

"No; Kiera."

Melissa was a little confused until it hit her. "Get outta here!"

"Yep," Eli nodded slowly. "I seen her today."

"Well, what happened?" Melissa asked fully aware of Eli's past with Kiera.

"Did you know she had a set of eight-year-old twins?"

"I think I heard something about it but it never dawned on me that you would want to know. I mean...the thought never crossed my mind."

Eli shrugged carelessly, "I guess it don't matter."

But it did matter. A man should have a right to know if he fathered children or not. And Eli wanted answers.

Chapter 5

Abe was delighted when he saw that Lovely and her best friend Robin had actually made it to the event. He saw them when they first came out of the building. Before they could take a seat on the crowded bleachers, he quickly walked over and greeted them.

"I'm so glad you showed up. I was getting worried for a minute there," Abe said.

"If it's for the kids I'll be here," Lovely said.

Abe noticed the young girl beside Robin as he reached out for a handshake. "Hey pretty girl," he said with a nice smile.

"Oh Grace, this is Dr. Abe Masters. He's our new friend." Robin stated as Lovely stood there with a smile.

Grace waved. "Hi," she spoke.

"Drop the formalities. You can call me Abe," he said to her with a smile on his face. He looked toward the separate seating area. "You ladies come with me so I can introduce you to a few others that you didn't meet last night."

Abe introduced them to his close circle of friends and family. When Eli looked at both Robin and Lovely something tingled inside him. Learning that Lovely was Abe's romantic prospect, Eli focused on Robin. She had fair skin with vibrant copper, colored hair pulled into a ponytail bun. She had full deep rose-colored lips and when she smiled she had deep dimples on either side. She wasn't a skinny woman, either. She was cornbread fed with thick thighs, wide hips, and a fat ass. Her demeanor and bashfulness was alluring to Eli. He thought she was beautiful.

Robin noticed the way Eli was looking at her. She thought he was rather handsome. When Abe introduced Eli as his younger brother it wasn't hard to believe. They resembled a lot except Abe's skin was lighter and he had blue eyes. She threw a smile Eli's way to let him know she was open to advances. He smiled with a slight nod, but that was about it.

When a deep pecan complexion young male with a neat fresh fade came over and sat down beside Eli Robin frowned. Eli only looked at the man and nodded as a way of speaking, but looked away. Robin sighed unsure of what Eli had going on. Was he straight, bisexual, or gay?

Humph, Robin thought. *Oh well, if he doesn't say anything then I'm not either.*

Lovely looked over at Abe. "Which one am I supposed to be rooting for?"

"The orange and blue one," Abe answered.

Lovely was drunken with his scent as he leaned in to talk to her. She looked at him. "You smell good."

Abe smiled. "Thanks."

Lovely smiled as she turned to focus back on the race. Lovely had been taken by Abe since he had asked her name at the Singles Mingles. After Robin described what he looked like, Lovely could only imagine how dreamy he was. He was really pleasant, attentive and the way he spoke was very soothing. She could tell he was very family oriented and friendly from the way he interacted with those around him and anybody that came up to him.

After sitting there for about twenty minutes watching Abe as he interacted with the people that walked up. They either wanted to talk business or just wanted to talk. Once the coast was clear she thought she'd try to squeeze in some talk time with him herself.

"So Mr. Abe Masters," she said, holding her hand in a fist with it up to his mouth like she was holding a microphone. "What's was the reason behind you opening up a place like this? I mean, what is TAV all about?"

Abe smiled, admiring the sweet, attractive tone in her voice, then said. "Well, I don't want any kid to go through what I did as a kid. I was a troubled youth, dropped out of school, and was trouble in the streets. Fortunately for me, I had people surrounding me that were persistent and never gave up on pushing me in the right direction. Shout out to David Batey of *Batey's Kuntry Kitchen*. What up dawg!"

Lovely laughed at his silliness. She got back into interview mode. "So how do you hope to impact these young people's lives?"

Abe continued like he was having a real interview with a beautiful host. "By providing them an environment in which they could turn to other than the streets or for the ones that's lacking in their home environment. Some parents just don't have the time or they just don't care. TAV is a handful of us successful members within the community trying to show these kids a little love, alternate paths, and hope. We have aftercare tutoring, computer labs and recreational activities...the kids love it at TAV."

Lovely put away her pretend microphone. "You seem to be this great guy."

Abe shrugged, "Some people tend to think that. I don't believe I'm that great. I'm just giving back since I can."

"Really?"

"Really. I'm simply doing my part."

"Hence, Takes A Village. I like that," Lovely smiled.

"You have a really pretty smile," Abe commented staring at her mouth.

"Thanks. Let's just pretend that I can see when I say so do you," Lovely said.

"So are we still on for tonight?" he asked, remembering he'd asked her out earlier.

"Of course we are," she smiled.

Lovely could feel the chemistry they shared. She could only hope that it continued unlike some of her other failed relationship attempts in the past. It was something about Abe that made her feel secure, both physically and personally.

————

Robin helped Lovely get ready for her date. Lovely was going with a simple cap-sleeved A-line dress that conformed to her figure and fell right above her knees. It was navy and she wore a denim cropped jacket with it. It was the middle of September and although it wasn't cold during the day, it had started to cool at night. On her feet she wore nude ankle strapped platform wedges.

Lovely looked at her image in the mirror one last time. "I'm nervous."

"Why? You look great and you're a sweet girl. What's to be nervous about?"

Lovely turned to Robin with a serious look on her face. "What if I fall or something?" she asked.

Robin burst into laughter. "Shut up Lovely! You know good and damn well you ain't falling. A big strong man like Abe won't let you fall anyway."

"I don't know. There's a first for everything," Lovely giggled nervously. Her face went blank. "Oh Robin what if I do? I'll never be able to look that man in the eyes!"

Robin was really laughing. Just like Lovely to poke fun at herself. As long as Robin had known Lovely, she had always been a fun loving, easy spirited person. Of course Abe would like Lovely. Robin felt a little jealous, but she was happy for Lovely nonetheless. Robin knew Lovely's story and knew that Lovely hadn't always been so lucky in love. It seemed like Abe and Lovely could use someone like the other in their lives.

Robin's phone rang out, *Ayy Ladies*, by Travis Porter. She did a little dance to it as she answered it. "Hello?"

"I need to see you," the smooth sexy voice on the other end spoke.

A smile crept across Robin's face. "Where and when? I'll be there."

"I'll text you in about thirty minutes."

"Okay. See ya in a few," Robin said seductively. She ended the call. She looked at Lovely with a grin. "Well you're not the only one that's gonna be having fun tonight."

Lovely gave Robin an unsympathetic look. "Really Robin? What have I told you about that married man? There's plenty of single men out there that would love to get with you."

"Single? Show me a true single man and I'll date him. Men always got a hoe on their arm. They just say they ain't tied down to just one but that don't make em single."

"I didn't say alone. Single is declaring exactly what you said. You have the freedom to see and date who you want to. A lot of guys aren't honest about it and lead women on to believe they're dating them exclusively. But when you find out the truth, separate yourself from the asshole."

"It's easier said than done, Lovely. Everybody ain't Miss Little Perfect like you."

Lovely chuckled taking Robin's words lightly. "I'm not perfect. I'm blind, remember?" Robin chuckled lightly. "But, I'm not willing to be a man's second choice. If I can't have access to you the same as you have to me then it won't work."

Robin wished she had something negative to point out about Abe, but truth was she couldn't think of one thing. Why would she want to hurt Lovely anyway when Lovely was being truthful. Robin just wasn't in the mood to hear it. She needed to get to her lover. "Well one day you might find yourself in a compromising position and doing what's morally right might be the hardest thing to do. There's such a thing as love, Lovely. You of all people should know about that. After all, your name says it all."

Lovely playfully threw one of the plastic cups they had been drinking out of at Robin. "As soon as the red flag shows up I'm out. But Robin, I definitely understand your perspective."

"I hope Abe is everything he portrays himself to be; if not I feel sorry for him. He's already had one heartbreak and you're about to give him another one."

"Surely he isn't expecting the presence of love tonight." She said now twirling through her hair. "And, I'm not in the business of breaking hearts but it goes back to what the conversation was about last night. Expectations."

There was a knock on the door. "Mama?"

Robin opened the door. "What you want lady?"

Grace said playfully, "I said *mama* not donkey."

Robin tugged Grace's ponytail making her head snap back. Grace grabbed her neck pretending to be in pain. "Mama! She gonna give me whiplash!"

Lovely asked, "What do you need Grace?"

"I wanna call Uncle Ceez and Papa Lu," Grace said.

"You're homesick baby?"

"A little," Grace answered, plopping down on Lovely's bed.

Robin gave Grace and incredulous look. "Homesick! You see this house you're living in? This house is like Disney World girl."

Lovely grinned. Her newly acquired property, 5108 Lotus Drive was her first huge investment. She got the house at a good price as it was in the process of being foreclosed on prior to her buying it. She purchased the house with cash as is and helped out the previous owners tremendously. Her god-uncle Cesar Pavoni, who had been pushing her to invest in something that displayed her wealth, had come in from Texas to help her purchase the house.

The house wasn't just three levels; it was actually four. There was a complete apartment suite with two bedrooms, one bath, and a kitchen on the third floor with a laundry room. There were four guest suites on the second floor, a guest suite and master suite on the main floor, and each bedroom had its own bath with the master having two separate for his and hers. The house contained several living spaces even with a conservatory. The pool house was a separate one bedroom and one bath within a laundry room suite. Lovely was thankful that the house came with an elevator already. If not, that would have been one of the first things she would have installed.

"I need to get a designer up in here so we can get this house hot," Lovely said exiting her bedroom. "You know Abe said he doesn't live too far from here."

"Is he rich?" Robin asked.

"Not sure. Don't really care," Lovely said heading toward the kitchen. She had her own money to be concerned with someone else's.

Grace skipped along behind them. "Can I call Uncle Ceez?"

"Sure," Lovely said. She asked Robin, "Will you be coming home?"

"I'm not sure."

Lovely's phone rang. It announced a call from Mr. Pretty Eyes. Robin saved Abe's name in Lovely's phone like that. Lovely shook her head. "Please change this before he hears that...Hello?"

"Hey Lovely, I have a question," Abe said without hesitation.

"Yes?"

"Your friend Robin...would she care to join us? I'm asking because I'm trying to get my brother out of a funk. If she could keep him company I would appreciate it."

Lovely smiled, "You know what. That would be an excellent idea. Hold on." She turned to Robin and pressed the phone against her chest. "Abe wants you to join us and keep his brother company. Say you will and cancel with that other man. Please, for me."

Robin was really looking forward to seeing her lover, but then again he was married. Robin should get out there and mingle with other people. Besides going out with Lovely would be fun as it always was. "Okay, fine." She said, feeling a little giddy inside.

"Abe? She said sure."

"Okay. We'll be there in about fifteen minutes," Abe said before ending the call.

Grace said, "So I guess I gotta go up there with Aunt Livy."

"Yep. Go on up there little girl," Robin said as she sent her lover a text.

"I don't know why y'all going on dates. Don't no men want y'all," Grace teased as she headed for the staircase.

"Since when did they make eleven-year-olds so sassy?" Robin asked with smirk on her face.

"When that one came out of the womb," Lovely commented as her phone rang announcing a call from Uncle Cesar. She answered, "*Ciao Cesar! Come stai?*"

"I'm fine, Lovely. How are things there?" Cesar asked.

"We're good. The house is awesome," Lovely stated.

"And you're fine with that?" Cesar teased.

"I'm okay. I was okay at Papa Lu's."

"I'm just saying. You know you've got a thing against us rich folk," Cesar joked.

Lovely giggled at the sound of Cesar's voice. He was half Italian but with a Texan accent. "I don't. I just don't agree with the lifestyle you rich folk have for myself."

"But you can't get away from it. You're surrounded by it. Now look where you are, but the house was a steal. Besides you have enough money to buy you two more of those houses if you wanted to."

Lovely thought about how much she was worth. Her grandfather, who was business partners with Cesar's father Luciano de Rosa was in the hotel/casino business. He left a substantial amount of money for his two sons and grandchildren. Lovely's parent's also put away money for Lovely in trust funds. When they passed away, Lovely was left with their insurance money as well. Combining all three sources, Lovely was worth enough that Grace's grandchildren wouldn't have to worry about a thing.

"So guess what Ceez?"

"What is it?" he asked.

"I'm going out tonight. Me and Robin both," she sounded bubbly.

Robin was on her phone texting her lover as she smiled, hearing how excited Lovely sounded.

"Really? And who might this gentleman be?"

"His name is Abe. Don't know a whole lot about him. I just know that he's nice and he goes to church. Met him last night at a singles mingle."

"Well, just be careful. Don't let him know too much right away. At least not until I can get a feel for him," he said always feeling concerned about her. "I want you and Robin to be careful. Have you heard from your uncle?"

"Mano? Yeah, his friend is the one that suggested the church we went to. Joyce is a sweet lady and I can see why Mano is taken with her."

Cesar chuckled, "Yeah she is. Hold on Lovely...This is Grace calling me. Let me answer her. You make sure you call me tomorrow and tell me how everything went."

"Okay," Lovely said. She looked toward Robin. "So this Abe guy is really hot, huh?"

"Yes he is Paris Hilton." Robin laughed.

———

"This ain't her house," Eli said staring at the three level brick home.

"It is," Abe mumbled, admiring the stately property. He wondered what Lovely was doing living in a house such as this. It was majestic and didn't quite go with Lovely's free-spirited personality.

The front door opened before he or Eli could ring the bell. It was Robin wearing a bright smile. Abe hoped going out and having someone as sweet as Robin would distract Eli enough not to be so focused on Kiera and the twins.

Robin was just as shapely as Lovely. Both women were the kind of thick one would expect of a woman from the south.

70

Ass, hips and thighs a couple of calories away from being labeled fat by a skinny woman. Lovely was slimmer in the waist than Robin but they had more of a pear shape rather than hourglass. If Abe had to compare them to someone they looked like the gospel duo *Mary Mary* just because of their hair color and shapes. Lovely was Erica all day long and Robin was Tina with the copper color natural hair.

"Well hello," Robin answered. "Do come in. Wait!—Y'all not vampires or anything, right?"

"No, but it would be too late cause you already invited us in," Eli said with a slight smile. He stepped in past Robin, admiring her cute style. He wasn't really looking forward to spending the evening with her, because he wasn't in the mood. Kiera had worked his nerves and seeing the twins which definitely resembled him had thrown him completely off. However, he did like Lovely and Robin. They were good wholesome girls.

Robin smiled at Eli, but still didn't know what to make of him. Abe whispered to her. "Don't worry about him. He gets moody."

"O-kay," Robin said closing the door behind Abe.

Abe stood in the foyer and just took in the elegance of the house. It wasn't a house. It was a mini-mansion. The detail of the wrought iron banister and stair railing was exquisite. He loved how the staircase split at the top into two different corridors. Abe noticed right away that the walls were bare. There was little furniture and personality besides the detail and finishes of the hardware of the house.

Lovely came from the great room to join them. Abe greeted her with a kiss to the cheek and took her hand in his.

Something felt right about how she felt. It had to feel the same for her because she behaved as if they had been together always.

After Robin went to grab her purse the two couples left. Eli and Abe rode up front while Lovely and Robin sat in the back teasing each other. They ended up at Bella's, an upscale Italian restaurant.

The hostess suggested particular wines to go with their food. Lovely was glad Abe didn't try to impress her by acting knowledgeable of the different wines. He knew enough but he didn't go all out with it. He carried on as if this was what he was used to. Lovely hated when average men tried to act knowledgeable only to make themselves look foolish.

After placing their orders Lovely asked, "If you don't mind me asking, but what line of work are you in?"

"Construction and real estate," Abe answered.

Robin asked Eli, "What about you?"

Eli answered, "I'm in whatever line of work Abe is in. He is my boss. I'm his 'do' boy."

Robin grinned. "Really? I'm the same exact thing for Lovely."

Dryly, Eli said, "That's great. We have a lot in common."

Robin wasn't going to let Eli's attitude get to her. She would enjoy this evening regardless. It also tickled her that her new lover was bothered that she canceled seeing him to be company of another.

Abe, Lovely, and Robin tried to have an enjoyable conversation. Eli would speak sporadically, but not steadily. Abe wasn't appreciating his sour mood either.

When the ladies excused themselves to head to the restroom Abe asked, "What's wrong with you?"

"How do I handle this Kiera situation?" Eli blurted out.

"Sit back and see what Kiera's trying to do. Is she even letting on that the twins could be yours?"

"Hell, look at them." Eli said, feeling unsure then definitely sure. "Well she text me saying we needed to talk. I didn't text her back."

Changing the subject Abe asked, "So what do you think about Robin?"

"She's plain."

"An ass like that ain't plain."

"Giving credit where it's due, she has a nice body. You think Dwayne might like her?"

"Our cousin Dwayne?"

"Yeah."

"He would, but she's on a different level. I wouldn't want to see her with somebody like him."

"She's pretty though," Eli admitted.

Abe eyed the ladies returning. "That she is."

Chapter 6

Back at Lovely's, Robin and Lovely gave the two men a thorough tour of the whole house except the third-floor apartment where Aunt Livy and Grace were. After the tour Eli and Robin went one way and Lovely and Abe went to her master suite.

They sat on her sofa in the sitting area. Lovely asked, "Do you want the television on? Or would you rather listen to music? You know, set the mood."

Abe smiled, "The music."

In a voice command, Lovely's room was filled with the soft soothing sounds of India Arie's Ready for Love. She fixed two wine glasses of cabernet sauvignon.

Once Lovely joined him on the sofa Abe asked, "How old are you Lovely?"

"I'm twenty-seven," she answered. "You?"

"Thirty-four. Your daughter Grace, how old is she?"

"Eleven. Yes I was a teen mom."

"I wasn't going to comment on that. But you do look really young to have a child that old. You kind of come off young spirited too."

Lovely frowned. "Is that bad?"

"I don't think so. It doesn't feel bad...it's just most women I date are uptight and refuse to crack a smile. Since I picked you up, you've been cheesing the whole time."

Lovely smiled big showing off two rows of perfect teeth. Abe admired how pretty her smile was even down to the narrow gap in between her top front incisors. He had that same nagging feeling that he had when he first laid eyes on her. It was something about Lovely.

"My daughter says I'm goofy."

"There's nothing wrong with goofy. Trust me, I know goofy. I'm surrounded by goofy people especially my brother."

"Are you goofy?" Lovely asked.

"It comes from nowhere most of the time. Random moments."

Lovely asked, "Do you have kids?"

"Nope. I want some. I'm getting old. Do you want more kids?"

"Sure when I'm married."

"I'm surprised you're not someone's wife already."

"I'm surprised you're not someone's hus...band...," her voice trailed as she realized her mistake. She remembered hearing that his upcoming wedding had been canceled. Surprisingly, everyone at the Singles Mingle was in favor of the cancellation.

Abe was tickled. "No. You're fine. It's not as sensitive as people make it out to be. I'm glad it didn't work out because you came along."

Lovely rolled her eyes playfully. "Cheesy. So tell me Abe, where do you and this lady stand?"

"She and I are going to remain friends but we are no longer a couple."

"So what did she do exactly?"

"Now Lovely, I know those big mouth women filled you in."

"Coming from them is hearsay. I wanna hear it straight from the horse's mouth. Hey, you ever wonder where idioms like that come from. Horses don't talk so...?"

Abe looked at her blankly then shook his head. She was a cute kind of goofy, and then he answered. "Anyway, I caught her with another man."

"Ew. That couldn't have felt good."

"It didn't, because she was the first woman I tried to have a real relationship with."

"Why is that?"

"I didn't date much in my twenties because of school and trying to get my company off the ground. I just didn't have time to dedicate to a woman. But I met Aisha and I felt like I wasn't getting any younger. I thought I loved her so after eighteen months I proposed."

"You said 'you thought'. What do you mean by that?"

"If I go into it then I'll have to go into other things that..."

"That you're not willing to share right now?" Lovely asked.

He shook his head. Lovely pretended to not care. "That's okay. There's things I'm not willing to share either. Now we're even."

Abe sat his drink on the wooden coaster on the glass end table next to him. He asked, "Do you mind telling me what a woman like you are doing in a house like this?"

"I won a settlement from the accident that caused me to lose my sight," Lovely lied. It was such an easy lie. She had already came up with that lie for when the question came up. She added, "And I have a really rich godfather. He insists that I have the best. This house was the only thing I gave in to. I kinda like how I can make this into a place of entertainment where I would never have to leave the house if I didn't want to."

"Yeah it has every amenity possible. You know what you need to do for the basement area?"

"What? Grace wants a bowling alley and a dance studio. She loves dancing."

"There's definitely enough space down there for both. But turn it into Lovely's Cabaret. I can see a stripper pole in the middle of that big space down there."

"What?" Lovely exclaimed in laughter. "A stripper pole?"

Abe chuckled, "Every woman has that inner stripper in her."

"You know all about that, huh?"

"No, I don't. But you got some powerful looking legs. I'm sure they could grip that pole real good."

His words made Lovely blush and become aware of how her dress had inched up her thighs.

Abe smiled. "Don't try to cover up now."

Lovely hit at him playfully. "Stop that."

"Can I get a kiss?"

Lovely blushed more. His voice had become soft and sexy. Just the gentleness of his voice drew Lovely to him. His lips seemed to be made out of magnet as hers were made of metal. They were drawing closer and the space in between her lips and his became shorter. Their lips met and they shared a soft sweet kiss but that wasn't what Abe was going for. He kissed her again, but it was more sensual as he parted her lips with his. Lovely reciprocated the same desire and the kiss went deeper. Her tongue was greeted by the aggression of his. Her hands went to his hair, his went under her dress to rub her thigh.

There was no denying the chemistry between them. The kiss alone awakened something within Lovely. Her gut quivered and her "girl" was aching and begging for attention. Attention that Lovely had deprived herself of for a few months. When they pulled away, Lovely wanted to jump Abe's bones. He felt so good being so close to her. He smelled wonderful. His hand felt massive, masculine and strong on her thigh. His hair smelled of coconut and it was soft to the touch. And his lips were soft and succulent. Lovely wanted more. Instead she cleared her throat and moved away from him. "That was good."

"It was. So why are you moving away from me?"

Lovely laughed nervously, "Because it was good and I don't trust myself."

———

Robin knew Eli wasn't interested in her in that way so going to her bedroom wasn't necessary. Instead they sat in the gathering room off from the kitchen. "Would you like something to drink or anything?"

"Y'all got something strong, like real strong?" Eli asked.

"I'll see what we got. Do you have a preference?" Robin asked as she walked toward the bar.

"Just strong."

Robin giggled to herself as she poured Eli a shot of tequila. She fixed herself a mixed drink. She returned to Eli giving him the shot. Eli stared at the glass. "What is this?"

"You said strong," Robin grinned. "Drink up."

Eli was hesitant. He hoped she wasn't trying to poison him or slip him something. He threw the shot back. "That shit hot. What is it?"

Robin giggled, "AsomBroso eleven-year-old Anejo tequila. You like it?"

He nodded. "What are you drinking?"

"It's got some Everclear in it but not a lot. This drink here is called a sloppy pussy. Wanna try it?"

Eli wasn't sure if Robin was throwing hints but a drink called "sloppy pussy" was kinda starting to sound a little appealing to him and quickly he nodded his head. "Sure."

"Just so you know, you've been warned," Robin said, sitting her own drink down. She quickly went to pour Eli a glass of the mixed drink. Returning to Eli, Robin asked. "So Eli, tell me something personal about you."

He took the drink from her. "What do you wanna know?"

"How old are you?"

"I'm thirty-two. Just had a birthday," he answered. He looked at her blankly. She stared back at him. He said, "Oh, I guess I'm supposed to ask you the question back?"

Robin shrugged sheepishly. "Just trying to make a conversation here." Her phone vibrated in her pants pocket. She retrieved it.

A text from her lover: **what u did was some bullshit, I owe u one**

Robin put the phone on the coffee table.

"Boyfriend?" Eli asked.

"No. Just some guy," Robin stated. "So, if you don't mind me frankly asking; why are you acting so stank on this date. I didn't think I was that bad."

Eli kind of felt bad for the way he'd been acting. "I'm just like that sometimes…most of the time." His brow wrinkled with confusion as he asked. "I haven't offended you have I?"

"Not really, well just a little," she honestly spoke. "I'm just trying to figure you out." Robin said very unsure of Eli's preference. He was a solid, very good looking man, but he was so pretty that he could possibly be just as attractive to a gay man as he would be to a straight woman. "So do you have a significant other?"

"If I had a significant other I would be with them instead of here."

"You have a smart ass mouth," Robin commented.

Eli smirked. "Glad you finally noticed."

"I been noticed. I've been wanting to slap you upside your damn head all night. How bout I pull that goddamn earring out of your lip so you'll think twice about the words you let slip out that mothafucka." Robin tried to keep a serious look, but couldn't under the stare of Eli's eyes. She started laughing. "Don't be looking at me like that."

"No, keep talking to me like that. I like that shit."

Robin straightened up with her serious face. "Who asked you to talk you attitudy bitch."

Eli started laughing. "Okay stop."

Robin laughed too. She said, "I think I'm getting tipsy."

"I think you are too. I see it in your eyes." Eli felt that same tingle from earlier in the day again.

They continued to drink and talk about different things ranging from children to their jobs.

———

The following morning Robin lay in bed staring at the back of Eli's head. He had really nice hair. His back was nice and strong with broad shoulders in the white tank tee he was wearing. His small slender frame was muscular and he was about six feet even. His complexion was a honey peanut butter and was smooth. Robin wanted to touch him.

Apparently after all of the heavy drinking they somehow migrated from the family room into her bedroom. They didn't have sex, because they both were still fully dressed. Or at least that's what Robin assumed.

Eli's phone kept buzzing. Robin wasn't sure if she should wake him. She had been awakened by her own phone. It was her lover calling and when she didn't answer, he messaged her. He was demanding to see her. She didn't understand what the problem was, because he did have a wife.

Eli moved. He reached over the edge of the bed and retrieved his phone. He looked at it. He mumbled something inaudible.

Robin asked. "Are you awake?"

"I don't wanna be," he mumbled. He flipped over on his back.

Robin eyed his chest. Her eyes went lower. He had serious morning stiffness. Eli caught her looking. He grinned and said flippantly, "Shit, it happens."

.

Chapter 7

Abe couldn't let Lovely and Robin get away without them accepting an invite to church. Lovely and Robin met them there and even sat with them. Afterward, Lovely was greeted by those who remembered her from Friday night. Some weren't surprised to see her with Abe. Of course others didn't like it. Aisha was one of them.

"Can I speak with you?" Aisha asked, tearing Abe away from the small group he was talking to.

Not wanting to cause a scene or come off as mean, Abe obliged. He excused himself and went with Aisha off to the side. "Can I help you Aisha?"

"Who is that?" she asked angrily nodding toward Lovely, standing with Robin and Eli.

"That is Lovely. I met her at the Singles Mingle on Friday. You shoulda came," Abe spoke casually.

Aisha glared at him. "So what is she to you?"

"Didn't you just hear me say I met her Friday? Right now she's just a friend who I happen to ask to join me for church today," Abe stated. "If you wanna argue you can do it by yourself, because I ain't got time for it."

"Wait Abe," Aisha said desperately. "Why are you punishing me like this? Baby, we need to work this out."

"The best thing we can do right now is take a break from each other. Now, I'm asking that you respect that and give me my space."

"How can we get back to where we were if we're not together? Do you want us to grow apart? And why you fuck me Friday if you were moving on with other females that quickly?"

Abe looked around to see if they had an audience. Of course they did. "Let's not do this here. I'll talk with you later." Abe left her standing there to rejoin his family and friends.

When he returned to Lovely, an older lady that looked a lot like his own mother was by her side. Lovely reached out for him, "Abe. This is the lady that suggested I go to the singles mingle, Joyce. Joyce, this is Dr. Abe Masters."

Joyce smiled extending her hand. "Oh I know who this fine gentleman is. I've been a member here at Greater Victory for a while now."

Abe shook her hand gently. "It's nice to meet you."

After chatting a little more with the ladies Abe invited Lovely and Robin back to his house for brunch. They accepted and followed him and Eli to his house.

———

Eli walking in the room caught Robin's attention and she found herself dazed out. She found him very alluring. Everything about him was sexy. His wild coils dancing about his head, his thick but shaped up masculine arched eyebrows, the eyebrow piercing, the lip piercing, the earrings in his lobes, the tattoos on his arms, his perfectly trimmed mustache that looked painted on…She sighed inwardly.

Eli looked in Robin's direction. He gave her a small smile and walked over to where they sat.

Since the others had arrived Kiera had been noticing how Eli and Robin had been exchanging subtle glances at each other. She wondered if Robin was who Abe insisted on going out with the night before to accompany Eli. The blind girl seemed to have Abe preoccupied, too. She had Abe cheesing. Kiera was feeling rather vindictive especially with Robin. Eli was hers if he was interested in pussy.

Kiera watched as Eli said something to Robin. She smiled and nodded. She was about to get up but Kiera interrupted them. "Hey Eli baby. I need to have a word with you. It's about…you know."

At first Eli was prepared to call Kiera out for being so rude, but when she mentioned the unspoken subject he softened. He looked at Robin, "Can you give me just a second?"

Robin looked disappointed, but she stayed put.

That's right, stay your fat ass seated bitch, Kiera thought.

When Eli was walking away with Kiera, Abe asked. "Can you grab a bottle of wine for me?"

"What kind?"

"Merlot or Pinot Noir. Anything ten years or older," Abe said over his shoulder as he joined the others in the gathering room.

Eli headed downstairs to the cellar. Kiera followed him through the downstairs maze until they got to the exclusive wine cellar. There was cubby after cubby with bottles of wine tucked away in them.

"Do Abe drink this stuff or is it just for show?" Kiera asked, pulling out random bottles and placing them back.

"Did you not just hear him ask for a bottle?" Eli removed the bottle she'd just pulled out from her hand and put it back. "What do you want to talk about?"

"I ain't never been down here. Didn't know it existed." She ignored him while admiring all of the bottles on display. Suddenly she noticed how quiet it had gotten.

Eli frowned. "What's up?" When she didn't respond Eli sighed with aggravation. "Here you go with this shit."

Kiera spun around to face him. She smiled with tease. "What shit Eli?"

"You playing. You said you needed to talk to me. I'm assuming it's about the twins."

"Maybe...No...I don't know."

"You play too much Kiera," Eli said. He began to walk away.

"Wait!" Kiera called out, grabbing his arm. "Why don't we set up a day and time where we can sit down and have a talk?"

"No, I don't think we'll do it like that. We are in one another's presence now. Why can't we talk about it now?" When she didn't have a response Eli shook his head with disgust and began to walk away again.

Kiera stopped him again. "Hold up. Whatchu rushing for? Let's play a little bit."

Eli gave her a confused look. "Play?"

Kiera loved his eyes. They were intense with eyelashes so thick it looked like he was wearing liner. Kiera said, "Remember that night?"

"I don't remember a damn thing about it," Eli replied snidely.

"I do," she grinned wickedly. "You said a whole bunch of shit, Eli. You said that it was good and that you really liked me."

"I wouldn't say that shit."

"Dang, I wish I could relive that night," she said with a dreamy faraway look.

Eli trapped her against the wall of wine and within the space between his arms. He looked into her eyes. "Why do you want me?" Kiera just stared at him intensely.

Eli averted his eyes away from hers. Kiera slid her hands up his abdomen in a slow tantalizing way. Eli looked back at her. She caught her bottom lip in between her teeth and focused on how she moved her hands up to his chest.

Eli thought there was something sexy about the way she'd act so innocent, oblivious to what she was doing to him. Furthermore, he found Kiera to be sexy. From her even caramelized sugar complexion, her succulent lips to her thighs and her fake bow-legged stance. But he knew Kiera was poison. Never trust a big booty and a smile and he didn't ever want to be in a situation like his brother.

Kiera placed her hand on the back of his neck, lifted on her toes and met his lips with a soft sensuous kiss. Eli returned the kiss with the same desire. His heartbeat quickened.

What am I doing, he thought. *I don't wanna be with this girl.* It didn't feel right in his spirit, but elsewhere it was everything he desired.

Eli pulled away. "I can't."

"Yes you can," Kiera said, pulling him by his belt. "You want me, don't you? I'm tired of you acting like you're not interested. You'll make a bitch think you're gay. Ever since that night, I've always understood your point of just wanting to get with one woman and settle down. You ain't settled yet, so why that woman can't be me?"

Eli shook his head emphatically.

Kiera smiled up at him with mischief. "What do you want Eli?"

"I'm confused," Eli admitted. He watched as she unbuckled his belt. His dick wasn't confused about the arousal. It responded as always. "What are you doing?"

"Something I've wanted to do since the first day I saw you when you came in the kitchen," she said, unfastening his jeans.

Eli pulled away from her touch and grabbed her hand before she could grab his dick. "Kiera, I need to go."

Kiera looked at him wickedly and shook his hand off hers. She went for the waistband of his underwear. Eli grabbed her again. "Stop. I need to think this through."

Kiera said, "Well let me leave you with something to consider."

Eli watched Kiera free his already hardened dick. Her eyes widened and she smiled with delight by the enormity of him. Kiera licked around his head and suckled it with the right amount of pressure. Eli let out a quivering breath as he shuddered. Kiera licked the length of him lubricating him with her saliva before taking him in her mouth. Gripping him by his waist, Kiera used no hands as she deep throated him.

Jesus! Eli screamed in his head. She was sucking him in a trance!

Maybe it was the excitement of doing something so sneaky and the fact she was so aggressive and giving him some mean head, but Eli wasn't able to hold back after about ten good minutes of her slobbing him down. "I'm finna cum."

Kiera didn't stop or waiver. She kept going until she tasted the thick substance in her mouth. She swallowed once her mouth was full. Satisfied she stood fully and smiled. "See you upstairs."

Eli fixed himself and followed her. "You a nasty bitch."

Kiera giggled, "I know!"

———

Abe watched Lovely, admiring her mannerisms all that evening. She kept a sweet smile on her face as she listened to everyone talk around her. She didn't say much but when she did it was a simple reply. He could tell she didn't like to be the center of attention.

Abe found himself fascinated by her delicate demeanor, her soft voice, the vulnerable position her visual impairment left her in, and her simple beauty. There was still something else that allured him to her. He hadn't figured it out yet. But he felt as if he'd met her before.

"She's pretty isn't she?" Aisha asked.

Her question snapped Abe out of his daze. He almost forgot she was present. He was watching Lovely from his breakfast nook. She was talking to David and Melissa on the terrace.

Aisha turned his face towards her. "You've been staring at her all day."

"I think I know her, but I can't pinpoint from where. It's like my mind won't let me peek inside the memory box she's in. I'm sure I know her," Abe said.

"She's weird," Aisha said nonchalantly.

"She's nice and reserved. She isn't weird," he defended.

"Whatever it is, you seem to be fascinated by it."

Abe said, "At this point I think I can be. I mean, weren't you fascinated with Michael?"

"You won't leave that alone will you?"

"It's hard for me too. Why are you here? I don't remember asking you to come by," he said with a hint of amusement.

Aisha cut her eyes at him. "I've always come over after church."

"That was when we were a couple, engaged to be married. So get this through your head Aisha. Unless I invite you over, don't come here."

Aisha could feel her eyes warm, but she refused to cry. To prevent herself from being emotional she thought she would throw an insult his way. "You ain't all that Abe. Why you think I went to him in the first place."

"If you're asking me why I think you did, I believe you did it because you a hoe. It's what hoes do. Now, if you'll excuse me. I have a guest to entertain."

"You only using her to get over me."

"Maybe I am," he said as he headed out to the terrace. He approached carefully, but Lovely turned and bumped into him.

"Oh I'm sorry," she said but quickly realized who it was.

Melissa teased, "Dang Abe, watch what you doing."

"You okay?" Abe asked Lovely.

"I'm fine. I was just about to go in," she said. "But now you're out here gives me a reason to stay."

Her smile was one of the most pleasant ones he had seen in a while. "If you could see, what would you be doing? I mean, like hobbies or interests?"

Lovely shrugged. "I don't know. Working for my godfather maybe."

"Your godfather...what line of work is he in?" Abe asked.

"Hotel and casino. They got them all over the place, more internationally," Lovely said. "Cesar is over operations. His father is still primary owner, but he's older so he chills here in the states. He lives primarily in Texas. Cesar is rarely in one place longer than a week."

"So they're wealthy?"

"Very."

Cesar and Luciano always had a bad habit of wanting to shower Lovely, Robin and then Grace with the best of everything. Lovely could do all those things on her own with her inheritance, but she purposely didn't live that lifestyle. Cesar knew that. He was always trying to get her to live the luxurious lifestyle. Lovely had an old country soul like her aunt Livy. She was raised modestly and to focus on humility. Livy instilled in Lovely the importance of living in one's heart space and being in touch with oneself and the effects on the rest of the world.

"So explain to me how you see," Abe said. "Am I making sense? This is just new to me."

Lovely smiled. "Trust me, I understand." She looked out into his backyard. "I can see all of this and how green your grass is. I can see the pool but I can't see the ripples. I can see you. I just can't tell you what shade your eyes are. I can't tell a person if that's four bushes over there or if it's just one big one. It's the details I can't make out."

"But you can always tell it's me without me speaking."

"I know you now. I know your body mass, your smell, the way your hair is. Even the way you touch me."

Abe couldn't deny that he really wanted to be with this woman. "You know I've been thinking of that kiss from last night all day."

Lovely grinned. "You have?"

"I have and I would love another one, but I'm pretty sure if I were to turn around right now I would see someone staring at us."

Lovely started laughing. "We have someone stalking us?"

"Yes. It's my ex. She came by, but I didn't invite her. She's in denial about our breakup."

"Oh."

Abe admired the softness of her face. Her eyes were focused on his face. He knew she couldn't make his face out but it was something about her piercing gaze as if she was trying to see beneath his outer shell. In that moment he felt as if he wanted to share his most inner thoughts and secrets. He had never felt like that.

As if he was realizing it for the first time, Abe had to speak up. "You are a very beautiful woman Lovely."

She blushed, "Stop that."

"I mean it. I feel something with you."

"Really? Like what?"

"Peace," he paused. "A calmness."

———————

Melissa rolled her eyes upward and sighed with frustration. Her husband always had a problem when she stayed out with her friends. Melissa felt he was actually jealous of her relationship with the Masters brothers. As far as she was concerned he needed to shut the hell up because he was barely home anyway.

"I don't want this shit!" Reggie spat as he looked inside the styrofoam box of food.

"Since when did you not like chicken," Melissa mumbled.

He cut his eyes at her as she removed her heels. "When can I get a meal cooked by my woman?"

Melissa carried her shoes in her hand and mumbled, "You have several. I'm sure somebody cooking you a meal."

Reggie scoffed. "You wanna go there?" He followed her out of the kitchen.

Melissa threw over her shoulder, "You ain't getting fat for nothing."

"You right. Cause what you won't do another woman will."

Melissa went to her bedroom ignoring his last statement. She went straight to her walk through closet and proceeded to collect her night clothes.

"Why the fuck am I your last priority?" He asked angrily.

Melissa stared at him blankly. Her husband was very attractive. He was a thick man no more than five ten. Although he wasn't cut up like Abe, he was a pretty solid guy. He thought he was a pimp and could pull any woman he wanted. He could if the women lived in low-income housing, frequented sleazy nightclubs, had low self-esteem, and was looking for a man with a job to keep her hair did. He was perfect. But if a woman wanted more, something meaningful Melissa's husband was not that man.

Lately Melissa was getting really tired of his ass. She wanted better for her and their seven-year-old son. She wanted to experience real love from a real man.

He shot, "And you wanna talk about fat? Why you so fucking fat?"

"I was this size when you met me. Probably a little bigger," Melissa pointed out. "So don't try that fat shit with me. Hell, I'm smaller than that orangutan you were fucking in your phone!"

"Why you always bringing that up?"

Melissa grew angry. "It just happened a few weeks ago!"

"That was a long time ago."

"You're an idiot. The time and date are in the damn phone stupid!"

"Why I gotta be stupid?" he asked walking up on her.

Melissa took a few steps back. "Get away from me."

Reggie wore a sinister grin. "You always wanna talk shit. Like you mothafuckin bad. Which one you fucking?"

"What are you talking about?" Melissa asked nervously. It wasn't the question that made her nervous; it was him walking upon her with that evil grin.

"I know you fucking Abe. You suck his dick on a regular basis. That's why you always working late and can't never be shit for me."

"You talking real stupid," Melissa stated angrily. "If that's what you wanna believe to make you feel better about the shit you're doing, so be it."

He jabbed her in her head with his fingers as he spoke. "You fucking him ain'tcha?"

Melissa pushed at his arms as he jabbed at her from both directions. "Stop! I'm not doing this--"

He grabbed her by her throat and snarled through gritted teeth, "Shut the fuck up! Let me find out you fucking any of 'em I will kill your ass and theirs."

Melissa struggled to remove his hand from her throat. Mekhi ran into the closet and kicked at him. "Leave my mama alone!"

He pushed Mekhi back, "Getcho ass back in your room!"

Melissa swung her arms and connected her fists with his head. With Mekhi returning his kicks and Melissa's blows her husband released her.

"Y'all wanna tag team on me!" he yelled. He started searching for something. Melissa didn't wait to see what he was looking for. She grabbed Mekhi by his hand and ran out of the closet. She went to the kitchen for her purse and ran to the garage door as her husband appeared.

Unlocking the doors to her Audi Melissa pushed Mekhi in through the passenger door as she almost squashed him getting in herself. She hurried and locked the door when Reggie came charging.

"Get out the car!" he demanded.

Melissa shook her head. She removed her phone and called her mother. "Mama, me and Khy are coming over."

"Okay. C'mon. Y'all done ate? I ain't put the food away yet," her mother said.

"Yeah, we've ate. Just need to get some sleep," Melissa sighed. She and Mekhi switched places.

Diane asked with concern, "Is it him?"

"Yeah. We'll be there in a minute." Melissa hung up glaring at her husband. She yelled, "When I get back you need to be out of my house!"

"Fuck you! I live here too."

Melissa brought her car to life. She opened the garage door with a push of the button. She backed out. She looked at him one last time and she was shocked that he was pointing a gun at them. "Khy get down and don't look at your crazy daddy."

"I hate Daddy," Mekhi mumbled.

Melissa pulled off as fast as she could. When she arrived at her mother's house she wasn't surprised her husband had called her mother looking for her.

After Diane put Mekhi to bed in his uncle's old room she joined Melissa in her old bedroom. "Melissa, why don't you just tell your brother and his friends?"

"Mama, he will be dead."

Diane shrugged nonchalantly, "So. That'll be one less problem for you."

Melissa chuckled, "Mama, that's not nice."

"Well it ain't nice how he treat you and your son," Diane pointed out. "Speaking of Khy, have you...."

Melissa shook her head emphatically. "I won't either."

Diane sighed giving her daughter a disapproving look. "You know one day you will have to."

"No I won't either. I shouldn't have told you," Melissa stated.

Diane laughed, "Listen...you wouldn't have to. I can clearly see that Khy ain't your husband's child. Everybody else can too."

"That's because he looks like me," Melissa pointed out.

"He's lighter than both you and him," Diane mentioned.

"Mama you're light skinned. Me and Jah got Daddy's complexion but Khy coulda got it from you. And Reggie is not that dark."

"Whatever you say. His real daddy know Khy's his son," Diane teased. She began to walk away.

"What does that mean?" Melissa called softly after her mother.

Diane didn't respond.

Melissa reached for her phone and went to her gallery. She studied a picture she had recently taken of Mekhi. There was no trace of her husband anywhere. Her husband was medium brown, round head, short, flaring nostrils, thin lips, and nice hair. Melissa was mocha brown, round face, very slanted eyes, small nose, medium thick shapely lips, and decent grade of dark brown hair that fell below her shoulders. People said she reminded them of a thick Latoya Luckett, one of the ex-group members of Destiny's Child.

Mekhi was light caramel, naturally curly hair, round face, almond-shaped light brown eyes, and shapely lips. Her husband said Mekhi looked like his own biological father. Melissa went along with that. She didn't argue and didn't rationalize in her head that Mekhi could be another man's child. If he believed Mekhi was his so would she. But what was Diane's last statement about?

Chapter 8

T he next morning, upon arrival of his company, before he even pulled into the parking lot Abe could see one of his office staff giving her boyfriend a hard time as usual.

"Do she have a bat in her hand?" Abe asked aloud. He watched out of his window as the short-medium framed, brown-skinned woman cursed at the person hidden inside the white Charger. She held the bat across her right shoulder, ready to swing at any moment.

"Bitch! Who the fuck is she?" Tawanda spat. She was losing her patience. She exhaled heavily. "Mothafucka, all your goddamn windows about to be bust the fuck out."

Jarrod saw Abe approaching. "Ay man...Abe, get'cho girl. Tell her it's too early for all this."

"Abe ain't gotta tell me shit! What you need to tell me is who the fuck that bitch was that just called your goddamn phone!" Tawanda said angrily. "Talking 'bout 'good morning baby," she mocked.

Jarrod looked at Abe for help. "She gon' make me late for work. I 'pose'ta been at the site."

"Where you working today?" Abe asked.

"At the river," Jarrod said.

Abe chuckled, reaching for the bat. He started pushing Tawanda toward the door. "You need to calm down and take your ass inside."

Jarrod called out. "Can I get my keys?"

Tawanda stopped at the door and look back at Jarrod. "Your ass better be glad Abe showed up. Ugly bitch! I oughta snatch your mothafuckin dreads outcho goddamn head." She tossed his keys beyond his car. "Go fetch mothafucka."

Jarrod started to say something but Abe cut him off. "Just get your keys and get to the site. I'll call Paul and let him know you on your way."

"A'ight," Jarrod mumbled, scrambling for his keys.

Abe went into the building. Most of his staff was in the reception area watching the drama unfold, including Eli. "Why didn't anybody stop that?"

"It's Monday and too early for that, but it's fun to watch," Eli commented with a light chuckle.

"Yeah. Especially when it ain't your own shit," Felicia, the receptionist stated.

Abe shook his head. For his company to be so professional, highly reputable and renowned, Abe had the most ghetto staff and crew members. He went to his office, ready to get his day started. Melissa and Eli both followed him in and took his respective seat in front of Abe's desk as always. Melissa started talking about an upcoming gala and reservations as Abe got lost in his thoughts.

With Aisha's craziness on his mind, Abe looked around at the setting of his posh office. *What was wrong with her?* He wondered. Why would she mess things up with him? He couldn't understand Aisha's actions. But then again, Aisha always said he was too needy. He didn't quite understand that either. Abe wasn't a co-dependent person. He didn't need her to function. He simply wanted a chance to love and for reciprocation to take place. He wanted love.

Abe's direct business line on his office phone began to ring. Eli paused on what he was saying as he answered. "Abe speaking," he said.

"Abe, will you please listen to me?" It was Aisha.

He sighed, feeling hopeless. "What Aisha?"

"I made a mistake. A huge mistake. I'm sorry."

"Okay. I know."

"Give us another chance. Give me another chance."

"We're not getting married," he said.

"Okay, we can postpone the wedding. We can work on us. Solidify our relationship so to speak," Aisha said desperately.

"Right now can I have some space?" Abe asked.

"I love you Abe...and I'm sorry I fucked up," she cried. "Please love me again."

Abe sighed. "Aisha, why should I love you after what you did?"

"I know Abe. I messed up. But I know you still love me. I know you do."

This was the first time Aisha had shown any emotion. She had been maintaining a flippant attitude like getting caught fucking another man was no big deal. She was beginning to realize Abe was serious and ready to move on.

"Are you at work?" he asked.

"Yeah but I'll quit. I'll come work for you like you wanted me to. I'll do whatever you need me to do...Please Abe?"

"Aisha...," he frowned. Now she was frustrating him. Now she wanted to quit her damn job. "Let me get back to you okay?"

"Can I just come see you?"

"I'm working."

"I can just sit there in your office. I won't bother you that much."

"That much?"

She snickered, "Yeah. I gotta bother you a little."

"I guess."

"Great! I'm on my way."

Abe ended the call. He looked at Eli and Melissa, "Do you feel like going to Batey's and work?"

Eli gave Abe a knowing look. "It's that skank?"

Abe nodded.

Eli stood up, "C'mon and let's get the fuck up outta here. This bitch worrisome."

As Eli followed Abe out of the office a certain presence caught his attention. He looked at Abe. "Go ahead. I'll be out there in a minute. Something I gotta take care of real quick."

Kris was looking dressier than what Eli was used to seeing. Kris was dressed in a crisp white button-down shirt with a black tie and grey slacks. Kris's hair was cut into its usual fade with a hint of waves on top. Diamond studs adorned either earlobe and the piercings that usually decorated Kris's face were missing.

When Eli's eyes landed on Kris his heart fluttered. It was a feel-good flutter. He was instantly mesmerized by Kris. The smooth caramel complexion, sweet innocent baby face, the neat fade, and petite short frame...Kris was just like Eli liked them. When Kris turned to face Eli their eyes connected. Eli didn't look away. He couldn't look away. He didn't want to hide the fact that he liked what he saw. It was bad enough he had to ignore Kris' presence at the fundraiser that past Saturday.

Kris bashfully smiled and looked away. Forgetting about Abe, Eli absently walked over to where Kris was standing. "Why are you here?"

"Damn, this my place of employment too," Kris chuckled.

"Yeah but you work out in the field," Eli said.

"So I'm not allowed to come here?"

Eli smirked, "You just came here to see me."

"And if I did?"

Eli leaned in to whisper. "I miss you."

Kris blushed. "Same here." Kris began to walk away with the human resource personnel to the back.

Eli gestured with his hand the notion to call him later. The message was understood with a nod of the head as Kris continued to walk away.

A small smile crept across Eli's face as he turned to join Abe. The scowl on Abe's face made Eli snicker. "I'm coming boss. Damn."

———————

Later that evening, Eli felt troubled as he and Kiera sat face to face. He could feel confusion creeping upon him. He found himself thinking of Robin more and more. She had forced herself into his mind on a daily basis. He also couldn't get out of his mind what Kiera did in the cellar. Then there was his "boo" of course that Eli swore he couldn't get enough of.

Those were his romantic troubles. His other trouble was Kiera's unwillingness to cooperate when it came to the paternity of her twins. She was being difficult. "I've given it some thought and I don't want their lives disrupted."

"How will it be disrupted?" Eli asked. "I just wanna know if I'm their father. And if I am, I want to start being a part of their lives as their father."

"No. Just leave things how they are."

"You're selfish Kiera," Eli spat. "You've always been that way."

That statement made Kiera angry. "Selfish? You of all people are calling someone else selfish? You only think of yourself Eli."

"I'm supposed to. Who else will if I don't? Shit, I love me and I always come first," he said.

Kiera rolled her eyes. "And that right there is why you're still not ready to be a father."

"I am if they are mine."

"They have a daddy. And his name is not Elijah Masters," Kiera said smartly.

"Whatever," Eli said. He turned his attention back to his laptop. He was at Abe's place working late. Abe, of course, was nowhere to be found because he was tending to Aisha's begging ass on the phone.

Eli looked at Kiera out of the corner of his eyes. She seriously needed to put on some clothes. Her ass cheeks were hanging out of the pink terrycloth boy cut shorts she was wearing. Her exposed golden buttery legs were enticing. His dick grew hard envisioning her nicely sculpted thighs straddled over his legs and riding him till the break of dawn.

"What are you looking at?" Kiera asked with a smirk on her face. "You must want some of this."

"Not really. But what was up with what you did in the cellar?"

"You know what that was," Kiera teased. She whispered, "The way you've dodged me, I thought you didn't like pussy."

Eli grinned wickedly. "That was your mouth, not your pussy."

Kiera cut her eyes. "You're full of shit."

"You started it."

Kiera smiled seductively, "I'm not wearing any panties."

Eli turned up his nose with disgust. "That's you! I thought Lulu was in there making mackerel or tilapia or something. Getcho stanky twat away from me!"

"Fuck you," Kiera spat.

Eli was cracking up with laughter.

Kiera cut her eyes. "You didn't think it was stinking nine years ago."

"I don't even remember that shit." He stuck to that no matter what. "But, for real though; they got medications for that. It's either antifungal or antibiotics. Whatever the case; you need to anti-something."

Kiera couldn't help the smile that crept across her face. This was typical Eli. Had it been someone else she would have been ready to fight. She snickered. "Boy, I can't stand your ass."

Abe walked back into the den. They both looked at him guiltily. Abe raised an eyebrow with suspicion. "What the hell y'all up to?"

Eli chuckled a little. "Oh nothing, I was just thinking of how wonderful it will be to get home to my King. It's too much distraction over at your place now since she's here." He rolled his eyes.

Abe chuckled, "You're so stupid."

Kiera side eyed Eli. "Whatever, boy."

"What was that?" Eli asked at the stank expression on her face.

"Like you don't know?" Kiera threw her hand back above her shoulder, clearly showing that she was disgusted with Eli.

Eli smiled smugly. "She just can't handle the fact that I don't want her."

Kiera waved her hand dismissively. Eli played entirely too much. However Kiera was willing to play right along with him. "You tell your "King" about us?"

Eli laughed. "Girl, I'm talking about my King size bed!" He said with a shake of the head.

Chapter 9

Almost two weeks had passed and it was FFA's annual Autumn Ball, always the third Saturday of September. Abe insisted Lovely and Robin be in attendance. Before long the ballroom at McArthur's mansion was buzzing with the sounds of a live band, laughter, chatter and utensils clanking against plates. The reflection of the lights gleamed off all of the crystal ware and crystal chandeliers. Lovely saw hues of golden lights. The tables were covered in ivory linen. Candles burned in the center of each table in a large hurricane vase. Lovely could make out the shimmer of gowns and the distinguished presence of tuxedos.

Lovely was familiar with FFA otherwise known as First Family Association. Her grandmother had been an active member that served on the Houston's chapter board before she became ill. Lovely remembered dressing up fancy to attend such events with her grandparents.

Lovely was in an elegant silver-blue form-fitting gown. Her hair had been straightened and sculpted into a sophisticated short hairdo that gave her swooping bangs. Kiera had done her hair. All night Lovely received compliments from every direction. She had to admit she felt good especially whenever Abe was close by. It was something about having him near. He made her feel secure and safe.

Abe dreaded these types of events. Having enough of the foolery before him, Abe got up from the table in search of his parents. They were more into this pretentious way of being more than he was. Sarah served on the FFA Nashville's chapter board and loved having brunch with all of the other affluent housewives. Abe just had to make appearances and network. Besides they always wanted to honor him in some type of way.

"Abe, you're fine as always," Celia Davis commented as she approached him. "Have you talked to that daughter of mine lately?"

Abe smiled at Aisha's mother. "I spoke with her briefly two days ago."

Celia sucked her teeth in aggravation. "I don't know what's gotten into her. She's losing her mind I believe."

It was weird because Celia always had a fondness for Abe despite his relationship with her daughter. Celia told Aisha she was a fool for messing things up with Abe.

Abe parted with Celia after talking briefly. He gave her an endearing hug before he walked off. He had his eyes on his mother and was headed to her table.

"Where you going?" David asked, looping his arm through Abe's and tugging him in the opposite direction.

"I wanted to say--"

"Not right now Abe," David chided quietly.

"I just wanted to ask my mama if daddy liked his birthday present."

"I'm sure he does. He's gonna wear it, drive it—whatever it is you got him every day," David said, guiding Abe back toward their table. Abe wouldn't fight David this time, but he was determined to speak to his mother.

When he got to the table mostly everyone had gotten up and left the table. Although she wasn't technically his date, he searched for Lovely wondering where she had gone off to.

Eli whispered. "Abe, I don't know how you're going to feel about this but...uhm..." And his eyes finished his sentence. Abe looked in the direction Eli was looking. It was a crowd of people.

"What am I looking for?" Abe asked.

"Over there," Eli pointed with an obvious effect.

Abe looked again and there she was in a form-fitting green gown that exposed her back and shoulders. It dipped very low in the front and would have been distasteful had she not been a b-cup. Her dark hair was falling over one shoulder. Her silky brown skin was radiant.

Abe closed his eyes remembering a time when love felt good. Kenya Childress. She was the one that got away; the one that he was unwilling to give the streets up for. She gave him an ultimatum, but he had to obtain at least another million before he was ready to walk away from that street life. He wanted her to understand, but she didn't. She had gotten accepted into Howard University and went to DC.

Abe used to say he would find her and they would be together, but she got married to some dude with money. Last time they spoke was about two years prior when she was visiting family in Nashville. They hooked up and shared two hours of passion. She had to get back to her husband and children. He had to get back to Aisha.

When Abe opened his eyes, Kenya was smiling in his direction. Abe smiled back.

Kenya made her way over to their table. "Hello everybody."

They all greeted her with the same enthusiasm. Abe gave her an endearing hug. "Why are you here?"

"My mom and dad begged me to tag along," Kenya said, staring into Abe's eyes trying to read him. No matter how pretty Abe's eyes were they lacked that sparkle. Kenya could detect he was still a troubled man.

"How long are you in town for?" Abe asked.

"A week or two," she said. Her smile faded. "However long I need."

Abe could sense something was bothering her. He asked, "Where's Calvin?"

"He's not here," she answered looking deeply into his eyes.

Abe shied away from her stare. Kenya started. "Where's that girl you were marrying?"

"We're no longer together."

Kenya smiled. She grabbed Abe by the hand. "Let's talk."

Abe followed her outside the perimeters of the dining tables close to the kitchen and serving areas. "What's up?"

"So I heard there's not going to be a wedding." Kenya said. "It is true."

"Who hasn't heard that?"

"I just knew you would be married."

"Well it's not turning out that way."

"Is she crazy?"

"I guess it wasn't what she wanted. It wasn't what you wanted either. Remember?" He reminded her.

"Abe, c'mon, don't do that. I did want you, but not that life at that time."

"But I changed my life and you still married Calvin." Abe pointed out.

Kenya sighed feeling defeated. "I thought Calvin was the better choice. But I was young and not basing my choice on love, but rather on logic and need."

"Had you given me another chance you would have seen I had way more to offer than he did." His voice remained soothing almost playful. Kenya smiled up at him.

"Abe, what if I got my divorce? Do you still have those same feelings for me?"

Abe looked out into the crowd. Lovely was talking to David's wife Vanessa and some other ladies. He said, "I still love you."

"But?"

"I don't know."

Kenya's mouth hung open. "You don't know what?"

Abe smiled. "Don't look like that."

"I'm divorcing Calvin," Kenya blurted out.

"Why?"

"He's a liar and a cheat. I just don't wanna deal with it anymore."

Abe was a bit shocked that she was being so candid about her marriage. "Just like that? You're going to walk away from what? Nine years of marriage?"

"Well, it's been building up," she confessed. "He's hardly ever home. When he is home all he does is bitch and complain. Sometimes I'm ready for him to go on a business trip. Then there are the texts and pictures in his phone. That's why I'm here. We had an argument. Me and the kids came to visit my parents."

"Oh." Abe quickly stated with a blank stare.

"What about you? Why did the breakup happen?"

"She cheated." He confessed. "But, I guess I wasn't feeling her like I thought I was because I could have gotten over it. I mean I'm over it now, but not to move on with her," he said eyeing the array of desserts on the table behind him. They were very inviting and delectable. It made him think of Lovely.

Abe slightly smiled. "Do you believe a person can fall in love within weeks?"

Kenya gave it some thought. "I guess it's possible. Why do you ask?"

Abe's eyes found Lovely again. He turned his attention back to Kenya. "I haven't been the luckiest man when it comes to a meaningful relationship. But there's this girl."

Kenya was surprised and rather insulted that Abe would be thinking of another woman with her present. "What girl?"

"Lovely," he said absently as he headed toward Lovely and the group of women she was talking to.

Kenya followed him eager to see what he was getting at. "What?"

112

"Her name is Lovely."

"You're moving on that fast?"

"I think she's what's missing in my life. She's what I want."

"Abe you're so complex."

Abe politely interrupted the group of women. "I'm so sorry, but I need to steal Miss Lovely."

"Go right ahead," Vanessa grinned.

Lovely eagerly went with Abe. He held her securely at her waist. "Kenya, this is Lovely. Lovely this is Kenya."

Lovely extended her hand out, "Nice to meet you."

"Nice to meet you too," Kenya said forcing a smile. It was as if Abe was throwing Lovely in her face. But Kenya had to admit Lovely was stunning.

Abe looked at Kenya, "If you don't mind, but I owe her a dance." He led Lovely to the dance floor as the live band covered Ronald Isley *For The Love of You.*

Lovely teased him. "I got my five-inch heels on."

"I can tell, but you're still short," he replied with a smile. He held her close and whispered how beautiful she was in Spanish. *"Eres la mujer más hermosa del mundo."*

Lovely whispered back, "I think you're beautiful too."

"So what are we doing now? What is this?" Abe asked.

Lovely smiled with uncertainty. "I'm not sure."

"Give it some thought." He said.

Lovely nodded before resting her head against his chest. *God, he feels wonderful.*

After going home to Alabama for a few days, Robin had come back to Nashville in time to attend the Autumn Ball. Her mother hadn't been feeling too well so Robin kept her company. While away she realized she wanted desperately to be with Eli. All she could think of while away was him and his slim tight body.

Robin found Eli talking to a group of people by the dessert table. "Hey stranger," Robin said from behind him.

"Hey," he said with a surprising smile. He looked at her as if he was trying to read her. "I didn't expect to see you here. How's your mother?"

"She was feeling a lot better by the time I left."

Eli looked her up and down. "You look nice."

She smiled coyly. "Thanks. You do too as always."

"Thank you." He smiled. "So how have you been?"

Robin shrugged. "I'm okay I guess."

There was silence. Then they started talking at once.

Eli said, "Go ahead."

"No you go ahead," she insisted.

Eli hesitated as he began to speak. "I hate to admit this...but I think we made a connection. Don't you?"

Robin smiled and nodded. She was about to say more until she noticed Kiera in a silver rhinestone spaghetti strapped gown approaching.

Kiera walked up to Eli with an attitude. "Really Eli?"

Robin's smile faded as she stepped back.

Eli saw Robin's stance change. Kiera leaned up against Eli. "You're supposed to be my date for the night."

Robin looked Kiera up and down. Kiera was proclaiming to be Eli's date for the night. *Really?*

Kiera cut her eyes at Robin as if to tell her she could leave now.

Robin looked at Eli. "Well, I'll see you around."

"Okay," Eli mumbled. He did like Robin and enjoyed the time spent with her. He hoped Robin wasn't intimidated by Kiera's shenanigans.

"So what was that?" Kiera asked.

"Nothing," Eli sighed in annoyance.

"No. Why was she all up in your grill?"

"She was just speaking. Damn, can't no other woman say hi to me? And why am I explaining myself to you. We don't go together."

"So when can we go together then?" Kiera wanted to know, placing both hands on either of her hips.

Eli scoffed with a little laugh, "Never!"

"You're a bitch Eli," Kiera teased.

"I know. But do me a favor Keke," Eli said sincerely.

"What?"

"Stay away from me like I asked you to," Eli said playfully.

"Nigga, you know you want this," Kiera joked as she poked him in the side.

Eli slapped her hand away. "Don't touch me. I feel molested."

Kiera stared curiously. "So, are you the bottom or are you the top?"

Eli paused and frowned. "What?"

Kiera was still unsure of Eli's sexuality and had never seen him with either sex on an intimate level. Seeing him talk to Robin like that definitely threw her for a loop. "When you're with your significant other are you the top or are you bottom?" She said, trying to clean it up after the awkward look Eli shot her.

Realizing what she was talking about Eli burst into hearty laughter. "Girl you stupid." He said, not caring if Kiera thought he was gay or not, because he really didn't want to be with her anyway. "Lemme get away from you!"

"What?" Kiera chuckled as she watched Eli's tall frame walk away. She stared at his legs. That nigga know he could wear the hell out of a suit. And those damn bowed legs! Kiera wanted Eli. She made up her mind in that moment she needed to feel him deep within her again.

———

Sarah gazed at Abe and Lovely swaying smoothly to the music. Her son looked nice with Lovely like they were a cute couple. Things were getting serious between them too. She had never seen Abe so taken with a woman. Sarah thought about years ago when she felt excited about love; a love that wasn't shared with her husband, either.

Sarah continued to eye Lovely and Abe. She wondered what was really going on there. Lovely wasn't saying much, but every now and then Abe would say something to her that she could only hear. Lovely would smile or blush. They looked really good together. Lovely would be something different for her son if he pursued her. First, he needed to get rid of Aisha.

"Don't they look nice together?" Mary asked wearing a smile as she gazed out at the couple.

Sarah remained indifferent. "I guess."

"Sarah, you have to admit. You have an amazing son. Look at him."

Sarah rolled her eyes. "I guess."

"Is that all you know how to say?" Mary asked.

"So where did this girl come from?" Sarah wanted to know referring to Lovely.

"Why don't you ask Abe yourself?"

Sarah shot her sister a stern look. "You know I will not do such a thing."

"Sarah, don't you think this is getting old? It's time you started speaking to your son. I swear you can be so stubborn," Mary fussed.

Sarah ignored her sister and continued to gaze out into the crowd. She wondered where her husband was since he was actually too busy to show up to the extravagant event. Knowing him, he probably had bumped into the hussy he was having an affair with and just decided to not to show.

Sarah knew Esau was seeing someone. She just didn't have the evidence. And quite frankly, Sarah didn't have the energy to find out either. She was too old for such foolishness, but she had something for Esau. Two could play that game.

––––––––

Melissa sadly watched Lovely and Abe. There was a chemistry between the two of them that she desired. Lovely's face was lit up and seemed to brighten every time Abe whispered in her ear. A few times she would blush, and her rosy cheeks were visible from even where Melissa sat. She had to admit, they looked really good together. Lovely would definitely be something different for Abe if they became an item.

"Where's Reggie?"

Melissa was snapped out of her thoughts by the sound of *his* voice. Trying to suppress her excitement, she responded dryly, "He doesn't like these type of functions."

"I don't either," Tomiko mumbled.

"It's not that bad," Ike responded.

Tomiko groaned, "Baby, I really wanna go. You can stay here and catch a ride with Eli."

Melissa could see the frustrated look in Ike's face. He said, "How about I leave with you and we can spend the rest of the night together?"

That panged Melissa's heart. Did he really want to spend the evening with Tomiko? Was his desire to make things work with Tomiko?

Tomiko said, "Nah bae; you stay. You do the networking thing for your job with your *brother's* company. I'll probably go to my sister's."

The slight in Tomiko's statement wasn't mistaken. Ike narrowed his eyes at his wife letting her know he was displeased. Tomiko could care less as she sipped her wine casually.

Melissa wondered what was wrong with them this time. Ike, Tomiko, and their two daughters had just returned from Japan. They had been overseas to be present for Tomiko's father's funeral. Melissa just didn't understand Tomiko. That woman shouldn't have any problems. Melissa considered Tomiko, the luckiest woman in the world. She had the best husband a woman could ask for; Isaac Masters aka Ike.

The Masters brothers were all well over six feet. Ike was the tallest at six-six. He was medium frame, thinner than Abe but his presence was still intimidating. Ike was a college basketball star, but a motorcycle accident ended his professional opportunities. Melissa remembered that accident too. She was by his side while he recuperated. Tomiko was there, but it wasn't at the top of her priority list.

It was then that Melissa realized she was in love with Ike. She would never be able to act on it though. Ike was deeply in love with Tomiko who was mixed with Asian. Tomiko was every man's dream. Melissa who always struggled with her weight was merely the chubby girl, the sister of Abe's good friend Jah and classmate of Eli.

As the years went by Melissa sat back and watched Ike be a wonderful husband to Tomiko and terrific father to their kids. She ended up with her own husband, settling into married life and motherhood herself. But there was still something there when it came to Ike.

Ike had the same chiseled looks as Abe, but Ike was nerded down. He wore black-framed glasses, his coily hair always appeared disheveled, and he wore the grungy five o clock shadow look. Only on special days like Sundays or events such as this ball, he would line his shadow giving it a neater appearance. He might even run his fingers through his hair once or twice. Like Eli and Abe, Ike had some pretty eyes too except his weren't blue or light brown but they were medium brown, and he had a dark caramel complexion.

Ike and Eli were supposed to have the same father which was odd being that Ike was the first child and Eli was the last child. However with the exception of Abe's blue eyes and lighter skin none of the brothers looked much different.

Melissa couldn't stand women who had great husbands and didn't appreciate them. Tomiko was one of them.

———————

After an eventful Saturday night with her circle of friends, Melissa went home to her husband and son. Melissa sat their takeout on the counter realizing her husband had company. She went to the door to the den. It was his brother Darius. "Hey, bae and Greg."

"What's up sis-in-law," Greg shot back.

Her husband looked displeased. He said, "Let me guess, leftovers from somebody else house again?"

"Technically, they're not leftovers. It's food I ordered," Melissa corrected.

"I don't want it if it came from that nigga's house."

"You are so ungrateful. Picky ass for a nigga who don't earn shit!" Melissa shouted. She headed back to the kitchen where she had sat her purse and keys on the counter.

He called out, "If I don't earn shit then maybe you ain't sucking Abe dick good enough. Bitch!"

Melissa cringed. She absolutely hated when he referred to her as a bitch. As a construction worker for Abe's company, her husband made decent money. Compared to what Abe paid her as his administrative assistant her husband earned pocket change.

Melissa grabbed her leftovers and her purse and left. She had absolutely nowhere to go. She didn't want to bother her friends or her brother. She certainly didn't want to go to her mama's for a lecture. Then it occur to her to go where she always liked to escape. Abe's downtown condo. It had the most beautiful skyline view overlooking the LP Field and Cumberland River.

Melissa got there and immediately unwound. She grabbed a glass of wine and sat out on the terrace. With her feet propped up the breeze swept under her dress and blew against the sweat in between her thighs.

After twenty minutes passed her phone chimed alerting her to a text received. It was probably her husband saying something stupid like: what?

Melissa reviewed it and was surprised to see it was Ike: **What r u doing?**

Melissa: **nothing**

Ike: **r u alone?**

Melissa sighed and replied: **as usual...what r u doing? Where's Tomiko?**

Ike: **club with friends**

Melissa: **is everything alright?**

Ike: **that's what I was wondering about you**

Melissa: **I'm good...HE will b back soon**

Ike: **home?**

Melissa: **yeah where else?**

Ike: **not Abe's condo?**

Melissa stood up and looked back into the dimly lit condo. Ike was sitting on the ottoman in the living room looking back at her. She was embarrassed for trying to lie. She walked inside. "What are you doing here?"

"I come here all the time," Ike said.

"Why? I mean you have that big beautiful house in Grand Ivy."

"And you got one in Northridge," Ike countered.

Melissa went to sit down but Ike reached for her. She knew she shouldn't take his hand but like a magnet she was drawn to it. Ike pulled her to him and held her close.

Melissa realized where this was going and tried to pull away. "Ike, we can't do this. I'm not doing this with you. Not again."

"Melissa, that was years ago and you know nothing has really changed since then."

Melissa glared at him, "I can't tell. You used me, then patched things up with Ming Ling. Y'all have been the happiest lil couple since."

"So are you saying you don't want me no more?" Ike asked.

"I'm saying I don't wanna be used again," Melissa retorted.

"This is what you said eight years ago and you're the one that pushed me away," Ike said. He let her go and got up.

Melissa followed him out to the terrace. He stood by the railing looking out into the night's bright lights.

"I did what I knew you wanted. I helped you out Ike. You weren't going to leave Tomiko. Not for me anyway," she said looking up at him.

"You don't know that cause you never gave it a chance. I left Tomiko, remember? I had moved in with Abe."

Melissa remembered. For two weeks she and Ike secretly hooked up right in Abe's old house. Ike was going through whatever he was with Tomiko and Melissa had only been seeing her husband who was just her boyfriend then for six months at that time.

Ike looked down at Melissa and asked, "How are things with him?"

Melissa gave a pouty half shrug.

"Must not be good. How come he leaves you home all of the time?"

Melissa shrugged again.

"You're not happy," he stated.

"I haven't been for a while. I mean I'm not happy with him. I'm happy around y'all and my son."

"How long y'all been married?"

"About seven years."

"I've been married to Tomiko for twelve." He drifted into a deep thought.

Melissa was curious and asked, "How many times have you cheated?"

Ike asked, "During the marriage or the entire time I've been dealing with Tomiko?"

"Just the marriage."

"Its been a few times."

"Is that the reason behind your strained marriage?"

"No. The reason it's strained is because I did what Abe was about to do. I married someone who I shouldn't have. Trust me, the times I cheated Tomiko didn't notice because she was too busy doing her own thing which led me to seek attention elsewhere in the first place."

Melissa digested what he was saying. He didn't sound hurt or anything. She asked, "So was that what we were about eight years ago?"

He didn't answer the question. Instead he said, "I think I'm ready to move on."

"Move on like how?"

"Divorce."

Melissa gasped in shock. "No separation? No counseling?"

"Nope. We've tried counseling. I really don't need to give any more thought to it. I'm just gonna do it. What about you?"

"I haven't thought that far ahead," she said. She grabbed her wine glass and went back inside. Ike followed closing the glass doors behind him.

Melissa went into the kitchen to pour more wine. She tossed it back in three gulps. Ike was making her nervous. He walked upon her. He towered her five-nine frame which she loved. She looked up at him. He had removed his glasses, and his eyes were extremely sexy, tight almond shape looking down at her. His lips were nice and shapely and coming closer to hers. Melissa's heart beat wildly as Ike covered her mouth with his in a passionate kiss. She returned it softly, sweetly. They pulled away to look at each other. Unspoken words were told by the way Ike lifted her up on the counter. The kissing returned deeper, hungrier as he slipped her panties off. Melissa wrestled with his belt and jeans.

No time for protection Ike pushed deep inside Melissa. She cried out holding onto him for dear life. He thrust inside her harder and harder making Melissa knock everything on the counter to the floor. He picked her up off the counter with every intention to carry her to the bedroom but forgot his pants weren't completely off. They tumbled to the floor.

"Dammit Ike!" Melissa exclaimed. She ended up on top of him.

Ike laughed uncontrollably, "I'm sorry."

Melissa giggled as she straddled him. She grabbed his dick and eased it inside her. She had to lean forward because Ike wasn't the type you could just sit straight on. She surprised herself because no way would she want to ride her husband let alone have the energy and passion she showed Ike. She took possession of Ike's mouth kissing him wildly. He grabbed her ass and pulled her down on him with forceful thrusts. Melissa pulled away from his kisses to scream as it was too much to bear.

This *affair* would be too much to bear. Melissa knew it would and it was why she would let this be this one time only.

Chapter 10

Abe was somewhat disappointed that he didn't get to leave the ball with Lovely. He was looking forward to spending time with her, but she'd swiftly left out of there like she was Cinderella. She didn't leave her shoe behind though. There was something about Lovely he was really feeling. However, with the way love had done him in the past he just wanted to be extra cautious. It was so easy nowadays to fall hard for a woman. He found himself extremely vulnerable and desperate to have a consistent special someone in his life. Which lead him back to the thought of Kenya. It was nice seeing Kenya again. There were feelings there that were undeniable, but he was still interested in what could become of him and Lovely.

Pushing thoughts of Lovely aside, Abe focused on his mother. Abe knew he was a glutton for punishment. When he asked Eli if he could ride with him the following day so that Eli could give their mother her birthday present, Abe said he wouldn't do or say anything. But it was something about seeing his mother every time that made Abe yearn for her. She looked so pretty and sweet as she laughed with her friends. Abe was drawn to her like a moth to a flame. The feelings his mother left him to deal with were so unhealthy, but she was his mother. He couldn't help it. Every time he saw Sarah he just wanted her to hold him and assure him everything would be okay.

Eli and Abe went around to the back of the home where their parents were entertaining guests. As usual Abe hung back while Eli greeted everyone. Esau threw daggers Abe way letting him know he wasn't welcomed. How could a man hate another man so much? Especially the man that kept him fed and provided the roof over his head. Abe didn't get it.

Mary, their aunt saw Abe and walked over to him wearing a big smile. "Give your auntie a hug."

Abe gave Mary a warm hug. She tried to step in during his younger years and be the mother to him that Sarah refused to be. By that time most of the damage had been done. Abe respected Mary, but in his teen years, he had become rebellious. Mary never gave up trying though. He appreciated his aunt for doing so.

Mary stepped back and side-eyed Abe. "Now whatchu come over here for? Why do you do this to yourself?"

Abe shrugged. "I'll never give up trying Aunt Mary."

"I really wished you would," Mary said.

Abe looked beyond Mary at his mother. She was a beautiful woman. She had a mocha complexion with simple soft features. He and his brother resembled their mother a lot therefore Abe having a different father wasn't as noticeable.

Abe called out to his mother, "Hey Mama."

Sarah ignored him. Abe said, "I hope you like what I got you." When she continued to ignore him Abe desperately pleaded, "Mama, will you please just look at me." He wanted to touch her shiny black hair.

Mary looked up at the anguish sketched across Abe's face.

Poor child, she thought. Her sister should be ashamed for tormenting this child that was now a man of thirty-four years old, all because of a dirty secret she was keeping from everybody. Mary knew, but as a promise to her sister she swore she would never tell.

"What you get her Abe?" Mary asked, pushing him toward the front of the house.

"I uhm...got her...," he was saying. His voice trembled as water began to build up in his eyes. He looked at Mary. "Why doesn't love me?"

Mary sighed, "I don't know Abe. I wished you stop doing this. Leave my sister alone. She ain't got a bit of sense. Just leave her snooty ass alone. You've done all you're supposed to as a son and trust me, God knows. He sees everything that you have become and he knows your heart. Why do you think he keeps right on blessing you?"

Eli joined Mary in trying to get Abe to leave. He pulled on Abe's shoulder. "C'mon Abe."

Abe didn't budge. He continued to stare at his mother as tears filled his eyes. His voice was above a whisper. "Mama please?"

———

The ride back home was quiet. It never failed. Abe always embarrassed himself when it came to Sarah Masters. To him it didn't matter. He would always try to get his mother to love him. He would always try to prove to both his mother and stepfather that he was worthy of their love.

With disappointment and hurt settled over him Abe felt a need for comfort that only a woman could provide. He couldn't disclose his past with Lovely just yet because he didn't want to burden her and possibly run her away. The next best thing to do was call his old love Kenya. She would understand him the most.

"Hello?"

"What are you doing?"

"Nothing," she said softly. "What's up?"

"Can I see you?"

"What's wrong? You don't sound like you're okay Abe. I mean I haven't known you that long and all, but I can sense when there is something wrong."

Abe was confused. He looked at his phone. How in the hell did he manage to dial Lovely's number anyway? She was sounding like Kenya too. He couldn't tell her he intended to call another woman. "I just need some company. What are you doing today?"

"Nothing besides sitting here. I'm a homebody, Abe. Don't do much without a driver. anyway. Robin is not here. And my Aunt Livy doesn't drive."

"How about I come to get you and we take a ride?"

"That would be great. I need to get out of this house."

"Give me fifteen minutes."

"Okay," Lovely said as they ended the call.

Lovely took the elevator up to the third floor where she entered the entertainment room. "Grace and Aunt Livy! Do I look okay?"

"Where you going?" Grace asked.

Livy smiled. "You look fine Lovely. Is your friend coming for you?"

"Yes, in about fifteen minutes," Lovely said. "Is my hair okay. Are these pants too tight? I don't wanna give off the wrong impression."

"Oh girl hush. You look fine. And ain't these the way y'all young people wearing britches nowadays," Livy said, fixing Lovely's blouse.

"Mama, you look like a hoochie," Grace teased. She pulled at the stretchy material on Lovely's legs. She was wearing newspaper print leggings with a red silk keyhole halter blouse. On her feet was a pair of red pointed toe pumps.

"Should I change?" Lovely asked.

"No. Shut up Grace. Lovely make sure you grab a jacket," Livy said, swatting at the young girl. "Your mama looks pretty as always. I just hate she cut all her hair off."

Lovely's hand went to her head to run her fingers through her curls. "It's just hair Aunt Livy."

"But it was so pretty. You know how many want hair like you had?"

"Aunt Livy, they want it and they get it," Grace said. "It's nothing to get a head full of weave these days."

"Besides Aunt Livy, it was a good cause. I'm gonna grow my hair back out just to donate it again," Lovely said. "Well, ladies I'm heading back down south to wait for my chariot to arrive."

"You be careful," Livy said as Lovely went back to the elevator.

130

Lovely went back to her bedroom to retrieve her purse. Just then the intercom buzzed. Lovely answered it. "Yes?"

"It's me."

Lovely could hear the thunderous purr of a motorcycle. Was he on a motorcycle? She let him in. She was at the door by the time he pulled up in what looked to be a black and white or silver big body motorcycle. Removing his helmet Abe asked her, "You ready?"

Lovely grinned. "So that's what you mean by going for a ride?"

"Yep. C'mon."

Lovely walked over to the bike. Before getting on, Abe pecked her lips with a kiss. "You look nice. Smell good too."

"Thanks," Lovely blushed as she straddled the back seat. She threw her cross body purse across her torso. She placed the helmet on her head and held on to Abe's muscular body. He smelled like heaven and felt so good to the touch. Lovely wasn't sure if she could keep up the good girl act too much longer.

They ended up in town at 360 Bistro for a late lunch. Lovely was still learning Nashville's spots. For a smaller southern city, Nashville had a very urban aristocratic feel in certain areas. Unfortunately only a certain class of people was privy to it just like any other urban city.

Sipping on her pomegranate martini Lovely asked. "Abe are you biracial? I've been meaning to ask you that."

"I believe I am. My mother is Black Hispanic, but I'm not sure what my father is. Never met him and my mother don't talk about him," Abe explained. He didn't want to divulge in what his father really was and what he did to Abe's mother.

"You speak Spanish?" Lovely asked, thinking about him telling her that she was beautiful in Spanish.

"I do, but only when I have to. I got a lot of Spanish speaking crew members so it comes in handy."

"I speak Spanish too. I made Grace learn it as well," Lovely said.

"Well I lived with my grandmama for the first six years of my life. English was her second language so she spoke to me in Spanish all the time."

"That's neat. So do your brothers speak it like you?" She asked.

"They speak it too. Their daddy is Hispanic too."

"Their daddy? You don't share the same father?"

Knowing he was speaking too much Abe sighed. "No we don't, but I don't really wanna talk about that."

"No problem. Ask me a question about me."

"What are you? You look biracial too."

"I'm Black and South Indian. Not Native American but across the water."

Abe smiled. "I can tell. You're a nice shade of brown."

"Thanks. You know I hate that I can't see what you look like exactly, but you feel good so I assume you look good."

Abe laughed. "O-kay. I'm just an average looking guy, though."

"Save it. I know you're fine. Robin have described you and I overheard the ladies at the singles night earlier this month," Lovely said. "I also heard your brothers are just as hot."

"You women sure do like talking." Abe grinned kind of blushing and glad that she couldn't see him.

"And men don't?"

Abe thought about how Eli filled him in on everything he's done with Kiera during the past week. "Yeah, I guess so."

"I know so. So what has Eli told you about Robin?"

"He says she's okay."

"Okay? Just okay?" she asked like she was appalled he didn't really like her.

Abe chuckled. "Okay, maybe it's more than okay. I really think my brother is going through something right now. From what I can tell I think he thinks a lot of Robin."

"I think I'll pull him aside and ask himself," Lovely said.

"I know you will."

"So what is your brother going through?" she pondered.

Abe chuckled, "You sure are nosey."

Lovely shrugged. "Hey, I just wanna know 'cause my girl really feeling him."

"And he probably is feeling Robin too, but my brother won't be very vocal about it right away. Not with me, anyway."

Deciding to change the subject, Lovely said. "So can we discuss business for a second? You talk about my house a lot. You have a lot of ideas. So, I was wondering if I could hire you to do the whole house. Your house seems to be really nice and Robin says it is. So what do you think?"

"The whole house?"

"I know it's a lot, but you could take your time. Be like a side project. Besides it'll be an excuse for you to be at my house all of the time."

"Yeah it would. I need to walk through it again. Are you sure you want me to do it?"

"I would love for you to do it. You can even work the stripper pole in there somewhere. Just give me a price."

Abe started cheesing when he heard her say that. "Okay, but what if the price doesn't have anything to do with money?"

Lovely blushed deeply. "What are you talking about Abe?"

"You know what I'm getting at."

"I'm not sure I'm following you." Lovely knew exactly what he was insinuating.

I can't, Lovely thought. *Steve Harvey says you must wait 90 days before giving up the cookie.*

"Lovely, I just want your friendship and companionship." He quickly said to clear the unsure look on her face. "I'm not talking about sex...although that would be favorable, too."

Lovely groaned with disappointment. "Darn. I thought that's what you were talking about."

Lovely tickled Abe. She was definitely different from the bourgeois, stuck-up women he was known to court. "You had sex on the brain, Lovely."

"I'm guilty. It's been a minute for me and Robin keep telling me this and that about all of this wild sex she had. And then I'm in the company of you...it can get pretty hard."

"What's a minute?"

134

"Several months."

Abe noticed her smile faded and she took on a somber expression. "Is this a sensitive subject?"

"No. It's just the last person I was with...well, mostly everyone I've been with back out of the relationship. I want to say it's because of my disability, but I don't want to believe people are that shallow. Grant it there are things I can't enjoy and I'm limited in what I can do, but that shouldn't make me be any less eligible as a good girlfriend. That's basically what my last male friend said to me."

"That's ugly. But I don't see any limitations in your disability. You see enough to function. You get around better than most people with normal vision. Besides I'm not thinking about what you can and can't see, I just want you to be able to feel."

"Is that right?" Lovely smiled slyly.

"It is." Abe said returning the smile.

"We'll see. They all say that you know," Lovely said matter of factly.

"I'm not 'they', I'm Abe. Get it straight."

Lovely laughed. "Okay...Abe."

Chapter 11

After their late lunch, Abe took Lovely to the Frist Center to prove a point. There was a contemporary art exhibit on display. With each piece of art, Abe would stand closely behind Lovely and describe it from corner to corner. It was almost erotic in the sensual way he spoke softly in her ear. A few times, he even placed a kiss behind her ear, one of her erogenous spots. Lovely was definitely feeling a strong desire for this man. Taking her to Frist proved to her that Abe could find a way to make anything that required vision enjoyable. With that, Lovely really appreciated his thoughtfulness.

Later, they met up with a few of Abe's friends at one of his favorite hanging spots. Abstract was a bar and lounge club used as a platform for up and coming new artist wanting to display their talents on stage. Talents could range from poetry, comedy to visual art. Lovely really liked the ambiance of the place. It was very casual and laid back. It played different genres of music when the live band wasn't doing covers of popular singles.

Lovely was unaware of the looks she received from the men and even some of the women. It made Abe feel somewhat proud to have her on his arm. Being with Lovely was nothing like being with Aisha.

However, there was one pair of eyes he didn't appreciate being on Lovely. Those eyes belonged to Reggie, Melissa's husband. He had been staring at Lovely all evening. Abe didn't understand why Melissa wouldn't just leave Reggie. He meant her absolutely no good.

"What's up with that nigga?" Abe asked Ike.

"Tey?"

"Yeah. He's been eye fucking Lovely all night."

"Really," Ike asked. He looked over at his wife, Tomiko who was engrossed by something Tey was saying. She was smiling big and giving Tey all of her attention. "I hadn't really noticed because her ass got a damn attitude as always."

"What's up with that? Y'all two okay?"

Ike sighed, "Not really."

"You wanna talk about it?"

As Melissa approached, Ike said, "Not here. But I'll fill you in later. What's up Lissa?"

"Nothing much. When we leaving?" Melissa asked. She watched Abe frown and walk away. He went to Lovely who was talking with Dewalis, Melissa's husband, and Kenya. "What's wrong with your brother?"

"Nothing," Ike said. He looked down at Melissa's luscious lips and wanted to kiss her. He said for only her to hear, "You looking good in this dress."

Melissa said, "Don't start that."

"You think I can see you tonight?"

"No. We ain't doing that again."

"That's what your mouth say. I bet her down there ain't saying that," he teased.

Melissa rolled her eyes. She smiled, "How you gon talk to me and our significant others are a few feet away." Men. Why did they have to be so animalistic? Fuck, eat, shit and sleep. That's all they knew.

"This is completely innocent. We interact all of the time just like they do," Ike said.

"Innocent my ass," Melissa smirked playfully.

"You're so beautiful. I wanna make love to you tonight. I ain't accepting no for an answer. Condo. Be there," he said as he walked away.

———

The lounge was full of patrons ready for a night of enjoyment. Lovely had a hard time focusing on anybody on stage or in her face because Abe was in her ear the entire time. He whispered, "*Quiero hacerte el amor con usted usar estos zapatos rojos.*"

Lovely giggled. He whispered. "Stop laughing before you hurt my ego."

"Okay," she giggled.

He whispered, "*¿Cuándo puedo hacer el amor contigo?*"

Lovely blushed. By the time the day would be over Lovely's cheeks would be aching so much from all of the blushing and smiling. Abe asked her when he could make love to her in Spanish and sounded so sexy. She was tempted to ask him if they could go back home and do it right then and there.

Lovely turned her head to kiss his lips sensually. She whispered. "*Usted puede hacer el amor conmigo, mi amor.*"

The seductive tone of her voice drove Abe crazy. He kissed her passionately.

"Ahem...," Melissa cleared her throat dramatically. She threw a napkin at Abe. "Y'all need to get a room with all that."

"Shut up," Abe spat playfully. He caught several men looking over at Lovely again. Abe hoped he didn't have to put any of these niggas in their place. When it came to a love interest Abe could be territorial unless she seemed to be interested in someone else. If it came to that, just as he done with Aisha, he'd cut her ass off.

The show was great. Abe nor could Lovely could wait to make it back to her house, but before going to Lovely's, Abe took the motorcycle back to his house to trade out with his car. They went inside for a minute before leaving.

"So you and Abe getting serious?" Kiera asked Lovely as she sat in the gathering room waiting for Abe.

"We're still getting to know one another," Lovely replied. She was kind of leery about Kiera. She wanted to like the girl, but there was something about her. It seemed that whenever Robin was around Kiera made a point to drag Eli away.

Kiera nodded. "He's a cool dude. You know he used to date my sister Kenya."

"Kenya," Lovely repeated. "Yeah. Wasn't she at the ball? I think I met her."

"Yeah, she was there. We're not that close. We have different mamas so we didn't really grow up together."

The doorbell sounded. Kiera shook her head. "Aw hell, I can guess who this is."

"Who?" Lovely asked as her eyes followed Kiera's body moving away.

"Let me go see. I'll be back," Kiera said. She went down the spiral staircase to the foyer and opened the door. "What do you want?"

"Where is Abe?" Aisha snipped.

"Aisha?" Abe was saying as he descended the stairs. "What are you doing here?"

"To see you. I told you I was coming over," Aisha said matter of factly.

Abe shook his head slowly. "I didn't tell you it was okay though."

Kiera headed back up the stairs to Lovely. She whispered to Lovely, "It's Aisha."

"Huh?" Lovely asked in disbelief.

"Yeah. That's her down there. She's always here. I think it's something seriously wrong with her."

Lovely wanted to know what Kiera meant by Aisha always being there. Lovely needed to see for herself. She wasn't as mad at Abe for abandoning her to speak with Aisha as she was mad that Kiera felt a need to tell her what was going on. Lovely followed Kiera to the landing of the staircase. Lovely heard them before she saw their bodies.

"I do love you, but you can't be doing this Aisha," Abe said.

"Doing what? You say you wanna move on, but you change your mind when I'm here. Baby, I know you wanna be with me. You're just afraid of what people might say. Fuck them Abe."

"That's not it."

"Well what is it?" Aisha kissed him. "What is it baby?"

Lovely made her presence known. She cleared her throat and called down to him, "Hey Abe, I think I should leave." She started down the spiral staircase.

"No Lovely. You stay," Abe said.

Lovely stood her ground. "No, I don't want to bother you. You're fine. I'll get Robin to get me or I'll just walk."

Walk? Lovely couldn't see and it was dark. No way would Abe let her walk. Abe shot daggers toward Aisha who was wearing the most innocent blank look. She had been texting him all evening. He replied to a few of them, but he didn't expect her to actually come to his house.

Still delusional, Aisha had been showing up at his house every other night wanting to talk. Now that Abe was openly seeing Lovely, Aisha worried that the chances of getting back together were slim to none. She was right. Abe had no intentions of ever hooking back up with Aisha. They were over with. Out of pity and sympathy he'd let her stay overnight just so she wouldn't make good on her threats of harming herself, but Abe hadn't been sleeping with her.

Lovely was on her phone. "Robin, do you think you can come grab me from Abe's house before you leave?...Okay. Thanks."

Lovely looked toward Abe. "What were you saying?"

"Don't go yet. I'll take you home. Call Robin back and tell her it's okay," Abe pleaded.

Aisha stood behind Abe. "Abe, what about the baby?"

"What baby?" Abe asked with exasperated confusion.

"That's what I've been trying to tell you. I'm pregnant baby."

"Great," Lovely said, throwing her hands in the air. She walked toward the door.

Kiera stood at the top landing of the stairs watching in silence.

Abe looked at Aisha like he could slap her. "Don't start that bullshit Aisha. If you are pregnant, it sure as hell ain't mine."

"Why wouldn't it be?"

"Getcho ass on the phone and call Michael about that shit," Abe said angrily. He looked back for Lovely. She was gone.

"We'll get a DNA test then," Aisha said.

Kiera cut in. "You gotta wait for the baby to be born."

"They can test while I'm pregnant," Aisha explained.

"Bitch you ain't even pregnant," Abe snapped.

"Bitch? Since when did you use such language, Abe?" Aisha asked.

"I call you a bitch all the time in my head. Like 'this bitch stupid as hell if she think she can put a baby on me'. Fuck you Aisha." He went after Lovely.

Aisha wore a crazed look. "That blind bitch ain't taking him from me. That I know. One way or another I'ma get Abe to love me again."

"But are you pregnant for real?" Kiera asked.

Aisha grinned devilishly, "Maybe."

———

Robin waited nervously. She looked around her hotel room. Everything was neat and in its place. She took a look at herself in the mirror. The red teddy and matching crotchless panties were enough to drive even a blind man crazy.

Her phone started ringing. She looked at it and frowned. "Hello?"

"Hey, what are you doing?" Eli asked.

"Nothing," she said, feeling awkward suddenly like she needed to cover up.

"I think I'ma call it a night and leave these fools alone. I was just calling because...you were on my mind."

Robin smiled, "Really? Like how?"

"I'm not sure what this is, but I feel an attraction that I can't really explain."

"Have you talked this out with Kiera?"

"Why would I have to talk this over with Kiera?"

"Isn't she your mate?"

"No. She's just--," Eli stopped himself. He was confused. "Why would you think that she and I were more than friends?"

"I don't know. It seemed like y'all were together at the ball."

"I did ask her to tag along, but she wasn't really my date."

"Can I ask you a question?"

"Sure." He said.

Robin was hesitant but she forced it out. "Are you bisexual or straight?"

There was a pregnant pause.

"Eli?"

Eli finally asked, "Can I ask you something?"

Robin listened. "Well...I guess, but I asked you something first."

"I know, but how much difference would it make if I was either?"

"It doesn't. I see you for being Eli and not by your sexual orientation."

"Are you interested in me beyond friendship?" Eli asked, ignoring the bisexual question. He always got that when he didn't want to sleep with a woman, but he had his reasons. He wanted a lasting relationship whenever he decided to get in one and nobody knew how to handle him at the moment.

Robin gave it some thought. "Maybe."

"Maybe," Eli repeated with thought. "We've been talking on the phone for a couple of weeks. You've come by my house. I've seen you at Lovely's and all I get is a maybe."

"Well, I'm not sure if you even like girls."

Eli chuckled, "I *don't* like girls."

"I mean women. You know what the hell I'm talking about."

Eli smiled. "If you need me to like women Robin, then I will."

"What kind of answer is that Eli? You know what? Don't answer that. Have you and Kiera decided what to do?'

"Fuck that bitch." He quickly spat. "She wants things to stay as they are now. I just don't want the twins looking at me and being resentful, because they didn't get to know me as their real father."

"So you're still convinced that her twins are your kids?"

"Have you seen them?"

Robin had definitely seen Kiera's children. They shared the same caramel complexion as Eli and had his same medium brown eyes. They even had raven black coils on their heads like his.

Eli asked, "So...is there any way you would feel like coming over tonight?"

"Well, I kinda got other plans going on."

"Oh. Well damn, that's what the fuck I get, huh?"

Robin snickered. "I may can come over much later or tomorrow."

"Just give me a call back if you can make it tonight." He said, just wanting to see her.

"Okay," she said as her hotel room door opened. Nervously she said, "Uhm...Let me call you back later." She didn't say goodbye or even wait for Eli to say it back before hanging up.

"Who were you talking to?"

"My girlfriend," Robin quickly lied to her company. "She wanted me to go out with them tonight."

He frowned, "Lovely?"

Robin nodded with uneasiness.

"You betta not be lying to me."

"I'm not," she said fretful of what he might do.

He grinned at her enjoying the sight of her. Not wasting any time he knelt down before her and pulled her to the edge of the bed. He spread her legs open. The crotch of her panties widened to reveal the fleshy moist part of her. Robin watched as he began tonguing her clit. She let out a quivering breath. "Ooh baby...that feels good."

Robin didn't care about nothing else in the moment. She just wanted a man to make her feel good. So what if he happened to be married.

———

Lovely heard the buzzer to the gate. She also knew who it was. She already told Abe she wasn't into sharing, she hated liars, and she wasn't a man's second option. Period. She was worth more; not just monetarily, but as a person to be a second best. Lovely was beginning to believe that being alone was her only option.

Her phone rang announcing Abe was calling. She answered, "What?"

"Are you not going to let me in?"

"Nope. Don't you have a baby mama to tend to?" she asked sarcastically.

"She ain't my baby mama. If she's pregnant it definitely ain't mine."

"But you've been sleeping with her right?"

"I did."

"So there's a possibility right?"

"I mean...there's always a possibility. If you let me in, we can talk."

"No thanks. I mean, you ain't my man, Abe. I ain't even mad like that anyway. It's just that this is my way of letting you know I'm not dealing with that. I mean what I say, and we can't see each other on a romantic level anymore. Other than that I still would like for you to do my house and we can be friends."

"Lovely, you're stubborn. You know that?"

"Maybe."

"Let me in please."

"No. There's nothing else for you and I to discuss except what color palette I prefer for my kitchen. Now, I don't wanna be rude and hang up in your face, but—"

"Aisha is desperate to get back with me cause she see me moving on with you. Right now she'll say anything. I've always been careful about not producing babies. I want one with the woman who becomes my wife and Aisha hates the idea of children. We always bumped heads when it came to that subject, but I knew that I would get my way once we were married, but it didn't happen."

"So she's lying?" Lovely felt her anger subdue quickly.

"Yes, she's lying."

Lovely didn't want to own up to the guilt she felt for being so mean and dismissive so soon. She was stubborn as Abe had mentioned before. "Okay. I accept that explanation. Now when you get the chance, please look into a time when you can come and do a walkthrough of my house and give me an estimate. Other than that, good night Abe."

"Lovely! Don't you dare hang up on me," he said.

Lovely covered her mouth to keep him from hearing her snickers. She composed herself. "What Abe?"

"Can I please come in? I need to be with you. That's all I've been thinking about all day. Don't do me like this."

"Abe, don't beg. It's not a good look." She pushed the keypad to open the gate.

"Thank you," Abe said.

Lovely hung up the phone. She giggled all the way to the front door. She opened it before he could ring the bell.

"I oughta bite you for putting me through that," Abe said as he walked toward her.

"Bite me?"

Abe leaned down to kiss Lovely. He wrapped his arms around her waist and lifted her off the ground. When he lowered her he said, "I'm gonna need a deposit on this job tonight."

Lovely grinned. "You so silly. C'mon."

———

Robin's phone lit up. She eased away from under her lover's arm and reached for her cell phone on the nightstand. Damn, it was Eli again. Ever since Robin hung up on him he had been calling her. Now that her lover was done for the night she decided to take a look at her phone. She silenced it completely before she started checking her texts.

Eli: **what's up with u? u hung up in my face and now u ain't answering**

Eli: **answer ur damn phone**

Lovely: **Can You Believe Abe Is Here?**

Eli: **r u with some other nigga?**

Why does he care? This made Robin smile.

"Who is that baby?"

Robin was startled. She thought he was asleep. "Lovely. She wanna know if I'm coming home." Robin placed her phone back on the nightstand.

"Tell her you coming home after you take care of Daddy one last time."

Robin smiled as he pulled her on top of him. He was hard already. She eased him inside of her.

"Damn girl, your pussy always wet and ready. You love me?"

"Yeah," she moaned. Did she? Robin didn't even know what love felt like.

"Fuck me like you love me then."

Robin rode him with purpose. She needed him to know she was just as good as the wife he was about to go home to. She needed him to believe that she would do anything he asked of her just so he would keep her in his life.

She hated when he climaxed and got his nut. She didn't get hers, but it was okay as long as he was satisfied. She just hated that he would be leaving her. He saw the sadness in her eyes and kissed her sweetly on the cheek. "I'll see you soon. Stop looking so sad baby."

"You know this the part I hate," Robin said.

"I know. But hopefully you won't have to worry about that soon."

Robin smiled. "You're still going to do it?"

He nodded as he gathered his things. He kissed her one last time before going into the bathroom to freshen up.

Robin grabbed her things that had been thrown about the room. Minutes later, he came out of the bathroom looking just as fresh as he did when he walked through the door. He gave her a light kiss before leaving. Robin hopped in the shower to freshen up. She thought she would give Eli a call back to see exactly what he wanted after she got out.

"Oh so now you wanna call me back," Eli said playfully as he answered.

"Well if you're busy I can call you back," Robin said coyly.

"You're fine. So was you with another man tonight?"

"Something like that. What about you?"

"I was not with another man tonight," Eli responded humorously.

Robin laughed. "Okay."

"You still wanna come over?"

"Sure. Give me fifteen minutes."

"See you when you get here. Bye."

"Bye." She said. She smiled. Then she laughed out loud as she plopped down on the hotel bed. What the hell was she doing? Eli was definitely starting to prove that he was a straight man. She felt herself falling for him so if he wasn't she was going to be pissed with herself for thinking he was.

Chapter 12

Lovely carefully entered her bedroom Sunday morning. She carried a tray full of breakfast foods fit for a king. The king was lying in her bed. Asleep. Naked. After what he did the night before, Lovely would proudly call him the king and serve him breakfast in bed.

Lovely had never been sexed down the way Abe put it down. She almost didn't let it happen still holding onto her stubbornness. The thing she liked about Abe was that he didn't back down easily. He was persistent, but so gentle and loving causing her to melt in his arms.

It started with him holding her from behind and kissing her ears speaking in Spanish softly. Lovely was weak for his sensuality. Every time she would try to pry away he would hold her tighter. Then his hands started to caress every sensitive spot on her body. He massaged her breasts with one hand and the other hand found its way to the junction in between her hips.

Abe led her to bed and prompted her to lie down. He took his time exploring Lovely's body leaving delicate kisses along the way as he undressed her. He was very gentle with her. He wanted to make sure she felt completely comfortable with him. But it took everything in him to pace himself. He had been imagining making love to Lovely all that night. The desire, passion and sexual needs were driving him insane.

Lovely groaned with disappointment when Abe pulled away. She loved the feel of being in his arms. She loved the way he softly kissed her. She felt cherished.

Hearing him remove his clothing Lovely softly spoke. "I can't see you like you can see me."

"But you can feel," he said. He removed his last article of clothing. He hovered over her positioning himself in between her legs. Kissing her, he took her hand and placed them on his face. "Feel me, Lovely."

Lovely wasn't as nervous as she thought she would be. Her desire for him drowned out her apprehension. As they locked in a deep passionate ravenous kiss, Lovely's hands familiarized themselves with Abe's body. She explored the softness of his hair, the angular lines of his face, his facial hair, his neck, his broad shoulders, his chest, his back, the muscles of his abdomen, and the bulge of his biceps.

Lovely let her hands travel down his chest, even circling his nipples with her fingers. When they became rigid and Abe let out a soft moan Lovely knew that was a sensitive area for him. Her hands went further down and caressed his lower abs and the lower part of his flanks. He shuddered beneath her touch and groaned this time. Another spot, Lovely thought.

"You can go lower," he whispered. Abe adjusted so that she could go further. His heart beat wildly as she wrapped her small hands around his dick. Her touch was sending him over the edge and he wasn't sure if he could contain his passion.

Lovely loved the way Abe felt in her hands. He was long and thick. Whenever she squeezed gently his manhood would jump. She caressed it, feeling its texture and warmth as she whispered. "You're beautiful baby."

He coaxed her onto her back. He placed kisses down the inner part of her thighs until he reached "her". He parted her slit with his tongue and proceeded to tickle her clit with the stiffness of his tongue. Lovely's legs fell open. She grabbed his head and thrust against his tongue. Abe spread her pussy lips and brought his lips around her bliss button while he suckled it gently. Lovely whimpered and moaned loudly. His tongue swirls caressed her clit just right to stimulate her into an explosive orgasm.

Lovely stiffened and cried out. When she couldn't take it anymore she shoved his head deeper into her pussy as she thrust her hips over and over to get every bit out. Bearing enough she clamped her thighs shut and pushed his head away.

Lovely let out a small quivering laugh. "Sorry," she groaned still feeling the aftermath of that eruption. "Oh God...," she called as her body continued to jerk.

Raising to his knees, Abe held her legs open with them on either side of him. He rubbed the head of his dick in the wetness of her, massaging her clit yet again. Lovely inhaled holding her breath and moaned massaging her own breasts. Abe leaned down to show her erect nipples a little attention. When he rose back up, he pushed inside her but she wasn't quite receptive to his entrance. Lovely inched back while crying out.

"*Relajarse, descansar mi amor*," he whispered. He continued to talk soothingly in Spanish as he short stroked his way in. The deeper he was able to go the more intense it got for him and her both.

Abe groaned. He couldn't even move because he was on the verge of cumming already. Lovely rocked her hips forward. Abe whimpered. "Oh don't move...shit, shit, shit..."

As he held still, marinating in her juiciness, he could feel her squeeze around him. It only made it worse. Abe thrust inside her aggressively. "Gotdammit fuck it!"

Abe stroked her deep and long at an even pace with deliberate movement causing her to moan, whimper, and shake. Lovely's pussy was wet, tight but deep. He loved her depth. He could sheath a lot more of himself deep inside her without her crying that it hurt. Before he could even bust his first nut he was convinced that he was in love with this woman.

Abe asked between breaths, "Can I go faster and deeper?" He slowed his pace for her to respond.

"Yes, just don't hurt me Abe."

"I won't. I promise. I just wanna make you feel good."

Lovely let him push her legs back. He drove deeper, faster, harder. Lovely's groans and cries got louder. She wanted him to stop, but she also wanted him to never stop at the same time. The way he was pounding her and the feeling it sent through her body

Abe whispered, "I wish you could see this shit." He watched his dick become covered in her creaminess. "You cummin on this dick baby?"

Lovely moaned loudly without reserve and let her eyes roll back as he sped up and went harder. She pushed on his hips to prevent him from going too deep.

"Move your hands," he demanded. She couldn't. Every time she moved them away she was putting them right back on his hips. "Hold those legs all the way back." He fucked her at an even pace; a method to each stroke. His agenda was to get her to orgasm.

Lovely gradually became aware of an aura settling over her, "Oh God! Abe...baby...what's happening..."

Lovely was climaxing, and the feeling was overwhelming. It was like something had invaded her body from within and filled her up, and now it wanted out. The only way it could get out was by way of explosion. Lovely screamed in a high pitch as her pussy walls contracted tightly around Abe. He felt her pussy walls forcefully convulse to the point it was pushing him out. She pushed him off her with her feet. Lovely's expression on her face was a look of mixed emotions as she let out a series of grunts and groans.

Abe watched her body twitched and locked up beneath him while a clear fluid gushed from her pussy glands. Hot damn! She ejaculated; not quite a geyser, but that shit was close enough. That drove him insane. When he reentered her his whole agenda was to make her do it again. And it happened again but the second time had involuntarily made him release inside her with profound force. Abe cried out in pleasure. Unable to control himself, he let the words. "I love you and this pussy," slip out. Realizing what he did, embarrassed him, therefore, he wanted to punish her pussy for making him vulnerable enough to say it.

He positioned her on her knees and hands with her ass up, head lowered. He had her pushed down in such a way that she couldn't crawl away. She tried taking it. Since she couldn't crawl forward, she would flatten her body to the bed when it became too much. Abe would fuck her like that for a while, but he would put her right back in position. He made her ejaculate a third time. By then she was spent and couldn't go on anymore. She collapsed onto the bed panting hard thinking of those words he expressed until sleep found her.

Lovely awakened early to find that she hadn't dreamed any of that. Abe slept quietly next to her with his arm draped around her. She eased out of the bed. She went to the bathroom to freshen up. She slipped on her floral kimono and headed to the kitchen. She called for Livy's help. Together they made biscuits, grits, scrambled eggs, breakfast chops, sausage links, sliced fresh fruit, fried potatoes, and freshly squeezed orange juice. As Lovely headed back into the bedroom, Robin came from her bedroom.

"I knew I smelled something good," Robin said eyeing the tray Lovely carried.

"I didn't even know you were here," Lovely said upon passing. "I would have wakened you."

"Is it enough for me Auntie?" Robin asked, going up to the breakfast bar. Lovely continued making her way to Abe.

"You got a young man in your room too?" Livy asked.

"Nah, not me," Robin answered sadly.

Lovely would have to remember to ask Robin what happened as she faintly heard her. She entered her bedroom and sat the tray down on the nightstand closest to Abe. She sat on the edge of the bed next to him. "Hey," she said shaking him. "Abe? Wake up baby."

"What is it?" he groaned.

"I fixed you breakfast. You smell it?"

156

Abe flipped to his side to face Lovely. He looked at the tray of food. "You ain't fixed me nothing. Your aunt did that."

"She helped me. But I cooked most of it. Believe it or not some foods can be cooked by smell and feel. You just gotta be careful or you can burn your fingerprints right off," Lovely joked.

Abe smiled playfully, enjoying her carefree attitude about life, even in her condition. "I'm gonna have to question your aunt. I don't believe you cooked most of this stuff."

She smiled. "I did. Stop tripping and eat it mister."

Abe sat up grabbing the tray. "Baby, this is a lot. You didn't have to do this."

"Well...you didn't have to do what you did last night either."

Abe smiled, "Is that what this is about?"

"I have no shame. Yes. It was good." She shyly blushed.

"C'mere," he said softly.

Lovely leaned in close enough so that he could peck her lips. "That's why I like you. You're not afraid to say what you feel and what's on your mind."

Lovely's phone rang. Thinking of the words he blurted out during sex she said. "Apparently you ain't' either." She got up to answer her phone.

Abe asked, "What does that mean?"

"Oh nothing," Lovely grinned. She answered her phone as it announced Uncle Cesar calling. "*Ciao!*"

"*Ciao mio caro! E 'bello sentire la tua voce,*" said Cesar.

"I've been waiting on you to call," Lovely said. "I know Grace has been wearing you out."

"It hasn't been that bad. Why haven't you called me young lady?"

Lovely looked in Abe's direction. "I've been preoccupied."

"Mmm hmm. That guy must be special. Yeah Grace tells me you're floating around that big house in love and all."

"Grace knows nothing."

"I'm going to have to meet this fellow."

"You'll like him. He's going to help me with the house. He's an architect," Lovely boasted. Abe grunted a laugh.

"Well that's good. Hey Papa wants to speak to you for a minute," Cesar said.

Seconds later, the smooth slight accented voice of Luciano Pavoni came on the line. The way he spoke reminded Lovely of Victor Newman from *The Young and the Restless*. "Lovely, my dear, how are you?"

"I'm good. How are you? Me and Grace need to come visit you."

"You sure do. Your grandfather would have kicked my ass by now if he knew I wasn't talking to you or seeing you on a regular basis."

"That's all my fault. I promise I will do better. Perhaps I could fly out to see you guys in the next couple of weeks. Maybe you could meet my friend."

"This guy friend of yours must be a special guy," Luciano said.

"He's cool. I like him," she said. Abe threw a pillow at her.

"Well that's good. Can I have his name? You know I like to do background checks."

"No Papa Lu," Lovely giggled. "I'm not giving you his name."

Luciano asked. "He's there?"

"Yes," Lovely laughed. She said to Abe, "My godfather and uncle are part of the Italian mafia and they gotta do a background check on you to make sure you're okay for me."

"What?" Abe asked incredulously.

Lovely said, "I know. That's what I said. Papa?"

Luciano said with a slight chuckle, "You know Lovely, I find out everything anyway."

"I know Mr. Nosy," she joked.

"I'm just doing my job and trying to look after you."

"I understand and I appreciate it. But I need to get back to my company. So if it's okay, can I call you back Papa Lu?"

"Sure my love." He said.

"Okay. Tell everyone I said I love them. Bye and I love you Papa."

Once Lovely ended the call, with a frown she turned to Abe. "Is Abe your real first name or does it stand for something?"

Abe eyed Lovely as she placed her phone back on the nightstand. He cleared his throat. "I don't really like talking about my name."

"Why? Were you named after an evil grandfather or something?"

"My name is Abram Miguel Masters. If you must know I had a legal name change because my mother named me something really fucked up."

"What did she name you?"

"It's in the Book of Revelations."

"The Book of Revelations," Lovely said with thought. Not one for arguing or nagging when someone was clearly bothered Lovely would leave the subject alone for the time being.

Abe grabbed his phone from the nightstand. He had eleven missed calls, eight were from Aisha. The last call came in at nine that morning. He had three voicemail notifications and seventeen text messages.

Abe deleted the three voicemail messages from her without listening to them. He reviewed the text messages starting from the newest to the oldest.

11:23 a.m. Eli: Where are you?

10:38 a.m. Mary: call me, this is your aunt

10:15 a.m. Aisha: Call me!

10:07 a.m. Aisha: where are u? We need to talk about this

10:03 a.m. Aisha: two wrongs don't make a right, I hope u didn't do nothing stupid like fuck that blind bitch...I love u

9:52 a.m. David: Give me a call son

8:35 a.m. Aisha: answer ur phone

3:04 a.m. Aisha: I hate u! U ain't shit!

2:13 a.m. Eli: make sure u call me in the morning...

1:34 a.m. Aisha: mothafucka at least I kept it real with u. U can't appreciate shit. U act like u so goddamn innocent. I know u fuck around with other bitches just like you probably fucking that blind bitch now.

12:38 a.m. Aisha: fuck u dumb bitch! That's y his dick is better and bigger

12:19 a.m. Aisha: u got ur goddamn nerves! How could you walk out on me when I'm telling you I'm carrying your child?

That one made Abe laugh out loud. This girl was crazy.

12:14 a.m. Aisha: I hope she give u AIDS and ur mothafuckin dick get gangrene and deteriorate

Again, Abe laughed.

11:47 p.m. Aisha: we ain't finish talking, call me back

11:20 p.m. Kenya: Hey! Call me if you can.

11.01 p.m. Aisha: where are u?

10:38 p.m. Aisha: I can't stand ur ass...that's why I did it!

He looked at Lovely and asked, "Are you crazy?"

Lovely frowned, "What kind of question is that?"

He chuckled thinking of Aisha. "Just wondering."

Chapter 13

When Kiera realized Dr. Abe Masters was Fyah it brought back a lot of memories. Kenya, Kiera's older half-sister was real close friends with Abe and the other boys that ran the streets. Abe had also been friends with David's son Troy. Back then Abe was part of a street organization that went beyond little boys trying to sell drugs. Those boys were true junior mafia. They were into racketeering, prostituting, dog fighting, beat downs, robberies and even murder. Abe got his name because he didn't mind putting fire to a nigga's ass whether it be by match or gun.

The Abe of today was nothing like the Abe Kiera knew back then. It was very surprising to see him all cleaned up, poised and polished. Back in the day he wore his hair in long cornrows, had a grill top and bottom, and wore white tees, jeans, and Timberlands. He rarely spoke but when he did it was to bark orders. He was eighteen telling guys twenty-five what to do. Abe's height, body size and facial hair gave him leverage and it gave him an older appeal.

Kiera walked into Abe's home office where Abe sat. "Lovely still mad at you from last night?"

Abe looked up from his computer's screen. He smiled, "Nah. She straight."

Kiera smiled back at him knowingly. "I bet she is."

Abe leaned back in his high back executive chair. "You still deal with Lo and Dante?"

"Not really," Kiera said. She took a seat in one of the leather chairs. "You know Lo still locked up."

Abe nodded. "Yeah I know. But Dante ain't. Is he the twins' father?"

Kiera shrugged. "He could be."

"Is my brother their father?"

Kiera stared into Abe's icy blue gaze. "No."

"He seems to think he could be. Kiera, don't be playing no games."

"I'm not. He isn't."

"They look like Eli more than they look like Dante."

"Uhm...isn't Eli and Dante cousins?"

"You need to get that figured out for my brother's sake. If those are his kids he needs to know. So while you're bullshitting and playing around you need to go ahead and set up a DNA test."

"This ain't high school, Abe. I'm a grown ass woman and you ain't finna chastise me like I'm a child."

"I'm not Kee. But, you know that shit ain't right."

"Naw, what ain't right is you forgetting where you came from."

"I beg your pardon."

Kiera broke out into a wide grin. "Where is Fyah?"

163

Abe rolled his eyes. "Fyah is long gone."

"Does Lovely know about Fyah?"

"No. It really isn't necessary."

Kiera smugly grinned. "I wonder how she would feel about you and the things you used to do."

Abe's brow furrowed. "What are you getting at Kiera?"

"Oh nothing," Kiera mumbled. She pretended to be engrossed by her fingernails.

Seeing where the conversations had taken a left, Abe grew mildly irate. "Baby girl, are you forgetting you're in my house? Now, I did this as a favor for your uncle. I love your uncle and he was like a father to me and still is. I'd hate to have to put you out and disappoint David."

"Put me out? You'd put me and the twins out?"

"If you try to start riffs in my personal affairs, I will."

"I understand, but how about we compromise. You get me a brand new Audi A8 or...or I'll have a nice conversation with Lovely about Fyah."

Standing to his feet abruptly, venomously he spat. "Bitch, don't play with me. Let me find out you running your goddamn mouth. Don't be bringing up my past to hold over my head. Don't forget who you trying to fuck with. I'll make your ass disappear. You understand me?"

Kiera had jumped back about two feet. In a nervous playful manner Kiera she tried to play it off. "Yeah but I was just fucking with you. I wasn't serious."

Abe sat back down and composed himself as if nothing happened. "I think I have a townhouse in the east area that would be perfect for you and the twins. It's in the Five Points area. You'll love it."

Kiera thought maybe it was best. Abe was crazy. Correction. Fyah was crazy. Abe was what everyone else saw. He was the nice, giving, loving man that everyone adored. Kiera thought he had grown soft, but that right there what he just showed her was enough to let her know that Fyah was just below the surface. Fyah hadn't went anywhere.

This wasn't the Abe that Kiera knew Lovely would like. If Lovely knew about Abe being this person she wouldn't have nothing to do with him. He would argue that that wasn't him anymore. Abe hadn't changed that much. All it took was the right stimuli to bring Fyah out.

———

Eli never realized within him, feelings had grown for Robin. It wasn't until hearing her being with another man did it hit him. Normally something like that wouldn't bother him because he would be doing him anyway. Lately doing him meant spending time with family, working for Abe, and enjoying leisure time with his own circle of friends including time with Kris. The more time he spent with Robin though, the more he understood what Abe found in someone like Lovely. Being with Robin was comforting. It felt good, safe.

Leaving Abe's office, Kiera had followed Eli to one of Abe's secondary bedrooms, the one right across from his master suite. Eli didn't know Kiera tip-toed behind him and was at the bedroom entrance listening to him talk on the phone.

"I'm over Abe's right now...Yeah, she's here...It ain't even like that and you know it...What do you want me to do?" He laughed. "When I get there you'll see...Yeah you will. Stop playing...You know you want it and I'ma give it to you...Okay...I'll be there in about...give me twenty minutes...Okay. Bye."

Kiera stepped in the room. "Ah! Talking to your boo?"

Eli spun around to see Kiera in her midriff white, off one shoulder, long sleeve tee with the word SEXY in red glitter and a pair of black glittered lips, black skinny jeans and a pair of black and white python stiletto pumps. He had to admit she was exactly what her shirt described. "What are you doing?"

"Being nosy," Kiera said, shoving her hands in her back pockets. As tight as her pants were Eli didn't think it was possible.

"Get away from me lil girl," Eli said, rolling his eyes as he sat at the foot of the bed.

Kiera seductively walked up on him until she stood in front of him. "Talk to me the way you did in the cellar that day."

"I don't even know what you're talking about," Eli said innocently.

"So you pretending like it didn't happen. That's cute," Kiera teased. She moved closer. "I can't keep you off my mind. I've been thinking about that big ass dick of yours and how it might feel in my wet ass pussy."

Uh-oh, Eli thought. He was roused. His heart thumped in his chest and blood rushed to his dick and it pulsated with life. He couldn't look at her. He focused on the black glitter lips on her shirt. He carefully said. "Kiera...please get away from me."

"Why?" She moved closer. Her lips touched his forehead.

Eli didn't want to touch her body. He knew Kiera was a freak. He enjoyed messing with her, but after the cellar incident Eli told himself he wouldn't let things go there. Not with Kiera. Even that day when he stuck his hand in her panties he was only teasing. "Please Kiera. You're scaring me."

Kiera smiled a bit amused. "Eli, are you scared of pussy?"

"Yeah...yours," he said dryly. He pushed her out of the way and got up. Without looking back Eli exited the room. He had to get out of there before he found himself in serious trouble. It was bad enough he allowed himself to get caught up and let Kiera do what she did in the cellar. But this was Eli's fault for leading Kiera on to believe he could possibly want her conniving ass.

After saying his goodbyes, Eli left. Instead of going home Eli found himself going to his "boo's" house; that's how Kiera would have put it. Kris answered the door with a wide grin. With no words exchanged, she grabbed Eli by the hand, shut the front door and locked it, then led Eli to the bedroom.

She pushed Eli back onto the bed, looking deeply into his eyes before taking possession of his mouth in a soft sensual kiss. "You taste good. Can I taste the rest of you?" She said, causing an anxious Eli to want her even more. She was the only reason why he could turn women down. He wasn't about to get in a relationship with a woman only to get his heart broken. He had to know it was real first. Kris wanted the same thing he wanted. Hot sex with no strings attached. And boy, did they have some very HEATED SEX. She wasn't bourgeois, or fashionable, but she was real and simple. He liked that about her. She didn't care what people thought about her, and neither did he. He knew the dick was good, but maybe she had her own reasons for fucking him, in hopes of never getting her heart broken by someone. Who knew, since there was clearly an understanding between the two of them.

Eli gave a slight nod. His heart rate quickened as he could feel a tug on his belt. It was quickly unfastened and his pants were unzipped with just one hand. Once Eli was freed, Kris's eyes widened. "Somebody's ready for this." Next thing Eli could feel was a set of warm hands stroking his hardened dick.

Kris kissed Eli one more time before taking the dive. Eli watched as Kris deep throated all of his swollen inches without a single gagging reflex. "Daammnn," Eli hissed.

His late night booty call moaned while bobbing up and down on his dick, and then pulled away long enough to ask in a very sensual manner, "Do it feel good baby?"

Eli nodded wanting Kris to hurry and return to the task at hand. Kris sucked him so good, it had Eli's eyes rolling up in his head. She gave the best head, hands down. Eli knew he was in love.

Kris didn't bring him to an orgasm. Instead she pulled away and started undressing, and then said matter of factly. "I want this dick in me. Now."

Eli was unsure because for some reason Robin kept popping up in his head. After getting that amazing head, he really just wished it was over. At least that's what he was telling himself. Why couldn't Kris stop at the head? Eli was about to object, but she was damn near naked already. Eli was mesmerized by Kris's body. It was perfectly toned in every way. So caught up in Kris's gorgeousness, Eli didn't realize she had started removing his clothes too.

Kris kissed all over Eli's bare chest after removing his shirts and stroked Eli's dick at the same time. "Step out of these pants."

Eli obeyed Kris's orders, admiring the low cut hair on her head that enhanced the beautiful features on her face as she batted her sexy eyes. As soon as Eli's last pant leg was removed Kris pushed Eli on his back and climbed on top of him. Before Eli could object Kris was descending on his dick. And oh how good it felt! A tug of war between rationality and stupidity begun inside Eli's head. Eli stammered, "Con...oh shit...we need...a condom...condom..."

"Ssh," Kris hushed him. "Don't you wanna feel it on your dick baby?"

Eli closed his eyes. Kris appeared. Then Robin. Eli tried to think about Robin again until Kris eased further down on him. He didn't know where Kris's freaky ass learned how to do what she did, but it had been mastered. It felt like she was working every muscle to grip his dick in so many different places at once.

"Kris...," Eli groaned.

"Eli," Kris breathed. She leaned over and kissed him, "Do it feel good?"

Eli cupped Kris's ass as it bounced up and down. He kissed her passionately on the neck.

She moaned as more dick was taken deeper inside her juice box. "Ooh, my ass finna cum all over this dick!"

Eli pulled Kris down onto him as he started slamming his dick deeper. Kris tried to stifle screams that were hard to hold back. "Shit nigga!"

Eli sat up keeping himself still inside her, he flipped Kris over on the back and started pounding relentlessly. Kris's screams and moans were like soothing music to his ears. It was what Eli loved to hear. He had to focus so he didn't let loose inside too quick because he felt it coming already. She felt so good. Mixed with the excitement of being with Kris was making things hard for Eli to contain himself. No matter how hard he tried, cumming was inevitable. He had cum in her way too soon.

She knew Eli had come from his movements and the intelligible cry of words that came from his mouth. It was alright. Kris wanted him to know it was okay. Eli whispered, "Damn, damn, damn, damn."

She went back down on Eli working him back into an erection. Kris bent over on all fours. "Come on and give me that dick."

Eli obliged. He plunged deep inside of her. She cried out in painful pleasure and then moaned taking in more dick.

"Ooh, baby you finna make me nut!"

Eli gripped Kris's narrow hips and slammed deep inside her without reservation. Kris hollered out, "Shit nigga!"

"Is this what the fuck you want?"

The venomous tone of Eli's voice sent Kris to another place. "That's it baby...Fuck me...Yes baby, I'm about to..." She let out a loud scream exploding in ecstasy again.

Eli came inside Kris again as her tight muscles convulsed all around him. Kris twitched and whimpered underneath him. Eli looked at the satisfied expression on Kris's face. He took a few minutes to compose himself. He was so disappointed in himself. Why was he mad though? No matter how much he wanted to pretend he didn't like it, he could not deny to himself that Kris had felt good. He thought three weeks back when he'd just told her that they had to stop this, only to find himself back for some more of her good fucking and for what? Was it because of the thoughts he'd been having about Robin? How did he really feel about her?

————

Abe was looking forward to being with Lovely this night as he did every night. He had made a habit of going home only to check on Lulu, but then would hurriedly make his exit to go to Lovely's. When he reached her house before he could exit his truck he got a call. This call was a pleasant surprise. He answered, "Hey Kenya."

"Hey Dr. Masters," she said brightly. "Am I catching you at a bad time?"

"No, I'm good. What's up?"

"Nothing. I had you on my brain and just wanted to reach out. That's all."

"Oh. I'm good. How about you?"

"Well, I'm here permanently. I've filed the divorce."

"Everybody's getting a divorce."

"Marriage just isn't what it used to be. You men want your cakes and eat them too. The vows you guys take are worthless."

"Hey. Don't group me in that category with them. I've never been married...," his words trailed as he had to remember he was about to get married to Aisha. He was so glad he caught her, because that would have been one of the biggest mistakes he could have made. "But, I wouldn't mind being somebody's husband. Me and Lovely talk about doing it all of the time."

"The girl I saw you with at the ball?"

"Yeah," he said with a smile thinking of Lovely.

"She's lucky. I hope she realizes it and don't do like that Aisha trick. Speaking of Aisha, someone told me she was pregnant by you. Is that true?"

"No it isn't. If she is actually pregnant she's pregnant by the man she was cheating on me with."

"Well, that's good to know. Abe?"

"Yes?"

"I wish I had come back sooner before you met this new girl. I really miss being with you."

"Well, everything happens the way it does for a reason."

"It does. She better not mess up though."

Abe hated getting caught up in his feelings over a woman. It reminded him of the love he couldn't get from his mother. He was so afraid of getting used to it only to be left alone; like what Aisha had done to him. But this Lovely; she had a hook on him he just couldn't shake. It was almost scary. Was this what obsession felt like?

Chapter 14

The October weather couldn't make up its mind. Today was a nice day though. It was in the seventies. Melissa decided she would take Mekhi, the twins, and Grace to the park while she enjoyed the nice weather while she had a chance.

With her Kindle, she decided to catch up on a few books she had been meaning to read. Working for Abe, she rarely had time to catch up. That's what Melissa was doing when she was joined on the bench by a handsome good smelling man. She smiled, "Hi."

He looked at her and smiled with surprise. "Oh hey! What a coincidence seeing you here. Right here on this bench."

Melissa laughed at Ike. "You're crazy. Where are the girls?"

Ike nodded out toward the playground. "They're with Grace, the twins, and Mekhi."

Melissa looked out to the playground. She hadn't even noticed. Ike had two daughters with Tomiko, fourteen-year-old Malaya, and twelve-year-old Shyann. When she and Ike agreed to meet at the park, Melissa asked Lovely if Grace would like to get out of the house. This would be Melissa's second time getting Grace which was funny because Grace still hadn't technically been informed that Abe and her mother had a thing going on.

Melissa asked, "You okay?"

"Yep. Are you?" he asked.

"I don't know," she mumbled.

"You don't know what?" he asked.

It was hard for Melissa to get her words out as his hand began rubbing her back. "I just feel like this is as a dead end as my marriage."

"So you wanna end it?"

She shrugged. Ike stopped rubbing her back as he fell into a deep thought.

"I'm tired of the emptiness," Melissa said somberly. She kept her face turned away. She didn't want him to see the water in her eyes. She didn't want his sympathy. He had been pitying her for almost a month.

"I'm sorry Melissa. Maybe I should have waited until all of this was taken care of. I guess I was tired of the emptiness too."

"And you used me," Melissa added.

"No, I wasn't. I'm not," he stated. He said softly, "Look at me."

Melissa cut her eyes at him, "Ike you have no intentions on divorcing Tomiko. I can see it in your eyes how much you want it to work. It was the same look eight years ago."

"No that's not what it is," he argued.

174

"Then what is it? Where the papers? Why do you still try to spend time with her if you want to divorce her?"

"Because she's my wife and I'm supposed to show concern and effort."

Melissa's feelings were bruised. "I think we need to stop," she said moving away.

"Don't," he whispered. He stopped her and tried to hold her.

Tears were rolling down Melissa's face as she pushed him away. She whispered yelled, "Leave me alone! Show some effort on that."

"No Melissa," Ike whispered. He wanted to hold her.

"Don't before somebody sees us," she mumbled.

"Let's walk then."

"No. It's over with," Melissa said wiping her face.

"Well just stay here with me," he said gesturing at the bench.

She reluctantly stay seated. He sat sideways so that he could face her. Softly speaking, Ike said, "Listen to me, baby. My intentions were not to hurt you. I love you, Melissa. I truly do. I would love to be with you. I should have made you my wife. But I was stupid, young and vulnerable when I married Tomiko. It was right after my accident, remember? It was you that came to the hospital every day. Shit. It was you who used to travel all the way to Michigan by yourself to visit me when I was going to MSU. You came to my games. When I was sick, you took care of me. You sent me all my favorite shit. Even when I came home, you catered to my every need. I was just too dumb to see it."

Melissa didn't know if the steady stream of tears running down her face was because he was saying he realized his mistake, or if none of this matter because nothing will ever be, or if it was because her husband should be saying these things to her.

"Don't cry love," Ike said as he wiped her face. His voice began to tremble, "I was stupid...I know all of this is too late but know Melissa that I love you."

Melissa was weak for a crying man. She removed his glasses. She whispered, "I love you too."

Ike whispered, "I love our son too."

Melissa turned away from Ike's words. She looked out at the kids grateful they were so wound up in their own activities to notice her and Ike. Her eyes landed on Mekhi. He was his father's son. Mekhi would be tall, and he had the same creamy peanut butter complexion as Ike.

"Don't start that Ike."

"That's my son Melissa. I'm tired of him not being in my life like Malaya and Shyann. I gotta watch him grow up from a distance with another man as his father."

"He's okay Ike. I don't wanna confuse him. He's only seven, and he knows you as Uncle Ike. He's crazy about you just as you are."

"Do you hear yourself?"

"I know what I'm saying."

Ike grew angry. "No, you don't. You sound crazy. That's my child, and he and I have a right to one another."

"Well, I tell you what Ike. Divorce Tomiko and you can have access to Khy."

"What about you and Reggie?" Ike asked. "You're staying married to that fool?"

"No. I'm meeting with a lawyer next week to file for my divorce."

There was silence as they both focused on the kids playing amongst other kids on the playground.

Melissa finally said, "He hits me."

Ike looked at her in disbelief. "He what?"

"Ike don't react all stupid okay. And please don't tell my brother or Abe. Just let things be until I can get my divorce. Then y'all can kick his ass."

"And in the meantime let him keep on hitting you? I don't think so. When I see him—where the fuck is he right now?"

"No Ike. I promise if you do or say anything I will go straight to Tomiko."

Ike was astonished that Melissa even let that come out of her mouth. "Melissa. He's hitting on you. I love you. What kind of man would I be to let you go through that? Is he doing it in front of Khy?"

Melissa didn't want to answer. She said, "Leave it be for now Ike. Please."

Ike was worked up. "I promise before the ink dries on your papers I'm kicking that nigga's ass. I can't stand that mothafucka. And when Abe and Jah find out that nigga is as good as dead."

"I know that. Which is why I don't want nobody knowing this."

"Shit," Ike hissed angrily. "Time won't hurry fast enough. I'm so ready for all of this to be over with."

"Me too," she said somberly.

Ike looked at her and smiled, "I love you."

Melissa chuckled inwardly. Every time she got with Ike she experienced every emotion possible. She went from being angry, despising him to loving him and never wanting to be without him. She said, "I love you too."

———

Takes A Village was a place for the children to go to release all of their expressive energy. Along with Shyanna and Malaya, TAV had become one of Grace's and the twins' favorite hang out spots.

"Where is Grace?" Lovely asked nervously. It was a lot of people at the center that Saturday morning.

"She's okay. I think they're in the dance studios. You know how Grace is," Robin stated. "She meets no strangers. By the time we leave here she would have made friends with everybody; even the lady at the information desk."

"Ladies," Eli greeted. He joined them on the bleachers of the gymnasium.

"Hey E," Lovely smiled.

"Hey Lovely...or should I say, Mrs. Abe Masters," Eli teased.

Lovely blushed. She looked out toward the gymnasium floor at the men in a game of basketball. Her Abe was out there. He was wearing an orange t-shirt with khaki cargo pants. She could recognize his massive body anywhere now. He was an incredible lover, and Lovely couldn't figure out for the life of her why Aisha would ruin a relationship with him. So far Abe had shown her nothing but goodness.

Lovely learned his body. She learned his mouth. She learned his touch. Every night they did more or went longer. He'd explore her body leaving a trail of kisses along the way. He would make love to her with his mouth. He loved to do that to her even if she couldn't reciprocate the same attention to him. He acted as if he didn't even want her to attempt it. Lovely had full lips, but her mouth wasn't big enough for Five Dolla. That was the nickname she had given Abe's member because she said he felt every bit the same size as a foot long subway sandwich.

Lovely loved the giddiness she felt in anticipation of his return to her bedroom. Since Lovely couldn't drive Abe had made it a habit to go straight to Lovely's house after work. Sometimes he would go home to check in on Lulu. Since Kiera was out of his house, going home was least of his concern. He had grabbed so many articles of clothing that Lovely's "his" closet was slowly filling with Abe's things. The "his" bathroom was also filling with Abe's grooming and hygiene products. This was a first for Lovely. She had never allowed a man that close or deemed him worthy enough to stay in her home like that. And Grace still had no idea a man had been staying in the house. But the house was so big it was possible for Abe's overnight presence to go unnoticed. Most of the time when Abe was there it was to take measurements of various things for the interior designing of the house.

Lovely could see herself with Abe for the rest of her life. He made her feel safe, protected, cherished and invaluable. She knew his feelings went beyond like because hers did. She looked forward to him coming home. He would tease her until she admitted she had been waiting on him. She helped Livy

179

cook just so she could feel like she was catering to him. He would be skeptical. Livy would vouch for Lovely and give her more credit than she deserved. She listened to him gripe about the demands of his job. Lovely didn't understand why he stressed himself by overworking. Although when he called her from work, it always sound like a party was going on in the background.

Lovely decided she should open up to him more. She wanted him to open up to her without him feeling like he was being invaded by her judgment. Between talks with David, Eli, Ike, Melissa and Lulu, Lovely pieced together that Abe hadn't always had clean hands. Abe had a past. None of it mattered to Lovely. She was in love with him for who he was in present time.

After the game, Abe walked up the bleachers to Lovely. "What's up beautiful?"

Her frown was replaced with a smile. "Hey. You're finish playing?"

Kiera smiled, "Hey Abe. I'm liking the townhouse, and you put me close to Eli. Thank you so much."

Kiera had such a mischievous attitude. Abe wasn't playing with her. If she wanted to enjoy her townhouse, she better get some act right. "Eli is moving away from there in a few weeks. Sorry."

"Where he going?" Kiera asked with a frown. She looked to Eli for an answer.

"He moving in with me," Abe grinned. He looked at Lovely. "When we get married I'm moving in with Lovely."

Lovely blushed but was surprised by his statement. They hadn't discussed anything like that. Abe helped her to her feet. "Come with me for a second."

Lovely smiled. The feel of being so close to him always warmed her spirit. "See y'all in a second."

Abe led Lovely down to the floor and out of the gymnasium. He kissed her softly on the lips. He couldn't help it. He had to touch her in some kind of way. "Are you okay?"

Lovely was hesitant about what was really on her mind at the moment. She was trying to not give Abe's ex much thought. However the more Lovely thought of her and Abe as being an official couple, the more the idea of Aisha being pregnant bothered her. "Well...Aisha insists she's pregnant by you. Abe are you sure you're not her baby's daddy?"

"I honestly don't believe she's pregnant."

Lovely shook her head with a slight smile. "You're that positive?"

"As adamant as Aisha was about not having kids right away I can't see her all of a sudden popping up pregnant at such a convenient time."

"I guess you have a point."

"I know I wouldn't mind getting a certain someone else pregnant though," he teased.

Lovely walked away and stood against the wall. She looked directly at Abe's face as if she could see him clearly. She said, "So you're talking about babies and stuff. You even mentioned marriage and moving in. We've been seeing each other for almost two months. The beginning of November will be two months. So what is this we're doing?"

Abe walked up on her, pressing his body into hers. "We go together. The hell you talking about?"

Lovely stood on her toes and wrapped her arms around his neck. "We do?"

Ms. Barbara, the center's director, came around the corner with two other ladies. She called upon passing. "You two get a room. There's kids around."

Abe smiled at the ladies as they all snickered.

Lovely smiled. "Why everybody always tell us that?"

"Because. they see I can't keep my hands off of you," he said. They shared a tender kiss. "You're beautiful."

"And you stink."

"And you love me anyway."

"I do," Lovely said.

Surprised by her response, Abe asked, "You do?"

Lovely nodded. Abe smiled big. "I love you too."

Lovely let her arms fall to her side. "So I guess I need to get this talk with Grace over with."

"What?"

"Grace. Take me to her. Robin said she's in the dance studio."

Abe led Lovely to the big dance studio where there were several kids crowding the dance floor. One of Chris Brown's latest songs was blaring. Abe spotted Grace right away. She was with a group of teen and pre-teen girls. They were trying to put together a dance routine. From the looks of it, Grace, who was not the oldest was the leader and instructing them.

"Hey, Dr. Abe," one of the girls called out. It was followed by a chorus of other's yelling out there greetings. Abe spoke back to all of the kids.

"Hey. Grace...can you come here for a second?" Abe asked.

Grace looked back at the others, "Malaya show them what I was talking about."

Abe was amazed because Malaya had no problem with following orders from an eleven-year-old. Grace looked up at Abe and glanced at her mother, "What's up?"

Abe looked down at the young girl, and something completely threw him off in that moment. There was an uncanny resemblance in her. It was like he was noticing how she looked for the first time. Grace was just as pretty as Lovely and even shared some features as Lovely, but she clearly looked more like whoever her father was.

Lovely reached out for Grace. "C'mere sweetie. Let me talk to you for a minute."

They stepped outside of the dance studio. Grace looked back and forward between Abe and Lovely. "If this is the official talk to tell me you two go together save it. I already know."

Lovely's mouth fell open in surprise.

Grace grinned. "Tell her Abe, I'm not stupid."

Abe chuckled. "Lovely, Grace isn't stupid."

"You kill me, lil girl," Lovely said. She asked, "So how do you feel about it?"

"If you're happy Mama, I'm happy," Grace said.

Abe asked, "So you're fine with if one day your mother and I get married and give you a little brother or sister?"

"Just do it before I turn fifteen cause I don't think I'll care for having a baby brother or sister by then. It would be like a fly; just annoying. And I'll go mad."

Lovely looked at Abe, "See why I love my daughter so much."

"She get it from her mama," he said.

Grace grinned slyly, "I knew about you and Mama getting serious when I accidentally came in mama room one morning. Well, I didn't accidentally come in. It was completely on purpose, but seeing you in my mama bed was an accident. Y'all were still sleep. I was like, 'Hey, ain't that the house fixer-upper dude.' Then I learned that you helped run the center. So I was like 'cool.'"

"Oh-kay," Lovely laughed. "What are you in there doing?"

"We just coming up with some dance routines," Grace said. "The OMG Girls ain't got nothing on us. We look better, dance better, and sing better."

"Let me be the judge of that," Abe said, grabbing Lovely's hand. "C'mon baby, let's see what they working with."

Grace smiled, "Abe, I bet you don't know Mama can dance too. She know all of the latest dances too."

Lovely grinned. "Don't tell him that. He'll wanna see and then I'll be looking like a fool."

"Lovely, you can dance?"

"Mama can do it all. Have you heard her sing? She can play the guitar and piano too. Mama got all kinds of hidden talent. Don't let what her eyes can't see fool you," Grace teased.

Lovely shook her head. "Abe, don't believe her."

"I wanna see this," Abe said leading Lovely back inside the dance studio. Minutes later, Abe found himself surrounded by a ton of rowdy pre-teens and teenagers trying to be the best at what they do. His family, friends and older other staff came inside as well, and it was like a lively party. Just like Grace stated, for a visually impaired person Lovely was a good dancer. She moved as if she could see like anybody else.

One thing Abe knew was that Lovely and Grace would make him one happy man as long as nothing from his past came to bite him in the butt.

Chapter 15

R obin looked down at her phone. The text read:
Meet me at the spot

Why hadn't she learned her lesson? She didn't want to be mean to him because he had been good to her. Besides, after listening to Melissa about the troubles she was having with her husband, the things Lovely would fuss at her about had started to sink in. Why would Robin want to deal with a married man when she had a perfectly good single man in her face?

"Who is that?" Eli asked.

She shook her head. "It's him."

Eli averted his eyes to prevent his true feelings from showing. He got up from his sectional. "You want anything while I'm heading in the kitchen?"

"Can you bring me more of that punch," she said.

Eli nodded. He let his eyes linger on her longer than usual. He looked at her phone then back up at her. He turned away and continued to the kitchen.

Robin text back: **I can't, I don't want to see you anymore**

The phone rang. It was him. Robin tapped ignore. She text: **don't call me anymore, I've met someone else**

Robin, I need 2 c u. dnt do this

Robin: **work it out with ur wife**

Please c me...

Robin: **I can't do this to another woman...if it hurts me I can only imagine how it hurts her**

Fuck her...I dnt even love her like I love u...besides we got plans

Robin felt a knot form in her throat. Why was she so weak?

"If it's that hard why don't you go on Robin," Eli said as he entered the den.

Robin looked up at him and sniffled. "It's not that hard."

"That ain't what your face says. You look like you're crying. If he means that much to you, go ahead and be with him."

"I'm where I wanna be Eli. It's just...I shouldn't have never got caught up with him in the first place."

Eli walked over and sat beside Robin. He handed her the drink she requested. "Why do we always want the relationships that mean us no good?"

Robin shrugged. "I don't want him though. I guess I'm just weak for people begging."

"He's begging?"

"He wants to see me bad," she said. Her phone buzzed again. **Please Robin**

Eli reached his hand out for her phone. "May I?"

Robin handed her phone over. Eli read over the previous texts between Robin and *Him*. Eli asked, "Him? Really?"

Robin giggled.

Eli text back: **this is Robin's new friend. Stop begging nigga. She's done. Call her or text her again I will come for you, I will find you, and I will kill you**

Laughing, Eli handed Robin her phone back. "Read what I sent to him."

Robin started laughing after she read it. "Eli! You can't be threatening to kill people. Not from my phone anyway. Hell, you think you the father from *Taken* don't you?"

Eli shrugged. "What the fuck he gon' do?"

"You're crazy."

"Not really. You know who's crazy? My brother, Abe. That nigga is undercover crazy."

Robin laughed. "Abe is sweet."

"Okay. You'll see one day. Once upon a time, Abe would have made good on a threat like that."

Robin's eyes widen. "Yeah right."

"Just put it this way. If you are in Abe's circle and in his good graces, I bet nobody will mess with you. Abe know people that can make your ass disappear."

"Shut up Eli. You're full of shit."

"Not shit. Maybe something else." He put it out there to see how she would react to something like that.

Robin wore an uneasy goofy smile but said nothing. Now why he go and say that, she thought.

Eli looked upon her face lovingly. "I really like you, but I'm afraid."

Robin appreciated his vulnerability. "What are you afraid of?"

"Liking you too much. I don't know what it is. Maybe I'm going through a phase, but I've never been so interested in a woman as much as I am with you."

As he spoke, Robin could sense he was being honest, but it was as if it was difficult for him to admit to. "Do you want to explore that?"

"I don't know."

"What are you afraid of?" she asked again looking him in his eyes.

Eli averted his eyes to his coffee table. "I'm afraid I won't be me anymore. I'm a free man."

"What's that mean?"

"I ain't never been tied down before. I don't do relationships."

"Really? And that's what you're afraid of?"

"Of other things too but...it's some really deep shit."

Robin said quietly, "Kiss me."

Eli's dick sprang to life instantly. He didn't know what it was about this woman in his presence, but he had a strong desire for her. Their faces slowly came close together, and they shared a simple soft kiss. He asked, "Do you wanna do this?"

Robin nodded. Eli went in for another kiss but was interrupted by Grace. "Robin!" She was coming down the stairs. Robin and Eli quickly moved away from each other.

"Robin, my friend wants me to come over to her house for the weekend. Mama told me to ask you if you will be here to drive me there," Grace said as she came around the sectional to sit in between Robin and Eli.

"Well if Robin can't, I can always take you."

"Great," she said. She looked at the television then at Robin. She nodded as she made her observations, "So y'all just chilling?"

"Yep," Eli said.

"Great," Grace stated, still nodding her head.

Robin snickered as Eli rolled his eyes impatiently.

"Well, I guess I'll go back upstairs and go to bed. Night Eli. Night Robin."

Eli waited until he didn't hear her footsteps anymore. Grace was good at being sneaky and eavesdropping. He looked at Robin with the same desire that was there before Grace interrupted them. She straddled him, possessing his mouth with hers claiming him for the moment. Eli surrendered and returned her aggression. She whispered, "I could rape you right about now."

Eli's hands cupped her ass as she wrapped her arms around his neck. "You would rape me?"

"Yes!"

Aunt Livy entered the family room humming a spiritual hymn. Robin groaned and fell out of his lap. "Are you serious right now?"

Eli snickered. "I guess I'll get going."

Robin walked him to the door. "I'm sorry about all of the interruptions."

"Everything is cool," he said slipping his jacket on. "It's just one of those things."

"Don't say that's not meant to be."

He shrugged and reached for the doorknob. "Call me okay."

She nodded as he exited.

Chapter 16

Thanksgiving was one of Lovely's favorite times of the year. She, Robin and Aunt Livy would start on Thanksgiving dinner the night before. They would rest, awake before the sun came up, and finish up dinner. Back in Alabama, the Bossiers would come over to Aunt Livy's, and everyone would have a good time. This year would be no different.

Lovely's house was 75% complete. There were a few bedrooms that hadn't been touched, and the equipment for her exercise room hadn't been installed. Lovely was not in a rush to get those things situated. Abe had enough on his plate as it was and he and his crew had done a tremendous job on her house thus far. Lovely's City of Sin was about 90% percent complete because that was where Abe was putting the most emphasis on. If Lovely didn't know better, she would think Abe was concentrating on the basement floor for his own pleasure. Lovely was sure of it.

Being that Lovely's seventeen thousand square foot home was big enough to accommodate everyone it was agreed that Thanksgiving dinner would take place at Lovely's. Guest were to include family from Alabama, Cesar and Luciano Pavoni, Eli, Robin and her mother from Alabama, David Batey and his family which included Kiera by default, and a few others.

Upon arrival, most of the kids went to the playroom on the second level. Guests took their assigned food items to the formal dining area's serving buffet tables. The house was flowing with chatter and laughter just as Lovely loved it.

"Lovely! Your home is spectacular," Celeste exclaimed. She walked up to Lovely to air-kiss her cheeks.

Lovely's face lit up. "Cece!" If Celeste was present, then Luciano and Cesar were too. "Where is Papa Lu?"

"I believe your sweetie got him and Cesar," Celeste said looking around the grand chef kitchen. Lovely was still putting finishing touches on some of the dishes. "This house is better than Lu's. Well hello, Olivia."

"Hey suga'," Livy said as she continued at her task.

"Who is this Lovely?" Robin's mother asked. She was helping out in the kitchen.

"This is Celeste. We call her Cece. She's Luciano's wife," Lovely said. "And Cece, the ladies in here are Melissa and her mom Diane, Vanessa, Robin's mom Brenda, Kiera...Do you remember Sandra and Karen, Livy's daughters? Jackie, I know you remember her. Jackie might be coming to stay with me in January."

"I am," Jackie smiled pushing up her glasses.

Livy grumbled, "Just you."

"Mama, don't be so mean," Sandra said.

"Them other ones need to stay where they at. Now if Reuben wants to come, he can. Them other grandchildren of mine needs not come," Livy griped. She stopped garnishing the turkey to say, "Where they at? They ain't here. Only one showed up was Jackie. That's cause she loves her Granny."

Jackie grinned at the recognition. She knew she was her grandmother's favorite. She was also Lovely's favorite younger cousin.

Lovely asked, "Where did Lu and Cesar go?"

"Abe, is your honey boo right? He led them down some stairs right off from the foyer," Celeste answered.

Melissa giggled, "Abe just love that basement don't he?"

Lovely excused herself to go find Luciano and Cesar. As Celeste stated, Abe had all of the men hostage in the basement recreational room that had turned more into a man cave than anything else.

"Ah! There's my sweet Lovely," exclaimed Luciano. He met her halfway to greet her with a warm hug and kiss to the cheek.

"*E 'così bello vederti!*" Lovely said sweetly.

Abe listened to Lovely in amazement. She could speak Italian, Spanish, and some Telagu, a language of her father's native South Indian roots. She had a beautiful singing voice, could dance like it was no tomorrow, cook despite her visual impairment, and could put in work in the bedroom. To top it off, she had a gorgeous personality, amazing body, and an overall beauty like no other woman Abe had encountered. If she kept it up, Abe just might have to put a ring on it.

"So I see you've met Abe. How you even know it was him?" Lovely asked.

"He knew it was us and he happened to be headed down here. He saw us come through the front door and told us to come with him," Cesar said. "He's done an amazing job with this house. I remember when it was bare."

Abe was at Lovely's side with his arm wrapped around her. She said, "I know. Everyone says it looks good. I really appreciate him for stepping in and doing it. If it was left up to me, it would still be like it was."

"Abe," Luciano said eyeing the younger man. "Can you show me the rest of the house while I have a word with you?"

"Oh-oh. You in trouble," Cesar joked.

"Am I?" Abe asked.

Lovely snickered nudging him. "Go on. Don't be scurred."

Abe proceeded to lead both men in a tour of the entire house. Abe was showing them every nook and cranny, even the hidden compartments and rooms only a few would be privy to. "You think like me," Luciano stated as they stood in the study. "You sure you're not a Pavoni?"

Abe chuckled, "I don't think so."

"First things first, is there a matter concerning Lovely's safety?"

There were few people that intimidated Abe and Luciano was one of them. It was something about his grandeur presence and confidence. He was an older man in his sixties and carried it well, no signs of deteriorating health. Lastly, Luciano's eyes were the same ones that Abe saw when he looked in a mirror. It was a bit eerie.

Abe said, "I'm just cautious."

"Men in our positions can never be too cautious," Luciano said.

"Lovely and Grace are very special to us Abe. We trust that you will keep her safe." Cesar said.

Abe nodded his acknowledgment.

"You know for years, Lovely refused to live a luxurious lifestyle because she didn't want the wrong type of attention drawn to her," Luciano explained. "She always felt like she would receive the same fate as her parents. Her parents Dharmesh and Naomi were like family to us...Lovely's father was a foolish man, but when they died he left Lovely a wealthy millionaire. For her to submit to the life you have offered her it shows that she really trust you. And Lovely don't trust anyone."

"What do you mean millions?" Abe asked.

Luciano chuckled, "Her grandfather Malik wasn't a fool. He left Lovely quite a bit. What he left her father went to Lovely after her parents passed. Lovely holds a thirty percent interest in the Bevy Company we own. She's my partner."

"So, in other words, I hooked up with a millionaire?" Abe asked.

"She haven't told you?" Luciano asked.

"No," Abe answered. He said, "Well I'm glad I know all of that now. I have to take some extra measures in ensuring her and Grace's safety."

"I'm curious Abe. How did she explain affording this house?" Cesar asked.

"She told me she won a settlement for an accident that took her normal vision," Abe explained.

Cesar laughed. "That was creative."

Luciano stated, "Don't be confused, Abe. I disclosed that info to you without Lovely's say so because I know she's bull-headed. She wants to be independent and care for herself.

196

She's a lady worth millions. She needs protection. You needed to be aware of her worth, so you'll know what you're protecting."

"Well I don't mean any harm, but without knowing her monetary value, Lovely is already priceless to me. I will make sure she's protected regardless," Abe stated firmly.

"I know you will," Luciano smiled. "Abe, I had you investigated. I know what type of man you are. I know what you used to be. I know what you are now. I know who your brothers are, your mother, your stepfather, your company's worth...even your old street name. I had to do my research if Lovely was going to be in your company."

Abe felt somewhat vulnerable. It never crossed his mind that someone would strip search him to discover who he was. Yet, here he was feeling naked. He could understand why Luciano would do such a thing. When Grace began to date, he was sure he would do the same to the poor fellow who was brave enough to date Grace. Abe chuckled to himself. There he goes again. Thinking of Lovely and Grace as if he knew deep down they were going to be permanent in his life.

Abe said, "It's understandable. So answer This Luciano-"

"You can call me Lu."

"Okay, Lu. Was there anything you found about me that might not be to your liking?"

Luciano smiled knowingly. "Oh no, not at all. You remind me of me." With that, Luciano gave Abe a quick wink of the eye.

———

Dinner was just about ready. The air was filled with delicious aromas of every sort of dish.

"Shoot!" Livy exclaimed. "I need more nutmeg. We're all out. Can one of y'all go get me some real quick? And don't bring me that cheap brand."

"I'll go, Aunt Livy," Eli said. "I'll go grab Ike to go with me."

"Can I ride?" Grace asked.

"Sure," Eli said.

On the way out, Robin's mother Brenda stopped them. "Where y'all going?"

"They're going to the store," Robin said. "You want anything back?"

"Can you bring me some Seven Up?" Brenda asked.

"You're still not feeling well Ms. Brenda?" Eli asked with concern.

Brenda shook her head.

"Well Mama go lie down back there in my room," Robin said.

Brenda chuckled, "I'm fine. You know I'm like the lil baby who refuses to go to sleep. 'Fraid I might miss something."

"Just nosy," Robin stated playfully.

Eli looked over at Robin. "Are you riding too?"

Robin smiled. "Well, I guess I could."

When they arrived at the local grocery store, they sent Grace and Ike inside for what they needed.

Eli looked at Robin. "How are you feeling nowadays?"

Robin shrugged. "I feel great I guess."

"You know I was thinking, you and I've been spending a lot of time together...And I'm enjoying myself. Are you?"

Robin nodded with a blushing smile. Although they still hadn't made it to the bedroom, there was still a definite strong sexual chemistry there between them. As of late, Eli didn't show the same interest in sex though. He pulled back. Robin assumed he had reservations about being with a woman since he hadn't stuck his dick in her yet.

Although he has yet to admit it and his responses on his sexual preference were always evasive, Robin was sure he was a gay man. How many times did she need to remind herself of that? Or maybe he was bisexual or simply struggling with his sexuality. Nevertheless, he had shown an interest in her. She was definitely attracted to him. Could it work?

————

Inside the store, Ike and Grace were walking the aisle to find the nutmeg and some other items Aunt Livy requested. "Don't forget to grab the *Seven Up*," Ike said.

"You want me to go ahead and grab it while you look for all of this?" Grace asked.

"Yeah—Hold up," Ike said in a hushed tone. He pulled her back onto the aisle they were on.

"What in tarnation," Grace said with a confused look.

Ike said in a lowered voice, "There's a light-skinned woman down there by the frozen section with long black hair. She's with a brown-skinned dude. Go down there and take a picture of them for me."

"What?"

"Just do it. Here, take my phone."

Grace casually walked down to the frozen section. There was more than one black couple. He said with long black hair. They both had long black hair! She would just take pictures of both couples. She tried to get close to the one couple as the other couple headed toward the end of the aisle. *Shoot!* Grace aimed the phone discreetly but realized the screen was locked. And he had a passcode on it. Great Ike!

The couple was getting away and heading towards Ike. Grace hurried down the opposite way. She said, "They coming. And I couldn't get a picture cause your phone was locked, dude."

"Shit," Ike hissed. "Just use your phone. I'm going to the restroom. I need you to be my spy."

"Wait! Is she wearing a brown jacket or black one?"

"Brown," he called back as he hurried in the direction of the restroom.

Grace stalked the couple taking plenty of pictures like she was paparazzi. Not seeing Ike anywhere she went ahead to the car to discover he was already there. He looked at her asking her not to say anything with his eyes.

But Grace just had to know. She whispered so that Eli and Robin wouldn't hear, "Hey, wasn't that—"

Ike interrupted her. "Yes, Grace."

"And wasn't that—"

"Yes Grace," Ike said casually looking out of the window.

———

Abe eagerly sought Lovely in the large home. He weaved and eased pass people just to get to her. She was in the family room with the older ladies. He went to Lovely, "Come here beautiful."

Lovely allowed him to pull her along. "Abe? What is it? You know I'm tired right?"

"I'm sure you are, but let me holla at you real quick."

Lovely snickered at his street jargon. She followed him to her bedroom door. He entered a code on a keypad to allow him access to it. Putting a lock and passcode on the door was Abe's idea. Lovely was impressed with the special attention and precautions he put into the house. He had her protected and guarded like she was royalty.

As soon as the door closed and was locked Abe lifted Lovely up cupping her by her ass. She wrapped her legs around his waist. Like two teenagers in heat, they wildly tongue tangoed, dancing a dance that only they were familiar with.

Abe carried her over to the bed. Before he went any further, Lovely spoke up. "I wanna talk to you about something."

"About what baby?" he asked as he softly kissed her on her neck. Abe turned her face by her chin to face him. He covered her mouth with his in a sensual seducing kiss.

Lovely felt her pussy jump. She moaned yearning to have him inside her. She found herself addicted to Abe.

Keeping their mouths on one another Abe's hand wandered down her pants. Lovely began to moan and widen her legs. He eased a finger inside her. Lovely murmured against his lips, "Abe baby..."

After juicing his finger up, he extracted it and rubbed the wetness on her clit. Abe learned that Lovely was very sensitive and it didn't take much before she would start to twitch. She whispered as he rubbed her clit gently in small circles. In between kisses he whispered. "You like how that feel?"

Lovely buried her face into his chest and gripped him tight as she began to climax. Although Lovely felt the sensation of her walls having spasms she didn't gush when her clit was stimulated. It was invigorating nonetheless. It was so intense Lovely clamped Abe's hand in between her thighs.

Abe kissed her, suckling her bottom lip. "I need my hand back baby."

Lovely pleaded softly. "Make love to me. I want you inside me."

He helped her out of her pants and panties. "Turn over."

Lovely did as she was told. Seconds later, Abe was deep inside her. Lovely whimpered with his entrance.

"Mmm hmm," Abe moaned. He whispered, "I needed this."

She could only reply with moans as his dick stroked her in a steady even pace. The wetness of her mixed with the sounds of her moans ignited the fire deep within Abe even more. He could live in Lovely's pussy all day long. He loved that her appetite for sex was just as insatiable as his. She never said no or denied him some type of sexual gratification.

He spoke to her as he went deeper, "Will you have my baby, Lovely?"

"Mmm hmm," Lovely moaned.

"I love you, baby."

"Love you...shit!"

Abe was dead serious when he asked Lovely about the baby. He was getting baby blues. He wanted a child. He wanted a wife. He was getting older, and those two things were missing in his life. He desperately wanted them. Now that Lovely was in the picture he was sure she was the one. He wanted this life with her to be forever.

After they were done with that quickie, they freshened up. Abe caught Lovely around her waist before she exited the room. "Wait. You said you needed to talk to me."

"Oh yeah," she said absent-mindedly. "I want you to move in permanently."

Abe was thrown. "Just like that?"

"Well, what are you doing now? You spend most of your time here. Your closet is steadily filling up with your stuff. It only makes sense."

"Are you sure?"

"I'm positive."

Abe smiled as he bent down to kiss her lightly on the lips. "I love you woman. C'mon before they start questioning our whereabouts."

When they emerged from the bedroom, Abe was surprised by a female's voice and laughter coming from the great room. When he and Lovely reached the end of the hall, Abe just stood there staring.

Mary saw Abe and grinned. "Hey, nephew!"

"Hey," Abe mumbled, staring at his mother sitting on the sofa. She glanced his way but quickly averted her eyes. She started talking to Diane and Brenda.

Lovely whispered. "What is it?"

"My mama is here."

———

If Sarah was present, was Esau too? Abe held onto Lovely's hand as he made his way over to the great room's sitting area. His Uncle Paul and wife Phyllis were present. Paul was Abe's chief of operations and also Sarah's and Mary's brother. Mary's husband, Larry, was sitting with them too. No sign of Esau, Abe's stepfather.

Abe smiled. "I didn't know you all were coming?"

"Yeah Aunt Livy, Eli, and Lovely invited us and told us what to bring," Mary said. "It sho' do smell good in here. Lovely's aunt put her foot in that turkey and dressing!"

Sarah agreed. "She did." She stared at Lovely standing next to her giant of a son. "Well Lovely, it's good to finally meet you in person."

Lovely smiled. She let go of Abe's hand to properly greet Mary and Sarah with hugs. "I'm glad you all came."

Phyllis smiled. "This house is gorgeous. And Abe I heard you're responsible for the inside. Paul, we need our den redone. If I had known Abe did all this, we could have been started."

"Babe, he's an architect. It's what they do. You shoulda asked," Paul said.

Luciano entered the great room from the butler's pantry with an announcement. "Aunt Livy has stated that Thanksgiving...dinner is...ready."

Abe noticed the slowing down of Luciano's words as he and Sarah did double takes at one another. Sarah cleared her throat nervously and looked away. Luciano quickly recovered and smiled at everyone. "She wants everyone to gather in the formal dining hall for prayer."

After everyone was gathered, Aunt Livy prayed over the food. Abe watched his mother googling Luciano. She was free to do so because Esau was not present. He was spending his holiday with the Masters. Abe focused in on Luciano, too. The man was definitely charming with his slight accent, tall, good looks, olive complexion, and low cut salt and pepper straight hair. He had a goatee, and the hair at his temples was completely white. Abe noticed how the older women stole glances at Luciano and Cesar, the same as they did him. Cesar, who was older than Abe by six years, had similar looks as Abe, and they could almost past for brothers. Abe was taller and bigger, but they shared the same European chiseled features. Cesar didn't have blue eyes, though.

Abe assumed two things with the way Luciano and Sarah were looking at one another: either they found a strong attraction to one another, but couldn't act on it because Celeste was present or they were already familiar with one another.

Abe pulled Ike aside. "Watch Mama and Lu."

"Huh?"

"Just do it and tell me what you think," Abe said before walking off to find Lovely.

Watch them for what? Ike thought. He looked up searching for his mother. She was at the dining room table staring at Luciano. Ike caught Luciano gesture with his eyes towards the foyer. When Sarah got up from the table to excuse herself, Ike abandoned his food to be nosy. Sarah and Luciano met briefly, a very quick passing, but Ike saw an exchange from Luciano to Sarah.

Ike found Abe downstairs and whispered in his ear. "They finna hook up or something."

Abe grinned, "I told you. What's that about?"

"I'm asking," Ike said.

"No don't ask, yet. She ain't gonna tell you nothing anyway. Mama sneaky."

Lovely cut in as she walked up. "What are you two talking about?"

"Nothing," Abe said quickly. "He was just telling me about a friend of ours he ran into."

Lovely smiled with a nod. "What friend?"

Jackie said under her breath. "What he look like?"

Lovely snickered, "Girl, don't be getting no ideas."

Jackie shrugged. "I'm just saying. Lovely, you didn't tell me you were surrounded by so many good-looking men."

"Well, I can't see good looking remember?" Lovely said.

"And you end up with Abe," Jackie said. "And what's with Robin and Eli? Gosh, I need the same luck."

"It'll happen," Lovely said patting Jackie's leg. "Just be patient."

Chapter 17

O n the drive home, Sarah took the time to reflect on some things. Her son who she hadn't acknowledged for years had been on her mind a lot. She saw him; his magnificent being. Sarah had produced a physically perfect son in Abe. She could see his golden skin, his silky black hair, straight nose, strong jawline, full pink lips, and icy blue eyes.

When Sarah gave birth to Abe thirty-four years prior, she thought he was the most beautiful baby. The nurses in the nursery along with her parents and sisters ranted and raved about how beautiful he had been. However, when Esau laid eyes on him, he saw his white complexion and grey eyes and determined Abe was not his child. Sarah programmed herself to hate her child because she knew it was the truth. Abe wasn't her husband's son.

Against her mother's wishes, Sarah named Abe what Esau thought was suitable for a spawn of Satan. They named him Abaddon. According to the bible in the book of Revelations Abaddon was another name to call Satan. Esau thought it was the most fitting because after all, Abe was a product of rape.

Sarah gave Abe to her mother to raise. Jolene died when Abe turned six. From there Abe returned to Sarah's and Esau's lives. Under Esau's direction, Sarah wasn't the best mother to Abe. His childhood wasn't exactly worth bragging about, but somehow Abe made it through. Of all the Masters children, he was the most successful. He was the most accomplished. He was a multi-millionaire, very giving and an influential contributing member in the community. His design and construction company, as well as, the realty subsidiary ranked amongst the top five companies in the area.

Sarah had always kept up with Abe through her other sons Ike and Eli. She never let Esau know. He wouldn't understand. He would get mad, but Sarah was beginning to feel a tug at her soul. All of these years she'd been mistreating Abe and for what? Because she was so selfish, hateful, and evil. It wasn't his fault that she'd had an affair and had gotten pregnant by another, only to lie about it like she'd been raped.

Sarah wasn't sure if it was a low tolerance for nonsense that came from old age, but Esau's blatant disregard for Abe's efforts were starting to disgust her. Despite how he had been treated, Abe took care of Esau and Sarah. They didn't work, lived fabulous, traveled, drove the best and wore the best.

But Sarah had actively participated in the abuse Abe suffered. Was it too late to mend their relationship?

Sitting in her driveway, Sarah looked down at the business card Luciano had given her. Seeing him at Lovely's had been a big surprise. This world really was small. She had to admit though, it was nice seeing him after all of those years.

Sarah went in her home and immediately unwound. She was glad she had given in to her sister's insistence and went to Lovely's. She really enjoyed herself. She wished she had had enough nerve to speak with Abe, but the shame and guilt wouldn't allow her. One thing for sure was that she was glad

Abe was happy. That Lovely seemed to be doing it for him. More shocking was the closeness that Eli shared with that Robin girl. She knew how he felt about getting into a relationship.

———————

The following morning Sarah was in a sour mood. Sarah couldn't believe the audacity of this man. He was coming home at inappropriate times for a man of fifty-five. Two o clock in the morning was just disrespectful. Who did he think he was? Furthermore, who did he think she was?

Sarah cut her eyes at her husband, Esau. Although he was quite the handsome man, Sarah knew him to be ugly. She couldn't believe after everything, over all of the years he had the nerves to cheat on her.

"Where are you off to now?" Sarah asked.

"Henry asked me to stop by," Esau replied without giving her eye contact.

Sarah scoffed as she moved around him. She headed toward her study as the landline began to ring. She didn't get in a hurry to answer it. Esau should pick up the line in the bedroom. It just kept ringing. She called out. "Really E? You're not going to answer it?"

Esau grumbled from the bedroom. "It's just your sister."

"Why didn't you answer it!" Sarah wished she could kick him in his gut. The phone rang again. This time Sarah was in her study. She snatched the receiver up from its base. "Hello!"

"What's wrong with you?" Mary asked.

"That damn Esau," Sarah said angrily.

"Well look, don't worry about him right now. I need you to get over here ASAP," Mary snapped.

"For what reason?"

"Just get here, and you'll see. Bye!"

Sarah shook her head. Mary was crazy too. But since Esau was leaving, she might as well leave, too.

"And where are you off to?" Esau asked following behind her. Sarah had her handbag, keys, and sunglasses in her hands replying to Esau with the sounds of her heels clicking on the hardwood floors. It reverberated louder once she got to the marble floor of the foyer.

"You're not answering me!" Esau called.

Sarah threw up a careless wave of the hand as she entered her car. Sarah would fix him. He wanted to be disrespectful and inconsiderate, so could she.

Arriving at Mary's Sarah pulled into the driveway of what used to be her mother's house. Abe's company had remodeled it with modern updates. It was really nice. Jolene sure would love it if she was still living.

Sarah noticed the shiny black Mercedes parked along the front yard. She wondered who that belonged to. Was that why Mary called her over here for? Abe bought Mary a new car?

Fixing herself, Sarah made her way to the side entrance of Mary's house. Surprisingly it was locked. Mary finally must be listening to her husband about keeping the doors locked. Sarah knocked on the door. Her many gold bracelets clashed against each other making just as much noise to announce her arrival.

The door swung open. Mary exclaimed, "You got here quick!"

"Well you said ASAP," Sarah said pushing her sister aside. She stepped inside the den. "What was so important that—"

What she saw shocked her beyond words. Sarah froze in her tracks. Was he really here? If so, why? After all of these years, he still had very radiant looks. His age barely showed with the exception of the grey peeking at his temples. He still wore his face close to clean with the exception of the thinned goatee. He was standing looking quite debonair in his grey Italian suit.

"Nice to see you, Sarah...again," Luciano said pleasantly. "I see life has been treating you good. You're beautiful as always."

Sarah glanced at her sister. She looked back at Luciano. "Why are you here?"

"Can we talk?" he asked gesturing back outside.

Sarah didn't want Mary knowing more than she was supposed to, so Sarah agreed to join Luciano outdoors. He suggested. "Take a ride with me."

"Of course," Sarah couldn't risk anyone seeing her talk to another man. Especially a handsome Italian man like Luciano.

Once inside the back of the Mercedes, Luciano ordered the driver to drive.

Sarah was unsure but quaintly smiled. "What is this all about? I thought we agreed years ago to stay out of each other's lives."

"I did. I was...until I came to visit my goddaughter for Thanksgiving. I hadn't seen her or Grace in a while. And yesterday..." his voice trailed as he tried to contain his anger.

He glared at her and snapped. "Why didn't you tell me about my son!"

"Because you don't have one! Well, at least not with me!" Sarah snapped back.

"Yes, I do. I saw him yesterday. He looks just like me. You lied Sarah."

Sarah didn't say anything. Sarah looked away with guilt as she gazed out of the back window.

Luciano was having a hard time understanding any of this. And the expression on Sarah's face was evidence there was more to this. "Sarah! Please explain what's going on? Abe looks like Cesar. Why did I not know about him? I never saw you with a blue-eyed boy. You showed me Ike and remember I said I believed he was mine, too. You denied it. You told me you thought you were pregnant again after we started seeing each other after that big blow up between you and me."

Sarah's voice came out soft. "That's when I got pregnant with Abe."

"The last time?"

"No."

"You didn't tell me. Why?"

"I need to get back to my car," Sarah said. She seemed on edge.

"Wait. I have to get all of this straight. If Esau is not Abe's father, who does he believe is his father?"

"Lu, I think we should just let things be. I don't want to discuss any of this any further."

Luciano wasn't satisfied. "We have a right to have a healthy father-son relationship. They should know their real father."

"They're grown. They don't need a new father in their lives. They have Esau." Sarah said defiantly.

"Sarah, I always thought, in the back of my mind, Isaac was mine and gave the thought of Eli being mine as well. I just never took the time to fight you on it. I wish I had."

"Fight me on it?"

"I know you, Sarah. The very thing I hated about you was the very reason I was crazy about you. You were sassy, vindictive, strong-willed and just bad. I would have had to fight you. But now that they are grown I can just go to them myself."

Sarah was horrified. "No!"

"No? Sarah, you can't really stop me."

"Oh, I'm asking you not to," Sarah said desperately. Luciano showing up in their lives would upset the way things were. Things would come undone. Her lifestyle could very well be cut off. People will hate her and condemn her. No. This couldn't happen just yet.

Luciano looked at her and wondered why there was so much desperation behind her plea. Regardless, she needed to know where he fully stood with this whole situation. "Sarah, who is Abe's father if I'm not and Esau isn't."

"I was raped."

"Bullshit. I know I'm his father. I just want you to say it."

"There's nothing to say. I was raped. I don't know who his father is."

Luciano scoffed, gazing out of the window. "This is crazy. I already knew you were Abe's mother. I didn't expect to see you yesterday, though. I didn't even expect Abe to look so much like me, but I had to see him in the flesh. He is my son."

"Lu, right now we should leave well enough alone."

"Why Sarah? Because you're selfish and you're afraid your son will stop doing for you?"

"No, that's not it," she lied. She knew very well once Abe found out that she knew who his father was all along, he would be terribly upset with her. She had grown accustomed to the lifestyle Abe afforded her. She wasn't ready to give it up just yet.

Chapter 18

Kiera's heart pounded with nervousness. You got this, she told herself. Kiera had never been so shaky about a man. She had to get it together. She was always the confident one and liked to take control. So why was she nervous? She didn't know what or who to expect on the other side of the door she stood at. Was he going to be playful or was he going to be grouchy and hateful?

Kiera rang the doorbell once and waited. She didn't see any cars in the driveway. Maybe he wasn't there. This was the right house, wasn't it? That's what she get for trying to show up unannounced. She lived just down the street and thought it would be a good idea just to stop and say hi. Of course, some other things were on her mind.

Kiera pushed the doorbell again as the door swung open.

"If you ring this doorbell one more time..."

Kiera looked him in his eyes with a devilish grin and pushed the doorbell just for the hell of it.

Eli looked at her blankly. "Why are you at my door? How do you even know my address? You ain't never been over here before. You stalking me?"

"Can I come in?" Kiera asked.

"No."

"Is your 'friend' here or is he coming?"

Eli chuckled. "You and them gay jokes," he said with a shake of the head. "Somebody coming here has nothing to do with why I don't want you in my house."

"Damn, it's like that?"

"What do you want?" He asked.

"To come in. Please? It's cold."

Eli sucked his teeth. "I guess." He stepped aside so she could come in.

Kiera looked around. "You and your brother and these damn downstairs foyers. Let me guess, Abe did these condos over here?"

"Shut up, and yes he did. Don't be hatin' on my brother," Eli said. He saw her wandering eyes. "Go ahead and be nosy."

Kiera could see ahead, there was a half bath and laundry room to the right. Straight back was a den decorated in neutrals with animal print everywhere. She went upstairs to the main floor. At the landing, there was the pristine white kitchen open to the great white room. The tiki wood flooring contrasted nicely with the white furnishing. The dining room was white too. Like the great room, there were splashes of color here and there. Kiera assumed no kids were allowed in these spaces. The top floor was the three bedrooms, one room served as a home office. The secondary bedroom was decorated in yellow, gray, and white. Eli's bedroom was red, black, and white. In Eli's entire house not one thing was out of order.

"You have a nice place," Kiera said.

"Thank you. Now, what do you want?"

"You. What else?"

Eli shook his head. "Nuh-uh. That bullshit you pulled a couple of weeks ago wasn't cool."

"It seemed cool to me."

Eli crossed his arms over his chest and gave her a doubtful stare. "How do you explain that, Kiera?"

Kiera grinned slyly, "Oh I see what this is. This is about Robin's little feelings."

"No, it isn't. It's about respect."

"So were you respecting her when you let me suck your dick?" Kiera teased.

"That didn't count. I didn't want that."

Kiera looked back at him with skepticism. She walked into his kitchen straight to the refrigerator.

"You ain't at home," Eli chided.

Kiera grabbed a soda and started rummaging through his cabinets. "So Eli...you miss me?"

"No," Eli said, watching her.

Kiera thought she would fuck with him by sitting the can down on the counter hard enough for some to splatter.

"Please get that up," Eli said.

"I'm not. You get it up."

"Get outta my house."

"Nope," Kiera said kicking off her heels.

"What are you doing?" Eli asked in a panic.

"I'm taking my clothes off."

"No, you're not!" Eli snapped angrily. He grabbed her hands to prevent her from lowering her pants.

Kiera grinned up at Eli. "You know I get my way. So stop fighting. The sooner you stop resisting, the quicker we can get this over with. You know you want to Eli."

"I can't do this with you no more," Eli said.

"Yeah you can," Kiera said freeing her hands. She caressed his face. "I'm sorry Eli. I wanna make it up to you baby. I wanna feel you inside me again. You know, like nine years ago. Shit two weeks ago."

Eli said, "I can't keep doing this with you. It's wrong, and it's crazy. Is sex the only thing you want? Then get it from those thirsty niggas that wanna fuck you and be in your face all the time."

Kiera wasn't bother by any of what he said. But she was curious about one thing. "Okay, so it's obvious you aren't gay if you're interested in Robin, but why shouldn't you love me? I can offer you more than she can."

"Like the twins that are mine."

"I'm not here to talk about that." Kiera quickly stated.

"You should be."

"I just can't get us out of my mind. It didn't help seeing you again. I feel like I'm in love with you."

"And you're basing this off of nine years ago?" Eli asked with a confused look.

"I remember it vividly," she grinned wickedly.

"I don't know why I let you in here. Bye Kiera. Get your shoes and come on," Eli said annoyed.

Kiera didn't budge. Her smile faded. "I'm sorry Eli. All I'm doing is making you hate me. And that's not what I want. I want you to want me as much as I want you."

"Why though when I don't want you?"

"You do. You just don't wanna admit it. Don't you?"

Eli still didn't understand Kiera's motives. He sighed in exasperation. "Maybe. But I can't offer you nothing else outside of sex. You're attractive Kiera. You're nice to look at, but I don't think I'd want anything serious with you. We'd just end up using one another."

"But I'm not using you," Kiera argued. "Like you said, if it's about sex then I could get it from those other niggas. I don't want them. I want you."

"You're not right in the head."

"I wish you'd stop saying that. I'm not crazy, just crazy about you."

Eli was tickled. "Kiera, I'm--," he was saying before being cut off by his phone ringing in the distance. "I'll be back."

Kiera could hear Eli talking on the phone upstairs. It sounded like he was engaged in a conversation with Abe. This would be the perfect time to fuck with Eli. Kiera stripped to nakedness and ascended the stairs.

Eli smiled as he talked on the phone. Kiera eased in his room quietly. Eli turned around and paused. He never got an opportunity to admire Kiera in all her nakedness even from nine years ago. Kiera was a sexy woman, Eli had to give her that.

Abe continued talking in the phone. "Eli! What are you doing? You ain't listening to me."

"What...huh...whatchu say?" Eli stammered as Kiera made her way to him. He shook his head at her.

Kiera went for his pants. Eli grabbed her hand.

Abe started again. "So when is this party?"

"Next weekend," Eli answered as Kiera grabbed him through his pants and squeezed his testicles. Eli had to stifle his scream. He pulled the phone away and mouthed to Kiera, "Let go! Please!"

Kiera whispered, "Move your hand."

Eli put the phone back up to his ear and let Kiera's hand go. Kiera immediately pulled his semi-hard member out and started performing orally on him.

Abe questioned him. "What are you doing? You messing around or something?"

"Oh...I'm distracted...I'm looking...Got-Damn!..." Eli grabbed Kiera by the hair to hold her still as he pumped in and out of her mouth.

"You looking at what? You must be on the computer."

"Mmm hmm," Eli had to catch himself. "I mean uh-huh. Yeah...I can't...Can I...can I call you back?"

"Go ahead and watch whatever...or fuck whoever," Abe said with a chuckle.

"Screw you nigga," Eli said hanging up. He tossed his phone on his bed. He grabbed Kiera's hair again and tilted her face up to look at him, "Next time you grab my nuts like that you will get punched in the jaw," Eli said factually.

Kiera pulled out his dick. "You would hit me?"

"I sure would."

Kiera stood fully before him. She looked at his lips and whispered. "Fuck me."

Eli surprised himself when he said. "I can't."

"Why not? Robin?"

"Stop bringing her up. I can't because I don't want this to continue on between us. What I need from you right now is to know what you plan on doing about the twins' paternity. Put your clothes back on." Eli fixed his own clothes.

"But Eli I've told you. You're not their daddy."

"Have you and this other man taken a DNA test?"

"We don't have to. He knows they are his."

Eli sighed with relief as his doorbell rang. He frowned, "Please put your clothes on."

Eli went downstairs to answer the door. He was surprised but also excited to see Robin.

She pointed back outside. "I see you have company."

"Yeah," was all he could offer her with a disappointed shake of the head.

"Well, I can come back another time," Robin said.

"Oh no. You don't have to go. She was leaving."

Robin couldn't stand Kiera. Just the sight of her made her nauseous. It was something very wicked about that girl that Robin didn't like. If Eli was secretly involved with Kiera, it was his business, but Robin wasn't going to be a fool and think his interest in her was genuine.

Kiera came down the stairs with her purse hanging on her arm. She looked at Robin and smirked. "Oh, it's you."

Robin cut her eyes.

"You can go upstairs and wait for me," Eli said to Robin. He watched her as she headed up the stairs.

Kiera gave him a look. "So you are into pussy now. Is that your girlfriend? She knows you let me suck your dick and you liked it?"

"You say that as if you're proud," he said.

"I'm good at what I do baby. You know that. That's why you can't resist."

"Get over yourself."

"How about you get over me," she teased playfully.

Eli rolled his eyes upward. "Anyway. I guess we'll discuss this again."

"Maybe," Kiera murmured. She added, "Maybe not."

Ike was surprised Tomiko was actually home so early on a Friday. However, she was moving around the bedroom as she got dressed for yet another night out with her "friends."

"Where's the girls?" Tomiko asked as she ducked inside the closet.

"At Abe's and Lovely's. Where are you going?" Ike asked as he sat on their bed.

"With my sister. It's our cousin's bachelorette party."

If there was a bachelorette party, then there had to be a wedding. Ike couldn't recall Tomiko mentioning having to attend a wedding. "What cousin?"

"Seiko's. I thought I told you."

"No. When is the wedding and who the hell is marrying her?"

"The wedding is tomorrow." She reappeared in black, red-sole platform pumps to go with the tight jeans and low cut black blouse she wore. Her black hair was hanging bone straight down to the middle of her back. She was slipping on her accessories. Tomiko was so sexy to Ike...physically. She lacked substance anywhere else.

"What time is the wedding?" Ike asked.

"Four. I gotta be there earlier cause I'm in the wedding."

"Tomiko, why haven't you mention any of this to me?" Ike asked angrily.

Tomiko shrugged. "I figured you wouldn't want to go. I mean damn Ike, now you know. You can attend it, or you don't have to."

"What do you want me to do?"

"Do whatchu wanna do," she said walking out of the bedroom.

"Tomiko!" Ike called.

"I gotta go!" she shouted.

Ike got up to follow her. "What if I don't want you to go? What if I need you?"

Tomiko scoffed with a laugh. "Seriously?" She crossed the great room to enter the kitchen.

"Stay here with me tonight," Ike pleaded.

"I can't. Don't you have friends you can hang out with?" She grabbed her purse from the kitchen counter.

"I don't want my friends. I need my wife."

"You need," she sneered. "You always fucking needing. Well, I need too! I need to get away from your damn needy ass!"

"Who the fuck is it?" he asked angrily.

"Who the fuck is who?"

"This one. What nigga you fucking now?"

Tomiko laughed in a jeering manner. She waved him off dismissively and headed toward the garage.

Just a few more months, Ike told himself. He waited until he heard Tomiko leaving. He sent out a text: **are u available tonight?**

Can get on it in about an hour.

Ike: *thanks*!

Another text came in as soon as he sent the last text. It was Melissa: **how u feeling?**

Ike: **okay**

Melissa: **u talk to ur mama?**

Ike: **yeah...evasive...no answers**

Melissa: **oh...r u going to Abe's 2moro? What does he think?**

Ike: **He thinks mama hiding something**

Melissa: **she knows something**

Ike: where's ur husband?

Melissa: *shrug*

Ike called Melissa. She answered, "What dude?"

Ike asked, "Can I see you?"

Melissa sighed, "Ike I was just reaching out to you. We agreed to slow things a bit."

"So you don't wanna see me?"

"I just think we should stop seeing each other."

"You did this eight years ago Melissa," he said with frustration.

"And you did the same shit eight years ago. I was a fool then. I'm just stupid now."

"Do you still think you're pregnant?"

"Oh so now you wanna ask," she said sarcastically. "It's been a week Ike and you ain't so much as looked at me."

"You told me you weren't fucking Reggie."

Melissa didn't reply.

Ike said, "I thought...I guess it don't matter."

"Yeah, it don't. I'm pretty sure if Tomiko could she'd be pregnant too."

"It wouldn't be mine."

"Whatever Ike."

"Melissa, the last time I fucked Tomiko it was in September. You know why we don't have sex often?"

"Let me guess. She fucking another nigga."

Ike was losing his patience. "You know what? Fuck this. Don't none of you mothafuckin' bitches appreciate a man who wanna do right by you. Instead, you want the mothafucka who is and who will always treat you like goddamn dirt." He ended the call. He was so angry he threw the first thing he could get his hand on. It was his phone.

When Melissa tried calling back, but it went straight to voicemail. Ike was so stubborn and always had to get his way. Melissa laughed inwardly. Tantrum. Really? Bitch? He called her a bitch.

Maybe she was being insensitive, but she was tired of putting everybody's feelings before hers. Melissa had enough of her husband's dogging ways, and she was tired of the emptiness Ike left her with. But Ike was still her friend, and she was very much in love with him. She tried his number again. Voicemail.

Melissa looked at Mekhi, "Come on. Let's get something to eat."

Melissa and Mekhi went to his favorite place, Mickey D's. Instead of going back home Melissa headed towards the condo. She could see the ninth floor before she got upon it. The light was on in one of the rooms. Ike was there.

Melissa and Mekhi went to the condo. Mekhi asked, "Who live here Mama?"

"Everybody," Melissa answered as she let herself in. When they entered Melissa felt the premonition greet her alerting her that something was off.

There was a female's blazer thrown over the back of the sofa. A pair of pumps were on the floor. Melissa heard voices coming from down the hall. She looked at Mekhi and whispered, "Stay right here."

Melissa headed down the hall to the bedroom with the lights on. Ike was sitting on the bed with just a tank tee on and his jeans. He was startled when he saw her standing there in the doorway.

"Melissa. What are you...," his voice trailed as he followed Melissa's gaze to the white woman that was coming out of the bathroom. Tabitha froze when she saw Melissa.

Melissa flipped out. "You low down mothafucka! You said you love me, but you brought this raggedy white bitch up here. You ain't nothing but a dog! Don't ever call me or talk to me!"

Ike went after Melissa, "Baby, it ain't even what it look like."

He saw Mekhi staring back at him. Melissa grabbed Mekhi's hand and pulled him.

"Come on Khy. Fuck this nigga too," Melissa said angrily.

"Melissa, stay, and I'll explain," Ike said. He looked down at Mekhi. "Stay so I can spend some time with him. Please."

Melissa looked past Ike at the white lady in the hall. She glared at Ike. "Fuck you!" And she walked out with Ike's son.

Ike looked back at Tabitha defeated. "That was Melissa."

"I thought so."

"That was my son."

Tabitha smiled, "I know. He looks like you."

Ike sat down on the sofa. Tabitha saw the sadness and frustration on his face. She said, "I gotta get going. You gonna be alright?"

He nodded. "Your services have been paid for. I'll be okay. Go."

After Tabitha left Ike pulled the photos from the orange envelope once more. He couldn't believe what he was seeing. Tabitha and her partner had been hired to trail Tomiko to capture her in the act of her infidelities. In doing so, they discovered who she was cheating with. Ike asked them to trail him too. Tabitha handed Ike some fresh photos as soon as she entered the condo. "Your man is a pretty popular guy. He get around."

Ike stared at the photos. Tomiko was having an affair with Melissa's husband.

Chapter 19

Lovely felt good about her decision. Letting Abe move in was a first step. Maybe not traditional or ethical in most eyes, but this was Lovely's life. Besides, Abe was at her place most of the time anyway. She loved him coming home to her.

"*Hey mi amor*," Abe said softly. He was inside the "his" closet of the bedroom putting his things away.

Lovely stepped fully into the closet. "Hey. Are you almost done?"

"Almost. Why?"

"Just wanted to know. Is Lulu settled in?"

"I believe so. She's about to make the fellas and me some food for the game."

"Oh yeah, that's right. You're having a men's day in the man cave today. I guess I'll call some ladies over to keep me company."

Abe stopped doing what he was doing so he could kiss on Lovely. "You must want some attention with your spoiled ass."

"If I'm spoiled you got me that way."

Abe lifted her up and placed her on the built-in island of drawers. He stood in between her legs. "There's something I've been wanting to talk to you about."

"What?"

"The truth about your money."

Lovely tensed up. Abe felt it. Soothingly he started. "We don't have to talk about anything you don't want to baby. But Lu and Cesar mentioned that your grandfather and your father left you an inheritance. They also said you basically live a low key lifestyle because you're afraid that you will end up with the same fate as your parents. Were they murdered?"

Lovely wore a look of uneasiness. She nodded.

"Okay. Just let me say this, as long as I'm around, you'll never have to worry about that baby. I will protect you like I'm supposed to."

Lovely spoke quietly. "That's what my daddy said to my mama the night they were killed."

Abe massaged the back of her head, letting his fingers bury in the thickness of her curls. He felt the scarring there. He asked, "How did this really happen?"

"I was shot. The bullet exited here, but not before it fractured my skull which damaged the occipital lobe of my brain," She said pointing to her right cheek. "It's the reason I can't see."

"You were meant to die I assume?"

Lovely nodded.

Abe sighed. "When did this happen?"

"Twelve years ago. I was fifteen."

"Do you know why your father was targeted?"

Lovely shook her head.

"Can I share something about myself?"

"I already know what you were in the streets."

Abe was a little thrown. "So you should know that no one will ever fuck with you right?"

"Being with you, I feel a little safer, but I still don't trust just anybody."

"Do you trust me?"

"Of course I do."

Abe placed a kiss on her forehead. "You better."

"Can I ask you one question though?"

"Go ahead."

"What's the deal between you and your mother? Why would she name you Abaddon? I used to think you and your brother were named biblical names. There was a theme. Elijah and Abraham but that's wasn't your name. I'm so glad you got a legal name change."

"So you figured it out?" he asked with amusement.

Lovely nodded.

Abe shook his head. "My mama always said that she conceived me when she was raped. She was already married to Esau. She didn't want to go through with an abortion. My grandmama said there was a possible chance I could still be Esau's child. She told my mama if I wasn't Esau's that she would raise me. It was obvious I wasn't Esau's, so my grandmother took me in until she died. They came back to claim whatever was left in the will. They allowed me to live with them only because of the house and money my grandmama left for me."

Abe paused and exhaled before going on to say. "Lovely, they treated me like shit. I was in a house that had been home to me for six years, and they turned it into hell. I wasn't even allowed my own bed to sleep in. Esau made me sleep in the den…on the floor. He would beat me for any little reason. Eli could have done something right in his mothafuckin face, but I would get the punishment. If Eli cried, I got smacked. My grandmama had been raising me to be loving and kind, mannerable and respectful. She drilled me with the philosophy of treating people the way you would want to be treated. So, here I was as a little boy thinking that if I continue to love them, they would love me back. If I was a good boy and done everything right, they would love and praise me the way they did with Ike, Eli and my cousins.

"I stood back many times watching my mama smother them with kisses and hugs. I wanted her to kiss me too. I wanted a hug. You know who would hug me and kiss me? My brothers. Although what was going on was too big for their little mind to grasp and understand they knew how to love. Grant it, they didn't do it in front of Mama and Esau because they were afraid of what was happening to me would happen to them, too.

He started to think back as he sadly reminisced. "I remember when I was about nine or ten and it was report card day…" Abe paused to keep from crying. "I don't know why I thought each time would be different. But, my last report card had a couple of B's on there, so I figured it wasn't good enough. I worked really hard to make sure I was on the principal's list this time. I couldn't wait to show Esau and my mama. They made big deals about everybody else's report cards although none of them had straight A's. I tried to show my mama my card. She kicked me and sent me flying across the room. Do you know how hard that had to be? When I hit up against the curio, something fell and shattered. Esau beat me with his belt. I was sent to bed early and didn't get to eat the little bit of food they had set aside for me. Eli and Ike snuck me food all the time, though.

"When I got about fourteen I was tired. I gave up. I still would respect them, but I knew my place. That's when it seemed like the evil manifested within me. At sixteen, I was bigger than Esau and dared him to hit me. I stayed in the streets a lot. They put me out. Out of the house my grandmama left for me. I dropped out of school in the twelfth grade. I was wild. I had become crazy. I became what they cursed me to be. I was Abaddon. I was Satan and didn't care about nothing. I did a whole lot of fucked up shit. I made a lot of money too. And even then I sent money home, cause I wasn't even living there. I was all over the place."

"So Abaddon represents the devil."

"Yeah. Revelations 9:11."

"So what was your turn around point?"

"My conscience started getting the best of me. I kept seeing my grandmama and how disappointed she would be in me. Kiera's uncle was always preaching to me, especially after Troy was killed. Then my aunt Mary would fuss at me too. I had more than enough money to quit the streets at twenty-one. I came back home, took my GED--yes, I got a GED--scored high on my ACT's and put myself through college. While I was doing that I invested in my uncle's little remodeling business. I started buying run-down properties, and with their skills and knowledge, they helped me flip them.

By the time I finished my master's degree, Masters Design and Construction and Masters Realty were both well-established businesses. David pushed me to get my doctorates." He smiled with a satisfying expression. "And, here I am today."

Lovely lightly smiled but felt very bad for Abe's childhood. "Will you ever forgive your mother?"

Abe shrugged. "I been forgave her. I just want her to love me."

"You know you wouldn't be where you are today if you hadn't gone through all of that. You wouldn't be so eager to love and willing to give. You are everything you are because of it, but it was your fate. Going through all of that molded you."

"Killing people? Robbing people?"

Lovely winced. "I don't wanna know about all that, Abe."

"But it's what I done Lovely. Does that make you uncomfortable?"

Lovely pulled away. "I mean..."

Abe lowered his head. "I asked for forgiveness a long time ago for everything I done. I tried to make amends with every person that knew I wronged them." He looked at her. "Let me ask you something."

"What?"

"The people that killed your parents and took your sight...do you forgive them?"

Lovely gave it some thought. "I did...but if I ever encountered one of them I would have absolutely nothing to do with them and have them immediately brought to justice."

"So you don't forgive them?" he said sadly said. "A lot of people probably don't forgive me. No matter how much I change for the better, no matter how much I give back."

Lovely held his head close to her chest. She hurt for him just as much as he hurt for himself. It pained her to see him struggle with his past.

"Abe, people do forgive you. They understand that people make mistakes. Nobody is ever perfect." She said in hopes of relieving some of his guilt. "You've changed. You're not that man anymore. The people that did this to my parents are thugs. They were hardcore with it, and if they're still living, they're probably nothing like you. I can't speak for them, but I can speak for you. I know," she said, rubbing her fingers lightly down his face.

"Is it bad for me to say that if I knew these men, I'd kill them."

"Don't ever say that," she said, grabbing his face by the chin and looking into his eyes. I would never let it come to that."

"But, how would you know?"

"Just please, stay the Abe Masters that I know. I don't want to know about your past or what you did because that's your past, but don't ever talk like that around me." She sincerely said. He'd changed his life too much to travel back down that path, and she couldn't stand by and let him make those same mistakes again.

"Well, do you remember anything about them?" He asked, almost ignoring what she'd said.

"Abe," Lovely called out with a shake of the head.

"No, I'm not going to do anything. I'm just asking." He said.

"I guess I wouldn't know if I saw them, of course. But," she paused. "I do recall how one of them looked from back then, but it's very vague. I'm not worried about it, though. I don't like to give it much thought. I used to think they would see me one day and wanna finish what they started. But with you being here, I feel so safe, so protected."

Abe smiled. "I won't let nothing ever happen to you again. I promise. If anything happened to you and our family, there's gonna be a lot of slow singing and flower bringing in the city."

Lovely laughed. "You're crazy."

"I'm serious."

Lovely cupped his face. "I wish I could see your face."

"Why? I'm ugly. You ain't missing nothing," Abe joked.

"Shut up. I know you're handsome, very handsome. All the ladies want my man, and they can't have him cause I got him and he loves me, and I love him, and we got it going on and—"

Abe pushed her hands away from him playfully. "Shut the hell up!"

"So you gon rough me up nigga?" Lovely asked comically. She started tickling his sides.

Abe moved away from her. "Baby stop. You know I can't stand that shit."

Lovely hopped down and grinned mischievously. "I know. Come here. Don't you run!"

Abe was already gone. Lovely laughed. "You big sissy!"

———

Was this what being in love was about? He sat at his office desk musing over the enjoyment he experienced being with Lovely. Abe didn't recall ever feeling this way with Aisha. With Lovely, it was like she was his respirator. Without her nearby, he felt like he couldn't breathe. That's why he was more ready than ever to make things official.

He thought about Christmas coming in the next few weeks. He was looking forward to spending the day with Lovely. He was going to ask her to marry him. That was his present to her. He had the turquoise Tiffany box hidden in his closet. In it contained close to four carats in brilliant round cut, rose cut, and paved diamonds and platinum gold.

Before Abe could propose he thought it only was proper to ask Cesar and Luciano for Lovely's hand in marriage being that they were the next best thing to being like a father to Lovely. He called Cesar.

Cesar answered, "Hello?"

"Hey, Ceez. Is this a bad time?"

"Abe! I'm glad you called. Papa wants to schedule a meeting with you about doing our next resort there in Tennessee. A mountain resort. What do you think about that?"

"Are you serious?"

"Yeah, you're family now. We always keep business family first, and then we go outside. Besides Papa loves your work," he informed him.

Abe smiled. "I'd be flattered. When do you wanna do this meeting?"

"How about that first week in January?" Cesar asked.

"I'll have Melissa look into my schedule and get back to you on that."

"Well, what do I owe the pleasure of this call? You called me, and I just started blabbering."

"Are you near Lu?"

"I can be. Hold on."

Abe waited a few seconds until he could hear Luciano talking in the background. "So what's up Abe?" Cesar asked. "He's here."

"I need to ask the two of you something?"

Cesar said to Luciano. "Papa, Abe wants to ask us if he can marry Lovely?"

Abe started laughing. "How do you know that's what I'm calling for?"

"I hear it in your voice. Besides what else could you be calling for and wanting to ask both me and Papa?"

Luciano could be heard in the background. "You have my blessing. Lovely is stubborn and don't take no mess. All I can say is be prepared."

Cesar chuckled but agreed. "I give you my blessing as well. We knew it was coming. We see the love you have for her and Grace. We couldn't ask for a better person for them."

Abe sighed with relief. "Thanks. I really appreciate it. I'm asking her on Christmas Day. Will you be able to make it here for the occasion?"

"If not both of us, one of us will be there."

The two talked a little more before hanging up. Abe was elated, but his excitement was short lived because Aisha called. Abe answered, "Yeah."

"Hey Abe," Aisha said sweetly.

"What can I do for you?"

"I just wanted to let you know that I go for an ultrasound to see what the baby is," she said.

"That's good Aisha. You tell Michael?"

Aisha laughed softly. "C'mon Abe. You and I both know that you are the father to this baby."

"Aisha, I'm not the father of the baby," Abe responded.

"You are, and you know it. Why you don't want to be a father now? It was all you used to talk about. Is it because of Lovely?"

"No. It's because I didn't get you pregnant. Aisha, honestly answer this. How long were you fucking around with Michael?"

"It was just that one time, Abe."

"Really?"

"Abe, c'mon. It was that one time because I needed to make sure if I was doing—"

"Save that shit Aisha," Abe interrupted. "The way you and him were fucking was like y'all had been doing it for a while. Besides if it was your first and only time y'all picked a hell of a time to do it. I had just taken you out for lunch. What was he doing? Waiting in your house until we were done?"

"No. He just so happened to stop by."

"You were supposed to be on your way to work. And why did he know where you live? See Aisha, I'm not gonna do this with you. And I'm not the father of your baby if you're pregnant at all. So stop bothering me about that."

"Okay, Abe. Even if I possibly slept with Michael more than once you can't take away from the fact that I was sleeping with you when I conceived."

"No, I can't. That part I'm not denying. But what I'm saying to you that it's impossible for me to be the father. I had a vasectomy some years ago. I couldn't have gotten you pregnant."

"Abe you don't have to go to that extreme. You can have babies. Stop playing."

Abe chuckled. This was amusing. "Lovely wants a baby. We're working on it. Ask me what she had to do this past Friday in order for us to have a baby."

"What did she have to do?"

"She got an injection to induce ovulation. Yesterday she went to get inseminated with sperm I had frozen. In two weeks we get to see if she got pregnant. I really hope she is, too."

Aisha was silent.

"Aisha?"

"What?" she mumbled. The cheerfulness was gone from her voice.

"I'm not making this up. I never told you, but you always acted as if you didn't want kids. I was going to tell you after we got married, though."

"Whatever Abe," she said. She was disgusted and annoyed.

"Call Michael and have a talk with him."

Aisha figured that the charade she was putting on was over. *Fuck it*, she thought. "I'm not pregnant any damn way. What I look like with kids?"

"That was my point exactly. It's nice to know you're not really pregnant. And by the way, I was just bullshitting about the vasectomy. The only tube my babies coming from is my dick."

"Fuck you," she said and hung up.

Abe enjoyed a good laugh off of that.

———

Instead of going home he went to his brother's house which used to be his house. When he got there, Ike was there.

"Is this a secret brother meeting I wasn't aware of?" Abe teased.

"No secret but I'm glad you're here," Eli said. "Need your opinion on something."

"What is it?"

Eli said to Ike, "Tell Abe what you just told me."

Ike sighed heavily. "I love Melissa. And I made a mistake marrying Tomiko in the first place. She was a hoe then and she a hoe now. And Mekhi is my son too."

Abe was shocked, "Khy? That's your...Well, he don't look like Reggie. He look more like Melissa though."

"But I can see it," Eli added. Eli smiled, "It makes sense now. I used to wonder why you catered to her son. So have y'all been messing around for over eight years?"

"No. That happened then. She didn't want to take it further. She married Dante. I stayed with Tomiko. We started messing around back in September when I got fed up with Tomiko. She ain't messing with me now cause she think I was fucking another woman," Ike said. "The woman she saw me with was a private investigator. I hired a private investigator to follow Tomiko so I can go ahead and file this divorce with the dirt on her. Find out she's cheating of course. Had her and dude followed or whatever. He's a married man."

"Who the fuck is he?" Abe wanted to know.

"Melissa's husband," Ike answered.

Abe fell out in incredible disbelief. "What? I hate that nigga! I didn't like the way that mothafucka looked at Lovely."

"Ike, whatchu gon do? I know you kicking Reggie's ass?" Eli asked.

"Not yet. I need more shit on Tomiko before I go confronting people. Right now I don't even care what the fuck she and he do. I stopped fucking Tomiko a long time ago. Fuck 'em both," Ike said.

"It's that serious?" Abe asked. "I always thought you and Tomiko were good. Hell, I envied you. I wanted what you had with her."

"It's been like that for a while now," Ike said casually. He showed no hurt over the situation. He grinned, "But I'm in love with somebody else who don't wanna be bother with my ass now."

Eli side eyed Abe. "What's your secret? I know you got one."

Abe fell silent. He turned to Eli's television and pretended to be engrossed in whatever was on the screen.

Ike teased, "You see that shit, Eli?"

"I can't talk about it," Abe jested. "It's classified. The least amount of people that know, the better."

"Shut the fuck up," Ike snipped playfully. "Me and Eli won't say shit to nobody. You know that."

Abe smiled. "It's nothing like what y'all going through. I'm gonna ask Lovely to marry me on Christmas though."

Ike and Eli exchanged looks.

Seeing the exchange, Abe frowned. "What was that about?"

Eli said, "I knew that was coming next. Me and Ike had a bet. I said Valentine's Day. He said New Year's so I guess he wins."

———

Robin rolled her eyes. She was annoyed with this man calling her all of the time. It was her fault though. After Eli threatened to kill him, he stopped calling or texting. On Thanksgiving, he sent her a message asking about her day. She responded taking the time to tell him she cared about him, but she could no longer see him ever again. He messaged back. Before she knew it, she was communicating with him behind Eli's back again.

Now a week later, He was asking her to meet him just to talk.

Robin felt like it couldn't hurt, but she told herself no sex with him.

She messaged back: I'll meet you

Same spot, same room

Robin called Eli. "Hey!"

"What's up?"

"I'm leaving Lovely's to do some shopping. You feel like coming out?" She asked.

"I think I'll have to pass on this one. Oh, have you called to check on your mother?"

"I called her earlier. She told me to call her back. She sounded better."

"Please call her back and don't stay out too late. Don't make me have to come looking for you."

Robin laughed. "Trust me I don't want that."

"I know you don't... Robin?"

"Hmm?"

He paused before saying, "Nothing."

"Okay. I'll see you later." She hurried and ended the call. She had grown really sensitive, and her feelings were a little bruised that Eli turned her down. She hoped that spending time with Eli would give her a reason not to meet her ex.

———

Robin arrived at the room to see her former lover was already there. He greeted her with a warm hug. "Hey, baby. I miss you."

"Hey," She spoke with saddened eyes.

"You don't miss me?"

Robin half shrugged.

"Oh yeah, I forgot you have a new man." He said, not happy about the idea at all.

"He's just a friend."

"How's that working? Is he good to you?"

"He's very good to me."

He shook his head with disappointment. "Is that right?"

"It is, which is why I shouldn't be here too long. Now, why you insist on seeing me?"

He tried to kiss her. Robin moved away. "C'mon baby. Sit down. You wanna be here just as much as I want you to."

"Not really. I'm serious about not seeing you anymore. I'm more than somebody's side hoe."

"But, I told you I was with my wife from the jump," He tried to explain.

"And I was stupid for seeing you."

"Admit it though. Have you not enjoyed being with me?"

Robin gave it some thought. "Yeah, but I can't anymore."

He scoffed with ridicule. "You know that you've enjoyed me and the perks I give you. Whoever he is could never be the man that I am to you. He definitely won't be able to handle that pussy like I do. You said it yourself that you ain't never had it as good as I give it," he boasted.

"First of all, do you even know how to love a woman the way she deserve? Look at how you do me and how you do your wife."

"Both of you live good; neither of you want for anything. Why are you complaining about it?"

"It gets old after a while. I get lonely and want my own man that comes home to me at night." She said.

"So you're desperate and is now spending your free time with a potential new guy?"

"Desperate, I'm not and how do you know I'm spending time with him?"

He chuckled. "You just told me that the guy is good to you so why wouldn't I think you're spending time with him? I'm trying to understand where you're coming from with this. We've been together for some time now, and it's been good. Don't start this."

"I'm not starting anything. I'm just moving on. I am really falling for this guy, and I want to be with him."

He looked at her with the eyes of a jealous man who wasn't about to give up. "Now I'm being nice Robin because I love you, but these are my rules. You know that. This ain't the time to be acting brand new. Don't go fucking this shit up."

Robin pouted. She didn't want to mess things up with him because he was actually good to her. She just didn't want to be the other woman anymore.

She got up to leave. "Well, I guess I'll see you some other time."

"Wait. You don't wanna spend time with me?"

Grabbing the doorknob to the hotel door, she said. "Call me when you get that divorce."

———

Eli's mind went to Robin. Although he was being entertained by Kris, he couldn't help but think of her. She sounded really disappointed when he passed on her invite to join her. The only reason he turned her down was because Kris had already beat her to the punch. Eli looked over at Kris. "Put your clothes on and make this bed while I jump in the shower."

Kris just stared at him blankly. "You think I'm your maid now."

"Kris, please. You know how I am."

She only cooperated because she wanted to please him. She hurriedly made the bed. Picked up the two used condoms and flushed them in the toilet. Kris went to Eli in the shower. "Hey, can I get in there with you?"

"Nope, cause you're trouble. You wanna keep on fucking."

Kris giggled wickedly and got in the shower with him, anyway. They fooled around, but they didn't have sex. Kris got out first and dried off. As she was getting dressed, Eli's phone started ringing. "Your phone ringing," she called out.

"Bring it to me."

Kris grabbed it from his bed. Robin's ugly mug was on the screen. She handed him the phone.

Eli answered, "Hello?"

Robin asked, "Where are you?"

"At home. Why?"

"You don't hear the doorbell?"

"I was in the shower. You're downstairs?" He nervously asked.

Robin sighed heavily. "Can I come in or do I have to stand out here in the cold?"

"You messing up my shower woman," Eli pretended to be annoyed. He really wasn't, but he had to put on for Kris. "Give me a second."

Kris watched Eli step out of the shower and wrap himself in a towel. Did he not realize how sexy he was? She was turned on with everything about Eli. His hair was curling up tighter from the condensation of the shower. His toasty skin was beautiful. Kris looked at him, and his long lashes looked like they belonged on a little girl.

"Finish getting dressed!" Eli snapped in a yell whisper. "You looking at me like you fucking retarded!"

Since he liked his life to be private, he wanted to keep it that way. Furthermore, he didn't want Robin knowing about Kris. Kris knew about Robin, though. Eli had felt a need to disclose the fact that he was seeing someone, "that he really liked." He would remind Kris that what was between them was purely a sexual arrangement that they both agreed upon. Eli also reminded her that he wasn't her boyfriend. Kris had always been compliant with Eli's wishes and never would want to expose their relationship.

He wasn't sure if he was pushing his luck, but Eli asked Kris. "Will you hide?"

At first, Kris was insulted. "Hide?"

Desperately Eli said, "Please?"

Reluctantly Kris gave in. "Where do you want me to go?"

"Go across the hall to the other room. Grab your stuff. Go." Eli threw on some boxers, lounge pants and t-shirt. He left

Kris there as he headed down the stairs to the hallway. He wasn't thinking clearly, but he didn't want to deter Robin. He really wanted her to believe he was genuinely interested in her, which he was. Kris was just a habit he couldn't break at the moment. He prayed Kris wouldn't act a fool and just go along with the flow. Besides what he had with Kris was simply a fuck thing...or so that's what he told himself. Eli let Robin in. Robin stared at Eli and smiled, "Hey."

"Hey," Eli grinned.

Robin frowned. "You have company?"

Eli looked outside thanking God that Kris' car was parked around back where the courtyard was. "No."

"So, I promise I won't be long. I just needed somebody to talk to. Well, I really wanted to be in your company. Were you finished with your shower? You seemed a little annoyed when I called." Robin asked when they got to the main floor.

Eli played it off. "I was finishing up, anyway. Sorry about that. Give me a second." He left her by the staircase landing and headed down the hall to his bedroom. His phone was ringing. He looked at it and frowned. It was Kris. He answered it, "Hello?"

"Eli, why are you doing this?" she whispered.

Eli lowered his voice, "Why are you calling me?"

"Are you fucking her? That's the only explanation for your behavior. Why you always seem to be protecting her little feelings?"

"No. It's just...I guess I'm just going through something. Don't take it personal."

"Personal? Shit, when she comes around I become invisible," Kris pointed out. "Shit, I know we have this lil arrangement, but I'm falling for you. I don't like her around."

"Don't start that shit," Eli said.

"I'm tired of this secret shit. What's the deal with this whole thing, anyway?"

"Why are you not whispering anymore? If she hear you I'ma kick your ass."

"E, can I at least kiss you again before I go? Come in here and pretend you're looking for something." She said.

"No."

"No? You know you like when I suck that dick." Kris said. "Is she sucking your dick?"

"No," Eli said.

"Bitch probably don't even know how," Kris said with a roll of the eyes.

Robin eased into Eli's bedroom. Eli's gaze locked on with hers. He said into the phone. "I gotta go, but you take care. Text me and let me know you made it home safe." Eli said before ending the call suddenly.

"I hope I'm not being too forward when I say that I want you... Tonight. No more waiting," Robin said seductively.

"Are you sure I'm what you want?" Eli asked for clarification.

Robin nodded as she peeled off her coat and let it fall to the floor along with her purse.

Eli smirked. "So this is the kind of company you had in mind."

"Absolutely."

Despite the two rounds he went with Kris, Eli was eager and ready to please Robin.

Curiosity got the best of Kris when she no longer heard Eli and Robin talking. Kris came out of hiding and carefully moved toward the bedroom door. She stepped into the hallway three steps toward Eli's bedroom, stopping short enough to get a view. Robin's back was to Kris. All she could see was deep wavy fiery orange hair. Eli was facing the door, but he didn't see Kris because he had his tongue down Robin's throat. He kissed Robin in a way Kris could only imagine. It was deep. It was passionate. Kris felt hurt, and at that moment she felt like she was really just a fuck thing to him, even though she wanted to try and change that.

Eli stood to his full height. Robin pulled his dick out of the fresh pair of navy underwear Eli had slipped on. A pang of jealousy ran through Kris. Eli's dick was Kris' dick. It repulsed Kris to see someone else handling Eli the way she did, but she had to give it to ol' girl. She had a mean head game; not as good as hers though as she stood there zoned out, watching the shit.

Eli looked up and saw Kris in the hall. Kris stood there with a hurt expression. Eli could only look back at her blankly. Kris knew it was time to leave. It was all in Eli's face. Eli had no respect for her presence. Feeling defeated and devastated Kris crept down the hall. She would respect Eli's wishes for now, but this would be the last time he'd step on her heart.

Walking to the car, Kris felt really low and humiliated. She dialed Eli's number. Of course, he didn't answer. It went to voicemail, and she left a message. "Eli, this is me. What you did was some pretty foul shit, and I can't take it, anymore. You wanna keep me a secret, but why? Cause I work for your brother and I'm not all glammed up like the thirsty women that hang around you? You know what? Nevermind. We've had this conversation a million times. I feel like you don't care about me any—"

The beep sounded indicating the recording had stopped. Kris called back again. This time to Kris' surprise Eli answered. He whispered, "Where are you?"

"I'm in my car. I was just leaving a message on your phone."

"Stop calling my phone. Okay?"

"Wait, Eli!" Kris yelled before the call ended. "Damn it!"

Chapter 20

This was another slumber party weekend that Grace loved hosting. She figured why let all of her mama's house go to waste. There was definitely enough room where she could have friends over and not disturb her mother and Abe. Naturally, Grace invited Bryce and Bria. She never wanted to leave them out.

"The kids couldn't wait to come over here to this big ol' house," Kiera said once they arrived.

Lovely didn't reply. She waited for Kiera to make her exit. Instead, Kiera came further into the house to admire how grandiose the Christmas tree was in the foyer. "I know Abe did this all by himself."

"Yep," Lovely said.

Kiera noticed a stack of framed portraits on the decorative chest in the foyer. "Who are these people Lovely?"

"My family," Lovely said. "I want Abe to hang them for me when he gets back."

Kiera picked up one of a young Lovely with a soft brown skinned black woman and an Indian man. Both older people looked very familiar to Kiera. "Are these your parents?"

"Yes. Dharmesh and Naomi Prasad."

253

Kiera commented. "You had such long hair. Can it still grow this long?"

"If I want it to."

"Your mother was beautiful, but you look like your father," Kiera said. "When you said you were Indian I always thought of the pilgrims Indian. You know over here, Indian."

"Yeah, everybody thinks that," Lovely stated thinking that Kiera was a little cooky.

Kiera looked closely at Lovely's father. A voice with a heavy accent came to mind. Kiera could see the store in her mind. She knew Lovely's father.

Kiera's mouth dropped open in shock. "Was your father rich?"

"My grandfather was. He was Luciano's business partner."

"What did your father do for a living?"

"Well, he had a chain of convenience stores and gas stations here in Nashville. My grandfather was into hotels and casinos. My uncle now runs the stores and stations and Luciano has control of the hotels and casinos."

"I thought he looked familiar. Did your dad have a store out North across from the projects? And they called him Pras?"

"I'm not sure where he had a store, but I know they called him Pras. Wow. You knew my father?"

"I remember your father," Kiera said. This was not good. This was really not good. Kiera wondered if Abe was even aware of who Lovely's father was.

"So why did you come back here?" Kiera asked.

Lovely hesitated afraid that she had spoken too soon. "I'm not sure."

"Really?" Kiera said placing the photos back down. "Well, I gotta get going. Take care of my babies will you."

"They'll be safe with me,"

Kiera left feeling queasy. Her discovery or what she thought was a discovery didn't settle right. However, until she knew for sure, she wouldn't be quick to jump the gun.

————

Abe hadn't seen Eric Barnes in a few years. So it was surprising when he received a call from Eric.

Eric was in town and wanted to catch up with Abe, as well as, pitch a business proposition.

Abe agreed to meet Eric for drinks at Bella's.

"Look atchu nigga!" Eric exclaimed happily when he greeted Abe. They shared a one-sided brotherly hug.

"Look at me? Nigga look at you. You clean," Abe teased.

"Im'a clean type of nigga," Eric said joining Abe at the roundtable. "What's up Eli? Ike?"

"Let me get that watch nigga," Ike said playfully in reference to the diamond Rolex on Eric's wrist.

Eric eyed Abe's blinding diamond Cartier watch. "Only if Abe give me that mothafucka right there! Man! That shit is nice!"

Eric looked over at the dark-skinned man with long dreads that accompanied him. "Y'all this my boy, Tee. My right-hand man."

They exchanged greetings. Abe asked, "So what's up?"

Eric, otherwise known as Ghost used to be one of Abe's partners in crime. They did a lot of dirty deeds together. Eric was about seven years older than Abe, and just like Abe, he was ruthless in the streets. He had ties with a lot of crime bosses and drug lords. He was the one Abe ran off with at sixteen and fell under the rule of Antino Mancuso. For five years, Abe along with Eric and Troy were beasts. They weren't big-time drug dealers fighting over their turfs. They were the ones a drug lord called on to handle their enemies.

They called Abe crazy. He was the youngest, but the tallest and well built. They nicknamed him Fyah as a joke, but it stuck. If they needed a job done quickly and didn't want the person hesitating or suddenly hit with a ball of morality and heart, they asked Abe to do it. He didn't care. It was his way of unleashing all of the hate, and anger within. Besides, the devil didn't contemplate wrongdoing, he just did it.

Eric was disappointed when Abe said he quit the streets. Troy had been shot and killed for something non-criminal unless fucking another man's woman was a crime. And Abe didn't succeed at killing that man, but he was paralyzed from the neck down. The only weapon Abe used was his hands.

"How's the family?" Abe asked to break into conversation.

"We good. Kam still give a nigga hell, but she ain't going nowhere. My two oldest are both in college. Nigga, what about you, though? Will you ever have kids? What are you now? Forty-five?"

Abe chuckled. "You gave me ten years. I ain't older than your ass."

"You still with that brown-skinned shorty?"

"Kenya? Nah, she walked away from me years ago. I told you that. Last time I saw you I was with Aisha."

"Yeah! That's right. Lil mama with those tight ass green eyes. Y'all married yet?"

"I ain't with her either, but I think the girl I'm with now might be the one."

"Shut the fuck up!" Eric hollered playfully in skepticism. "Nigga you full of it."

Eli cut in. "Nah, he serious. He's awestruck and whipped."

Abe side eyed Eli. "For real?"

Eli laughed. "You are. Ask anybody. We ain't ever seen your ass like this over no female."

Abe waved him off dismissively. "Anyway...well...I guess I am whipped. I'll give it a few more weeks to see how things continue to go. I'm positive I want her to be my wife, so be looking out for your invitation."

Eli asked in an unbelieving tone, "Abe, you really wanna marry her?"

"I shouldn't?" Abe asked.

"She's wonderful wife material. It isn't her I question. It's you." Eli stated.

"When can I meet this special lady?" Eric asked.

Abe was still stuck on Eli's comment. He decided to let it go for the time being. "How long you in town for?"

"We'll be here until Monday. I gotta visit with her family and mine and shit."

"Come by Sunday after church. You can meet Lovely then."

"Cool," Eric said as they spoke briefly about life, then on to his business proposition. An hour and a half later, the meeting was over.

————

Eric hoped Abe considered his nightclub proposition. He was relocating his family back to Nashville. A lot of his money was going to be tied up in opening his luxury car dealership. Abe had more than enough to back the nightclub. Anytime a man wore a quarter of a million dollar watch for no reason he had plenty of bread.

Abe was smart. He saved his money when the rest of them splurged on cars, parties, women, and clothes. Abe let his money make money. Then going into land development, construction and real estate had proven to be a lucrative business move.

Eric had money, but not like Abe's. With Abe in Nashville, Eric knew that's where he needed to be. Partnering up with Abe would put him back where he needed to be, but Abe didn't seem like he was biting on the nightclub idea though. Eric had forgotten that Abe had became a good ol' church boy on him.

"I'm hungry," Kam snapped.

"What's up with your attitude man?" Eric asked.

"I don't have an attitude," Kam mumbled looking out of the passenger window.

Eric let it go. He never won with her any damn way. "What the fuck you wanna eat?"

Kam shrugged.

"You shoulda ate over my auntie's house."

"Nah Daddy!" Sanchez exclaimed from the second-row seating. "Your auntie food was nasty. I didn't even eat. I pretended to chew and spit in my napkin."

Kamella added. "Yeah, it was gross except the candy."

Kam snickered.

"What the fuck you laughing at," Eric said trying not to laugh, too.

"Bae, c'mon now. You know I wasn't fixin' to eat that macaroni and cheese. And I love macaroni and cheese. It was more cheese than noodles," Kam commented.

"That shit was thicka than a mothafucka! It wasn't no noodles cause she cooked the hell of them bitches," Eric said with a laugh.

"We shoulda went by my mama's," Kam stated. She got excited when she saw Batey's up ahead. "Bae! That's the place your friend took us to that one time. Let's go there. Everything I had in there was good! The catfish was so damn good I wanted to go over my mama house and smack that bitch."

"Yeah, that is Abe's lil spot. Some of his people own it."

As anticipated, Batey's didn't disappoint them. In its upscale, but family-oriented atmosphere the Barnes were more than pleased with what Batey's offered their appetites.

Eric was on his phone discussing money as usual when he happened to turn to look toward the back of the dining area. He did a double take with a frown. The woman in the back looked familiar. He turned his head, not wanting her to notice him then he took another look. He'd never forget a face like that, no matter how many years it had been.

That couldn't be, he thought. *That bitch was supposed to be dead. What the fuck she doing here?*

Eric glimpsed back at her again with a nervous shake of his right leg. It was definitely her. She was sitting at a table with another female and three kids. She was laughing and chatting it up. Eric didn't believe this shit!

"Bae, you done?" Eric asked after he ended his phone call.

"Hold up," Kam said slurping the rest of her mango iced tea. "That shit is delicious."

Eric threw his hand up at David as they exited. Once in the car, Eric dialed Abe.

Abe answered, "Hello?"

"You busy?"

"I'm at a board meeting with my enrichment center staff. Why? What's up?"

"Remember that last lick me and you did together? Right before you did a one-eighty on a mothafucka."

"Yeah."

"The girl ain't dead!" Eric exclaimed.

Kam shot him a look and nodded back at the kids. Eric was paying her no attention.

"What do you mean? And how you know this?" Abe asked. His relaxed tone changed to a tensed one.

"I just seen the bitch. Me, Kam and the kids stopped at that spot you took us to eat. She was in there at a table eating. Man, it's her!"

"Eric are you sure? We put a bullet in her head."

"She alive nigga!"

Abe fell silent in his own thoughts. Abe was hit with a wave of nausea as a flood of memories crashed in his mind. "Leave her be."

"She knows who you are. Didn't she see your face?"

"It was brief. I don't think she really saw me, though." He said, feeling sicker and sicker as he listened to Eric continue. "It was a long time ago. Just let it go."

"Fuck that Abe! Whatchu mean? That bitch ain't finna take me down. My family depends on me. They need me. What about the life you want with your new woman?"

"I'm leaving it in God's hands. I love my lady and want nothing more than to spend the rest of my life making her happy. But if I have to be punished for something I done in my past then so be it. But that's me, Ghost. Do whatever you feel you need to do."

"What the fuck is you smoking?" Eric laughed.

Abe snickered. "Nothing, I just don't want all that chaos in my life. I've been living right and my hands ain't been dirty for almost twelve years. I have done a lot of fucked up shit. Horrible shit. Shit, I don't even wanna think about like the shit you bringing up now. I'm not trying to revert to that."

"A'ight," Eric said. "I gotta call and make some moves, but I'll get back with you. If not, I'll see you Sunday."

"Eric?

"Yeah?

"Leave that girl alone." Abe insisted. If she lived, it was meant for her too.

"I just wanna check some shit out."

"Like where she work? Live?" He asked.

"Yeah."

"Don't fuck with her. I'm serious. Just come by Sunday." Abe said.

"A'ight," Eric said ending the call. What the fuck was wrong with Abe?

Eric called Tee, anyway. "I need you to do a favor for me. Meet me down here at this place called Batey's."

————

"Will you be mine forever? Yes or No?" Grace read aloud. She rolled her eyes. "Why do you and Abe do corny things like this?"

Lovely shooed Grace away. When Lovely received the flowers, she was elated just as she was the other umpteenth times Abe sent her flowers. She didn't bother calling him this time. She would wait until he got home to thank him.

Abe was running later than usual, though. Lovely continued to wait until she couldn't wait anymore. She went to bed.

Lovely thought she was dreaming when Abe asked her if he could make love to her. He was whispering in her ear the way he always did. Between each question, he would plant a soft kiss by her ear and down her neck. Lovely moaned. He kissed her shoulder. His hand rubbed her thigh, caressed her stomach and groped her breast.

"Quiero hacer el amor contigo mi amor ... Te quiero tanto. Te necesito mi amor."

Lovely could smell the liquor on his breath and wondered what time it was. Was he drunk? He had to be. He was undressing her, and she could feel his nakedness.

"You feel so soft." He said, feeling intoxicated.

His hand found its way in between her thighs and rubbed her there. Lovely whispered softly, "Abe…"

"Hmm?" He continued to kiss down to her breasts and over her stomach. He went lower.

Lovely grabbed his head to stop him. "Abe…What are you doing?"

"Let me Lovely."

"But I just went off my period. I'm not really ready yet."

"I don't care about that shit. Just relax baby," he whispered as he kissed her inner thighs. He held her legs open. With the tip of his tongue, he tickled her clit. Lovely inhaled and caught her breath. His lips closed around her clit as he gently sucked it. Lovely gasped without releasing the first breath. Then Abe's tongue caressed every inch, every fold of her pussy back up to her clit. Lovely had moved her hands away, but they were right back on his head as she wiggled under him thrusting back against his tongue. He inserted his tongue into her opening and tongue fucked her. His tongue found its way back to her clit. He stayed on it beating it with a systematic rhythm. Lovely's breathing labored as she felt herself climaxing, "Oh Abe…baby…I'm about to cum…Oh God…"

Lovely thrust wildly, holding Abe's head in place as her pussy walls convulsed. His tongue was still applying pressure on her engorged and now very sensitive clit. Not able to bear any more, Lovely pushed his head away and clamped her legs tight.

Abe kissed her softly, tenderly on her still twitching body. He hovered over her watching her face as she recovered from her orgasm. He whispered. "You're beautiful."

Lovely wished she could see his face. She reached out and touched his shoulders. Her hands glided down his arms. They went to his face again. She caressed his face lovingly reacquainting herself with the shape of his nose, the fullness of his lips, his long lashes, even his ears.

Abe covered Lovely's mouth in an aggressive passion-driven kiss, obsessively searching for her tongue. Everything was almost perfect until the head of his dick pushed through her opening. He was too rough. In his excitement, he forgot to be gentle, but he had been pushed over the edge. Lovely knew this, so she bared the roughness he delivered. It was such a feel good pain, so intense that she didn't mind. Whatever was troubling him to the point of being aggressive, she would let him unleash it on her.

When he was finished, he simply admired her beauty. He held her close.

Abe rubbed her hair back off her face. "*Eres tan hermosa mi amor.*"

Lovely knew whenever Abe used Spanish he was feeling passionate. He just didn't speak it often; therefore, no one would know he spoke it fluently.

Lovely smiled, "You're so sweet to me."

"I'm supposed to be. Would you love me if I wasn't?"

Lovely shook her head. "You wouldn't be here."

Abe contemplated his next questions as he stared into her honey-colored eyes. "Lovely, you say you know about my past, but do you know exactly what I done?"

Lovely thought, why would he ask her that now and they decided to take things to the next level. "I've already told you I know enough."

"And you still felt okay with letting me live with you?"

Lovely nodded. "Your past is what it is."

"I did things. Horrible mean things."

"I know. I don't know the details, but David and Lulu painted the picture for me."

"They did?"

"Yeah. I don't want to know the complete details, but I've been waiting for you to open up about it. I didn't want to stress you by prying, so I talked to them about it. Lulu said you used to be a gangsta."

Abe laughed, "A what?"

"That's what Lulu said. She said you were a gangsta," Lovely giggled.

"Lulu need to stop that shit."

Lovely snickered, "Yeah." She got serious. "So did your stepdad abuse Ike an Eli too?"

"He did. It wasn't as bad as what I got, but either way, he was wrong," Abe answered.

"What about your mother?"

"She loved on Ike and Eli. She hated me."

"Why do you still try?"

Abe shrugged. "I don't know...Sometimes I just feel like if I can get them to accept me..."

"You don't need them to make you feel valid, Abe. You got tons of people who accept you, love, and appreciate you. I'm one of them."

"What am I supposed to do?" he asked trying to blink back tears.

"Not cry, cause you're gonna make me cry," Lovely joked.

Abe smiled. "I'm not."

"I can hear it in your voice," she teased then said. "Fuck them. Live for you and worry about those that have your back. In thirty-four years, they ain't got over what happened then something's wrong with them. You endured enough of their abuse as a child. It's time to cut that shit off and let go of the hold it have on you. They take and take and take from you as if they're entitled. You've turned your life completely around. You owe no one, and the only people you answer to are God and you. Whatever you've done in the past is between you and God. If He has forgiven you and saw fit to bless you as he has, then it's gotta be a purpose behind it. Don't question it. Go with it, but lose the baggage, i.e. Sarah and Esau Masters and your past."

"How long have you wanted to say all that?" Abe asked.

"Since October when I used to sit and listen to you rant and vent about random stuff."

Running his fingers through her hair, Abe massaged the back of her head. He felt the hardness of the plate under her scalp. "Can we talk about this some more?"

"No."

"Why not?"

"Because everything I just said to you I gotta apply it to me and my situation."

Abe laughed. "Well do it."

"It's not as simple."

"Well, talk to me about it. Maybe we can come up with something together."

Lovely turned away from him. She sighed. "Some days I can't get past what happened to me."

Abe reached out for her. "Come here. We don't have to talk about it."

"Everything happened at the same time," she blurted.

"What did?"

"My head injury, my mama's death and the rape."

"Rape? What rape?" he asked confused. Maybe it was the liquor, but Abe didn't recall Lovely ever mentioning a rape.

"That same night. I was raped. Me and your mother have something in common. You and Grace have the same thing in common. Grace is a product of rape. She doesn't know it, and I don't want her to ever know it. Unlike your mother, I saw Grace as a blessing and wouldn't dream of mistreating her the way your mother, did you. I named her Grace because Aunt Livy said to me that it was by the grace of God that either of us survived that night when clearly I should have died."

Knowing this was sickening for Abe. It was the liquor, too. The nauseating feeling was overwhelming. This news mixed with the phone call he received from Eric was too much to bear. He hurled his body across the bed and vomited on the floor.

Lovely was disgusted. "Seriously Abe?"

"I'm sorry baby. Don't be mad."

"Don't talk. Just lay back down. How much did you drink?" Lovely was fussing. She got out of bed and grabbed her kimono style robe.

"Baby, I'll get it up. I—" he was saying before he vomited more.

Lovely started laughing. "You sound atrocious."

Chapter 21

Eli was elated that Robin had come back after visiting with her mother in Alabama. He missed seeing her face. He missed her fiery orange hair against her fair skin. Making love to her was everything he imagined it would be. It pushed thoughts of Kris out of his head.

But, then there was Kiera. She was in an upbeat mood. She smiled brightly and pranced around in her whore red platform pumps. The lipstick she wore matched the shoes and the belt around her small waist. Her medium length weave had been styled off her face giving her a more sophisticated look. The grey pencil skirt she wore made her upside down heart shape ass delectable. It was something about Kiera's allusive way she behaved and dressed that turned Eli on. He thought Kiera was sexy, but she was poisonous.

"What's up with that?" Robin asked in his ear.

"With what?" Eli asked.

It was Sunday evening, and mostly everyone was at Abe's house for dinner. Their aunts with Lulu's help had cooked. Eli was sitting on the sofa beside Robin. Kiera had walked by.

"You staring at her every time she walks by," Robin teased. "Do you want her?"

Eli side eyed Robin. "Hell naw. She the last person I would want."

"Mmm hmm," Robin hummed. "Sure. Tell me anything."

Eli smiled. "I can tell you that I wanna tear that pussy up again."

Robin blushed and had nothing to say.

His phone indicated he received a message. It was from Kris: **call me**

Eli quickly responded: **I can't**

Kris: **are we done?**

Eli pondered the thought. He wasn't ready to give up Kris. He knew he had hurt Kris with that fucked up move he made, but he would try to make it up to her.

Eli: **no, just be patient with me. I'm just really stupid and unable to think clearly right now. I'll make it up to you I promise**

"Who you're texting?" Robin asked.

Whoa, Eli thought. She was being nosey, and he didn't like that. Eli hoped Robin didn't think she was privy to his personal business because they fucked once. Eli replied, "A friend."

"Oh," Robin said. She got up. "Well, I'll give you some privacy."

Kris: **stop feeding me half-truths and empty promises**

Eli: **believe me, please**

Kris: **see me tonight then**

Eli: **I'll call you when I'm on my way**

Kris: **okay. I love you baby**

Eli studied those words. Saying I love you was like signing his life away. As always he responded with: **I love me too**

He walked towards the family room where the others were. Kiera passed him again and smiled. Something was up with her. Eli could sense it. She had been extra cheerful and nice. She was up to something.

Robin came back by catching Eli's eyes lingering on Kiera's backside too long. She gave him a look.

"Where you going?" Eli asked, ignoring the look she was giving him.

"On my way to answer the door. Abe's friend just arrived." Robin said, continuing her journey toward the front of the house.

Eli continued to the family room.

"What's wrong with you?" Abe asked.

"Nothing," Eli mumbled sitting beside him.

"Relationship troubles," Kiera teased with a smirk walking into the room.

Eli frowned in Kiera's direction said, "No, I'm fine."

"Where is Lovely?" Melissa asked. "She's been gone for a minute."

Abe heard Eric's loud mouth before he saw him. "I feel like I'm in Hollywood or something!"

Eric was impressed with Abe's home from the design to the decor. "How's everybody doing?"

Kam stood at his side in complete awe. Sanchez and Kamella were looking around in amazement.

"Y'all wanna go where the kids are?" Robin asked the kids. They nodded. "Is it okay if I take them downstairs?"

Kam said, "Yeah, they can go."

Abe introduced Eric and Kam to those who may not have known them. "This house is bad. Can I get a tour or something?" Kam said.

Melissa jumped up, "I'll do it. I'll be your tour guide."

As the women left, Eric lowered his voice and asked. "Who is them two with the fat asses?"

Eli shook his head at Eric. His wife was there, and he was asking about Kiera and Robin. *Nigga, your best bet is to focus on your chicken head wife,* Eli thought.

Abe shook his head shaming Eric. "Man, you crazy. The one in pink is Kenya's sister and David's niece. You remember Keke nigga. She all grown up."

"Keke?"

"You know the lil girl that we used to get to watch people for us. She used to steal shit all the time. Keke."

Eric gave it some thought. He started laughing. "Get the fuck outta here!"

"That's her."

"Your lady looks like that, too?" Eric asked.

"Body-wise, yeah. My lady's a little thicker." Abe grinned proudly.

Better than that box body wife of yours, Eli thought.

"What about the other one? Shorty got a man?" Eric asked.

Abe asked Eli with a sneaky grin. "Is Robin dating?"

"Robin ain't seeing nobody, cause she's practicing abstinence, took a vow of celibacy and don't believe in premarital sex," Eli lied flatly.

Abe chuckled knowingly.

"I know that ain't Kiera's case though. That ain't the shit she be talking with me." Eli said, matter of factly.

"You've been with her?" Eric asked.

Eli didn't want to put his business out there. "Nah, It came close though, but I think she holding out for Rico. He scared to fuck with her, though."

Eric was confused. He tilted his head to the side, "Damn, ain't you...gay?"

Eli went from zero to one hundred. "I wish the hell y'all quit asking that goddamn shit!"

Eric and Abe started laughing. "My bad nigga."

"Fuck you," Eli spat under his breath. "I bet I can get way more pussy than you can and have a bitch hooked. Don't let the swag fool you." He raised his voice a little.

Ike interjected, "Kiera is a hoe, anyway. You don't wanna fuck with her."

Abe commented. "A bit harsh are we?"

Ike laughed, "Calling it like I see it."

Abe asked Eric quietly. "What did you do about that?" Abe was trying not to let Eric's news bother him. He had come too far for things to crumble now. But what if his life as he knew it presently was in danger because of that girl? What if she remembered his face? She was staring at him when he came into the room. Why had her blindfold not been on properly? Abe thought nothing of the girl seeing him because she was supposed to have died.

Abe looked at his left arm covered in a 3-D style tattoo where his skin appeared to be peeled back and torn to reveal an arm built like a machine. Several years ago when he decided to walk down the straight and narrow path, he went through the long process of having his old street tattoos removed. When they were barely visible, Abe decided to get the tatted sleeve to cover the remnants of those tattoos.

Abe didn't know what Eric's plan was, but he didn't want any parts of it.

"Nothing yet, but my man know where she lives. Said she stays in some big ass house. Well, at least that's where he followed her to."

What they talking about, Eli wondered.

"My nigga, Tee handling it. I thought you weren't worried."

Abe said, "I'm not. I just thought maybe you would change your mind."

Eric laughed heartedly. "Mothafucka you got your nerves. Fyah wouldn't have changed his mind."

Ike shot Abe a suspicious look. He looked over at Eli, and they shared a knowing glance. They knew of "Fyah," and that nigga died several years ago. There was no need for a resurrection when Abe was finding peace in his life.

Abe winced at the mention of that street nickname. "That was then."

"If it came down to it I bet Fyah would come out," Eric teased.

"Fyah need to stay where he at...Dead," Eli said bluntly.

Eric asked. "What's up with that? Dead? That nigga ain't dead. Let some shit pop off. I have seen Abe go off. It ain't pretty."

"I have too," Eli said pointedly. "But that Fyah shit need to stay where it is. In Abe's past."

Abe sensing hostility in Eli spoke up. "Calm down E. Ain't nobody reverting to that."

"I'm sorry it's just that I don't wanna lose my brother over some bullshit," Eli said with a softened tone.

"I know," Abe said.

The ladies could be heard returning.

"Baby! I want a house like this," Kam said coming into the living room. "It's different."

"Well if you get one like this it wouldn't be different, anymore," Eli said smartly.

Melissa looked at Eli with surprise as she tried to stifle her laugh.

Abe didn't know what was wrong with Eli, but he'd made a mental note to get to the bottom of it.

Kiera eyed Eric. "What's up Ghost? Ain't seen you in forever."

"I didn't even know it was you until Abe had to remind me. You done grew the fuck up; I know that," Eric said, taking in the sight of her.

Trifling, Eli thought, thankful that Kam was so consumed with the house she wasn't paying her husband any attention.

Still grinning, Kiera glanced at Abe. Kiera asked Eric. "You met Lovely, Abe's lady yet?"

"No, not yet," Eric said.

Abe spoke up. "She ain't here. She left with Aunt Livy and Lulu."

Kiera cut in. "You show Eric what she look like?" She gestured to Eric to follow her. "Let me show you what Lovely look like. You passed her portrait."

As Eric stared at the portraits in the foyer, he thought this was some type of joke or something. Abe was on some fucked up shit for this. It took everything in Eric to compose himself.

The girl with the jet black hair looked the same as she did twelve years ago. She was definitely thicker in the portrait with her and a little girl who was almost her exact image. Damn! Eric remembered wanting to fuck her after Loco was done, but Loco's shit had damaged the girl enough. Eric had wanted to fuck the then fifteen-year-old girl when he pretended to be cool with Pras. He would see Lovely quietly move through the house like she was a pure angel. Her body was far more mature than what her young mind could handle. With her long hair, honey colored eyes, and a thick bronze beauty Lovely could have manipulated anything out of every man she encountered.

"This is some fucked up shit Keke. Abe with this girl for real?" Eric asked in disbelief.

276

"So I assume you know who she is. Look at the man. Abe so in love he don't recognize none of them," Kiera whispered. "She has a visual impairment, so she can't make out what people really look like."

It was apparent, Abe was in love with the girl. Abe didn't even know who she was. As fucked up as Eric could still be—still street, still money focused, and also very envious of Abe—he still had a lot of love and respect for Abe. Eric felt sick. He could say nothing at all and let Abe enjoy happiness, but if it was him, he would want the truth. He had to let Abe know without Lovely suspecting. Then it dawned on Eric. "Shit," he hissed. He pulled out his phone to call Tee. It went to voicemail.

Eric turned to leave the foyer. "Where you going?" Kiera asked.

"I gotta tell Abe who she is," Eric said. He frowned at Kiera. "Why in the hell ain't you said shit?"

Eric went back into the den and tapped Abe on the arm. "Show me around this big mothafucka real quick. I need to talk to you about some shit, anyway."

Eli glared at Abe to let him know he better not be on some bullshit. Abe got it but was tickled that his brother was adamant about Abe, not backsliding. Abe had enough money that his grandchildren's children would be set. There was no need for a life of crime.

Eric didn't say anything right away because there were people in damn near every area of the house. It wasn't until Abe showed him the garage that he took the opportunity to tell Abe.

Eric sighed heavily. Abe could tell Eric was troubled. Abe asked. "What's going on?"

"Look...I don't know any other way to say this but to just come out and say it," Eric was hesitating. "Lovely is the girl."

Abe wasn't following him. "What girl?"

Eric held up his finger for Abe to give him a minute. He dialed Tee on his phone. "Don't worry about that...Nope. Some shit just came up...Let her be."

Abe still didn't understand. "Eric, you better tell me what you're talking about."

Eric looked Abe in the eyes. "Lovely was Mano's niece. She's the one that was there—"

"No Eric," Abe cut in, shaking his head emphatically. Denial set in quick.

"Nigga, that's her. That the same girl that Lorenzo raped right before you got there," Eric assured.

"Raped?" Abe frowned. It was like he was hit with a bolt of lightning. Why hadn't this all come to him prior to now? Everything had led up to this, and he was the one who could see but was blind to the fact that Lovely was that girl. That's why she always looked so familiar to him. He stomach cringed inside as he thought back.

————

Abe showed up to the home invasion as it was in the middle of going down. The guys should've been in and out. He looked around and noticed that the husband and the wife were already dead so why was it taking them so long. He became upset and started giving them orders.

"Get to the gotdamn vault! Stop all of this other bullshit. *Y date prisa!*"

The teenage girl's blindfold had moved out of place. As Abe spoke, she could clearly see on his wrist a tattoo of a demonic creature that she would always remember. Her eyes fluttered to his face. The scowl on his face reminded her that she wasn't supposed to see him. She looked away quickly, but it was too late.

"Why the fuck is her blindfold off. What the fuck is wrong with y'all?" he barked.

Lorenzo slapped her so hard that Lovely felt like her head would snap off. She cried softly not wanting to upset the invaders. She kept her head lowered, not wanting to look up anymore.

"*Este estúpido coño hizo,*" Eric said in reference to Lorenzo who had just raped their young captive.

Once the vault had been emptied of all of its contents, the invaders put a bullet in Naomi's head and then one in Dharmesh's, just to make sure that they were dead. Lovely let out a blood-curdling cry, and she knew she was about to die. At that moment, she may as well accept it. Her spirit was so violated she didn't even react when the gun pressed up to her head. There was hesitance. Then Abe ordered that they go ahead and set fire to the house. The girl thought, for a brief second, they would let her live.

Then Abe said with no feeling whatsoever, "Kill that girl, too." Before he walked away, Lorenzo shot her in the back of the head. Everything went black.

———

Abe refused to believe what Eric was implying. "You got her mixed up. She might look like her, but that ain't her."

"It is Abe."

Abe shook his head. "Damn man, Lorenzo raped her?" He said, feeling bad as fuck for the woman he loved. "This can't be real." He said, with misty eyes. Eric had never saw Abe in such a vulnerable stated.

"I watched Lo put a bullet in her head. I guess she survived that shit, Abe."

"Don't say that," Abe said with devastation. He felt sick and oxygen deprived. "Please don't say that shit. We didn't do that to her. She was in a..."

"You can't recall what she looked like cause Fyah didn't give a fuck. I know cause I used to be in Pras' house. His wife was Lovely's mama. Abe..."

"That ain't her!" Abe yelled. He was ready to knock the hell out of Eric. Instead, Abe leaned over the trash can in his garage and vomited. In all his adult life he had never felt that sick. It felt like his life had ended. He didn't want to believe any of this was true. He was sure the universe had done something wrong. It made a mistake. Eric was mistaken. His thoughts were misleading.

Eric's heart ached as he watched the reality sink in Abe. Eric felt like crying with Abe.

"Abe, I'm sorry," Eric said apologetically. He tried to comfort Abe.

Abe angrily pushed him away. "Get the fuck off me!"

"Abe."

"I don't wanna hear no more! Get your family and get out of my goddamn house!"

"I'm sorry, but I couldn't sit back and—"

Abe lost it and his fist connected with Eric's mouth. Through greeted teeth, Abe said definitely. "Get outta my house."

Eric was stunned as he grabbed his mouth. "Mothafucka, you made me bleed!"

Abe stared at him coldly. Eric understood his rage. He damn sure didn't want to get into a brawl with Abe. Eric walked away.

When Eli saw Eric returning with his two kids in tow, he knew something was wrong.

Eric called to Kam. "Bae, let's go."

Kam complained, "We just got here."

"I said come on," Eric said firmly.

Kam asked. "What happened to you?"

That's when Eli noticed Eric's busted lip. That wasn't there before. Eli jumped up on defense, "What the fuck happen between you and Abe? Where is Abe?"

Eric ignored Eli leading his family towards the foyer.

Lovely, who just showed up with David, Lulu and Aunt Livy asked, "What's going on?"

David, Ike, and Eli went searching for Abe. They found him in the garage sitting on a bench. His forehead rested in his palms, elbows on his knees. He was agonizing over something.

"Abe, what's wrong?" Eli asked sitting beside him.

"Leave me alone," Abe mumbled.

Hearing him sniffle Eli knew Abe was crying. "Why is Eric leaving with a busted lip? Y'all got into a fight?"

"Didn't I tell you to leave me the fuck alone?"

Eli got up and moved away from Abe, "I don't want no busted mouth."

"Abe, tell us what's going on!" Ike demanded.

Abe raised and stared at Ike, "I ain't telling you shit. Now get away from me."

"We just wanna help. We're concerned," David reasoned.

"I wanna be left alone. Please leave me alone," Abe pleaded impatiently.

"No, not in the state you're--"

Abe grabbed a nearby bucket and slung it forcefully. It cracked against his truck. "Goddamit, I said leave me alone!"

Eli put more distance between him and Abe. Eli was too pretty to be a victim of Abe's rage.

"Mothafucka, if that shit would have hit me..." Ike started.

"Or what!" Abe challenged by standing fully. His fist were balled.

In beast mode, nobody wanted to fuck with Abe. When he was enraged, he seemed about six inches taller and fifty pounds heavier. In his wild street days, Abe was known for the damage he could do with just his fists.

"C'mon man," David interjected. "No need for any of this. Ike leave him alone."

Abe sat back down. He returned to his devastated distressed heartbroken state. He said in a softer tone, "I just need to be alone."

"You want me to get Lovely?" Eli asked.

Abe started to sob at the mention of her name. He cried, "No. She's the last person I wanna see."

"This is about Lovely?" Ike asked. "Eric told you something about her."

"I don't wanna talk about it," Abe cried.

Why was this happening? She survived, and twelve years later she had found her way into his life; into his heart. A woman he'd helped out and fell in love with, he'd also hurt, violated and intended to kill. This was God punishing him. Abe always wondered how he glided through life unscathed. He grew richer, obtained love and admiration from so many, and had no worries. God's irony was not amusing at all. The woman, whose life's struggles were brought on by him, was the woman whom he loved. If this is ever come to light how could she forgive him? Why would she ever choose to continue to love him?

Just the thought of it all made him sick all over again as he looked up to see her standing there.

"Abe baby, are you okay? Talk to me," she sincerely said, rubbing her fingers through his hair. Abe didn't respond. He couldn't respond. "Whatever has you so upset will seem like nothing once you hear this news." Abe still couldn't face her as he held his head down. "I'm pregnant."

About the Author

Ada Henderson brings her imagination to life as she writes amazing urban romance fiction under the pseudonym Ivy Symone. Writing has always been a passion of hers even before she realized that's exactly what it was: passion!

The urge to put daydreams to paper began for her at the tender age of ten. The impulse to write was sporadic over the years; but as an adult she picked writing back up, and it served as a therapeutic outlet for her. It wasn't until late 2013 that her mother encouraged her to get published.

Ivy's first debut novel was Why Should I Love You. After that, came Why Should I Love You 2 & 3, Secrets Between Her Thighs 1 & 2, Never Trust A Broken Heart, Crush 1, 2, & 3, Hate To Love You, Stay, If You're Willing, Bad Habitzz, and The Bed We Made. Ivy humbly received two AAMBC awards: 2015 Ebook of the Year and 2015 Urban Book of the Year for her phenomenal Crush series.

She currently resides in Nashville, TN with two of four children in her home. When Ivy is not reading or writing, she's enjoying cooking, watching horror movies all day long, and spending quality time with her friends and family.

CPSIA information can be obtained
at www.ICGtesting.com
Printed in the USA
LVHW04s1543240918
591190LV00011B/1033/P